Alyssa—

Thank you so mu[ch]
your enthusiastic interest & sup[port]
appreciate what a positive friend
been to me, and can't wait for
more years to come!

H O͘ M E

Enjoy the
Story!

by

Nicholas Cassady

This book is dedicated to:

You.
So many of you. There are so many people who have pushed me, and supported me along the way that your names outnumber the constellations in the stars.
If you are reading this, in some way, this book is for you.
-N

v.1

4

I: The Savior

I am a child born of two Homes. I am a child born of two worlds. My story is fantastic, and in no way conceivably possible.

So I have been told, creation is merely a fable of man; a device used to explain that which could not be understood...The Beginning. The Bang: energy forged from life, life forged from energy. For fractionless time we were two, however, the collapse forged the one.

The Bang placed chaos among order into the Known Universe. Beautiful child of light followed by a heart of darkness crept upon mortality; and so it was written. It was written as fate, predetermined to set off something greater; a purpose even greater than the Writer could have imagined. Imagine. Utopia and Hell at once: a Home, a dream, a birthright of burden.

So it is in the End, as it was in the Beginning.

Hollow words passed down by blind divinities. However, their nearsightedness could not be their fault. As mortal creations, that was their flaw. I stand before them, destined as "*He*: The One", and they stand for me as "*Them*: The

Guardians". The words given unto man, "Life" preceded by "Death" are ours to escape.

The Son of the Seventeenth Savior of Man will be born for this Universe as the child blessed with the capacity to move humanity back to the path of righteousness.

I am a child of two Homes. I am a child of two worlds. My story is fantastic. And in no way conceivably possible.

Or so I'm told.

Monday — 13
Joshua & Joycelyn Blake

The wind rustled the curtain resting its back on the open windowpane. The cold air crept into the darkness of the room, and proceeded to make its way to the sleeping occupants of the bed. Voices, screeching, sorrowful voices filled the air as it brushed passed his face, breathing fear into him.

Joshua Eason Blake was a complex man. Not by first glance, nor even really by personal reputation; Joshua Eason Blake was a simple man outwardly to many, but at the core of his being, he was a rather complicated man. Among other things, he was also my father.

I was led to believe that my father was born and raised to be a man of 47 years old. He met my mother at the tender age of 17, and the two star-crossed lovers married within a year. He was a go-getter; he had plans, designs…a purpose.

From such a young age he was sure to be destined for greatness. He put his existence on the map twenty-five years ago when he founded the Blake Genetic Industry. Back then, he was a naïve twenty-something with something to prove, or so he let the world think.

His mind wrapped itself around such concepts as biogenetic engineering, digital logarithms, DNA base-coding and made sense where no other trained mind could. One of the world's most gifted minds—an accolade he had come accustomed to—however, he preferred more simply, father, to myself and brother.

Now that I look back, I understand what they mean when they say that "hindsight is 20/20". I could have known...more importantly, I *should have* known.

*

"GRID detections! We have incoming!" Her voice was high pitched and shrill as she screamed to make herself heard among the explosions.

"They're rocking the boat!" He fell to his knees as the structure was struck, the lights dimmed for a moment and a computer screen exploded in the background. He steadied himself on a sturdy console. Peering into the abyss of space was a lone glass aperture which ominously overlooked all of them at the front of the mechanical marvel. "Lock, load and let 'em fly! There are no wait commands here! Keep your Pekor faces on, now go, go, go!" his voice was so familiar and so commanding.

"Fire in the hull!"

The marvelous center in which they stood was dark and glowing red intermittently. His face reflected in the glass covered top of the computer console on which he had earlier steadied himself. My father stood with a worried confidence exuding from his body. The explosions of traded fire ignited in front of them, shaking their craft. As he studied the positions of the enemy ships against his own and his battalion, my father strategized his next movement. "Give me a lateral bump on the port. New heading, come about to 45 mark 73 mark 0."

"Operations confirm, new heading: 45 mark 73 mark 0!" there was a stocky man strapped into a seat at the front of the rustled center who called his new order out over his left shoulder.

"Sir that will put us directly in line with enemy fire!" Another man's voice called out in a screech.

"No time for questions, Guth," my father called to his left. "Conn, execute command," he directed the stocky man in front of him. "Load tubes zero through thirteen—as soon as new heading is confirmed: let 'em fly! Open communications!"

"Heading confirmed!"

"Tubes are loaded, rounds away, sir!"

"Communication open."

"This is the Allied Starship..." the ship took a heavy hit to the starboard side. My father was reduced to his knees as the ship swayed across space.

"Sir your efforts are futile, they refuse to respond! GRID is detecting more closing in on our position. They are trying to surround us..." sparks flew in the silence following this last exchange of words.

"Send out the call. Bring Prodigious Abstract Fusion online." My father's voice hinted at defeat.

"Sir, there aren't enough available system resources..."

"Divert it all. I'm not dying today." He was concrete in his declaration.

"Shutting down Diminutive Abstract Fusion, bringing Prodigious core online...Awaiting execute command."

With a heavy sigh he breathed out his next word: "command."

*

The word echoed endlessly through his sleeping mind, as it resonated through his being, he jumped, waking himself from the nightmare. His muscles were tensed and he was soaked in sweat.

"What is it, Joshua?" My mother sleepily asked rolling over and putting her hand on my father's bare chest.

"Nothing. It's nothing, sweetheart," he picked up her hand and kissed it as she slipped deeply back into slumber. The digital clock on his nightstand shone on his face, it read Monday – 4:23AM. He picked up his phone lying next to the clock and scrolled through the contacts; he pressed call. The phone dialed, and rang once before a perky voice answered. My father sat for a moment paused in thought before he finally responded, "Vexandrees, the deadline is Wednesday." He hung up the phone and coaxed himself back to sleep.

My mother awoke what felt like seconds later to the disturbing buzz of my father's alarm clock. "Joshua, turn that off," she said brushing the curly brown frizz from her face. When my father did not obey my mother's request, she asked again patting his side of the bed. She scrunched her eyebrows and opened her eyes startled to see that my father was not in bed with her. "Joshua?" The alarm continued to buzz in the background.

"Joshua?" My mother called down the stairs and into the foyer. She received no response from my father again. Scurrying down the stairs, she made her way through the foyer, the formal dining room, sitting room, and into the kitchen. She was surprised to see that it was also empty, with a pot of coffee brewing on the hot plate, and a dirty mug in the sink. She walked to the refrigerator, and scrolled through the messages on the LCD screen on the door of the fridge. She rested her palm on the final message, which was as predicted, from my father.

It simply read: "Duty calls, my love."

My mother studied the message for endless seconds. When she finally felt as if she had taken the correct meaning from my father's words, she proceeded out of the kitchen and back up the stairs to their bedroom. Once at the top of the stairs, she took a detour to her left and down the hall to my brother's room. She tapped on the door lightly and stuck her head in, "Deavon, sweetheart, its 6:50..."

My brother kept his head buried under his pillow, and kept himself buried in the mess of clothes upon his bed. He reached his hand out from under the pile of slop and waved my mother off. She knew that motion all too well. After nearly eighteen years of waking my brother, my father finally left the task to my mother. My dad knew that my brother would never strike her as he struck my father in the morning. Deavon was not a morning person.

She continued on her morning path and made her way down the hallway bypassing their room again and onto the opposite end of the upstairs hall, where my room was. As she tapped, the door nudged open, and she pushed it a bit more. Peering into my room, she could see that I was laying in bed still fast asleep with my back to her. "Sweet..." she started but immediately stopped when she noticed my sleepy ramblings.

Out of all of the mostly unintelligible ramblings of which I spoke while still fast asleep, there was one word that my mother caught with absolute certainty that struck her in a very wrong way. The word slipped out of my unconscious mouth so innocently, but my mother knew its place: "Corona".

Terror struck her face as she gasped and closed the door. The disturbance was enough to wake me. She hurried back down the hall to her own bedroom, and shut the door behind her. Tears welled in her eyes as she covered her mouth. "It couldn't possibly..." She cleared her throat and did her best to regain her composure. "Shower, 80 degrees," the sound of water in the background captured her attention briefly. "Coincidence..." she said the word aloud as if trying to convince someone or something other than herself.

*

Across town, my father was growing tired of his work as the day was already pressing upon him with great pressure. His office had been infiltrated with upset geneticists, and other colleagues from the moment he stepped foot onto Blake Genetic Industry's campus. When he was disturbed yet again, by another knock at his door, his patience broke and he screamed in response: "What?!"

11

"I am sorry to bother, sir," A slender blonde-haired woman entered his office carrying a clipboard snug against her body. She adjusted her black-framed glasses and stood apprehensive to address my father again.

"No bother, Vexandrees, I must apologize."

"No apologies are necessary, sir."

"What may I help you with?" He asked turning his attention back to the work that was laid out upon his desk.

"Sir, I know that you have already talked with Norman and Areul, but other department leaders are quite skeptical that they will be able to meet the new deadline..."

"I am aware of such concerns, but we must continue to press on," there was something in his voice that hinted that he was approaching a level of agitation that he had not previously ever conveyed.

"Sir, they are scrambling."

"All departments knew that there was a possibility of moving the deadline. There should be no surprise."

"Why now, sir?" The woman my father addressed as Vexandrees broke.

"Pardon?"

"If I may ask, why such expedience now, sir? For near to twenty years, you have worked so diligently at perfecting the compound, and now when it is in the final phase, you will deny final testing in order to meet a new deadline..."

My father listened to her words frozen at his desk. He broke his blank trance and looked directly into her eyes. "Last night, I almost made it Home, pal," his words were heavy.

12

Vexandrees' eyes widened. "Tell Areul and Norman that there is no room for error." He went back to his work.

"Understood, sir," this was not a lie. She truly understood my father's fear. She exited his office leaving him to his work.

My father's admission disturbed him. Something stirred inside of him, something that he had not felt in some time. He dropped his work, and turned his desk chair around to face the large series of windows behind him. His office sat at the top of Blake Tower, and overlooked much of the city. He stood from his chair and stepped closer to the cold glass. Pressing his hands upon the window he spoke: "We are at war..."

"Captivating." A mysterious voice came from behind my father's back.

"You are dead," my father responded to the one-word statement without turning his attention away from the city landscape.

"And you are severely observant, young Joshua."

"I haven't lost my touch," my father retorted.

"Get on with it, young Joshua...you were saying something about war?"

"Get out."

"If I remember correctly, it was those words, was it not? The words that started it all..." The voice behind my father was very sinister.

"If memory recalls, it was the strike on Pandine that started it all..." my father said crossly. He whipped around to stare the intruding individual down.

An elderly balding man with a striking resemblance to my father was standing just on the other side of the desk. He chuckled at my father's remark, "if we're going to get technical about it, Joshua, then technically it was the Klondaessian moon that started it all..." Slouching as he stood, the elderly man was wearing a brown suit with a mustard yellow undershirt and stared just as crossly back at my father. The mysterious stranger took a step forward, stopping short of my father's desk. My father did the same.

"You should not be here," my father said between his gritted teeth.

"Physical and dimensional impossibilities aside, I am, Joshua." The old man shifted his focus to the outside world showcased just behind them. He smiled, "I love what you've done with the place."

My father blinked and when his eyes opened again, the man was gone. He stood startled at the elderly man's absence.

"Truly spectacular," his voice cut into the silence and jarred my father's attention. Turning around, my father saw the man standing at the windows admiring the view from the tower's top.

Shaking his head, my father's blood boiled, "how *dare* you take his image!" he screamed.

"Now, now, child," the elderly man turned to face my father. He looked at him with a sinister tenderness, "why all of the aggression, son?"

"You are *not* my father!" he slammed his hand against the glass window.

The man standing in front of my father, claiming to be his own father, leaned in closely and stared him in the eye; "You cannot be so easily rid of me," he smiled maniacally.

"And you are in no position to fight me," my father said brushing his hand through the man in front of him; he was merely a ghostly apparition. He leaned in closer, so the two of them were nose to nose, "he will be the end of you."

"How wrong you are..." the old man raised his clenched fists and shook them in my father's infuriated face. He slammed them down to his sides and disappeared in a smoke-like collection of clouds billowing away into the ether.

***

Monday – 13
Angelica Johnson

"I want you to know that I've been here. Every step of the way," his voice was soft and full of sorrow. He looked upon the sleeping blonde girl, tucked into her bed, unaware of his presence. "Bad things are coming my dear. I'm going to fight just as hard as I always have. You will never know what you mean to me..." his fingertips began to trace down her cheeks.

The door to her room whipped open. There was the sound of a pop, and Angelica Johnson was awake. She may have been an angel in sleep like any other, but in waking life, Angelica—Angel—Johnson found herself crushed underneath the chip on her shoulder. The converging sounds shook her awake in panic; her brown eyes ripped open, and she immediately turned her attention to her now open doorway. Her mother, Loren, was standing in her door's place in a grey pantsuit and her curly, dirty-blonde mane pulled back in a ponytail. She lifted her coffee mug to her mouth, taking a sip with a smile, "Morning."

Angelica scoffed at her mother's offer, "Oh my God. Would you wipe that damn smirk off your face?" She pulled the pillow from under her head and chucked it at her mother. After eighteen years, Loren was a pro and prepared for such a feat. She reached out and grabbed the hurtling object, taking another sip of her coffee. "Lucky catch," Angelica growled.

"Lots of practice," Loren remarked sardonically. She crossed into her daughter's room, and stood at the foot of the bed. She set the pillow down on the bed carefully, and turned to Angelica, "Now, I would just love nothing more than a tiny little..."

"Miracle from your little *Angel* of a daughter..." Angelica finished with a dull sarcasm. "Spit it out."

Loren sat for a moment in patronized defeat, before she dropped her act and cut to the chase, "Look, please...please just try not to stir any trouble this week, okay? I've um...I've been working really hard," Loren looked away for a moment out the window, stealing with the glance a second of serenity. "This week is just really important, okay?"

Angelica sat for a moment, pondering her mother's request, "Yeah, yeah, I get it. I'll see what I can do...but *no promises!*"

"That's all I ask." Loren exhaled, stood and straightened her clothes. Before she could leave, Loren wrapped her right hand around the back of her daughter's head, and placed a sweet kiss on her forehead.

16

Angelica sat for a minute pondering her day and thought, "I need a cigarette." She waited for her mother to leave the house before she finally rolled out of the bed. She pulled the secret pack of cigarettes from under her mattress pad and withdrew a single menthol cigarette. She walked out of her room and down the hall into the bathroom. She started the shower, and opened the window. As the bathroom filled with steam, she puffed away on her cigarette and pondered her day. She inhaled the cool sweet smoke and exhaled her already building anxiety. After fifteen puffs or so she had taken what she needed from the cigarette and threw it out the window into her yard, near a pile of other cigarette butts.

The clock on the wall read 7AM; she slouched, groaned, and proceeded getting ready for the day. After mere minutes in the shower, she straightened the sleep out of her unwashed hair, traced on a thick layer of eyeliner, pulled her hair back into a tight ponytail, and threw on her school uniform. She hastily grabbed her backpack and jacket and slammed the door to her room, walking directly out into the great room that was their living room and adjoining kitchen. Loren had left Angelica just enough coffee behind for a small thermos full. Angelica poured it and capped it and noticed a note on the fridge: "Have a good day my Angel. Love, Mom." Angelica ripped it off the fridge and crumpled it up. "Barf," she said aloud, throwing the wad of paper into the trash. She walked out of her house with jacket in hand, backpack on her back and thermos safely secured on the counter top.

She carelessly tossed her backpack into the messy back seat of her dilapidated red car. She slammed the creaky door

17

shut, and turned the ignition—her car not requiring keys. Over and over again, the car continued to struggle to turn over. Like a dying animal, her car cried out as she continued to struggle. "C'mon!" she screamed slamming her hand down on the wheel. She pumped the gas to the floor, and turned one last time. The car roared to life, screeching the minute it ignited with activity.

After minutes of rummaging through her purse, she finally found the lipstick she had been searching for. She pulled down the visor and slathered the deep red onto her lips pursing them as she finished, making an audible 'pop'. She threw the vehicle into reverse and whipped out of the driveway not caring to look behind her. She peeled out of her driveway, rolled down the windows and pumped the morning radio show as she cruised down her street.

As she continued on, she blew through stop signs, ignored right-of-ways and managed to offend several elderly with her middle finger. Miraculously she managed to make her way unscathed to the home of her former boyfriend, Nathan Thomas. Putting the car in park initiated its annoying screech again; just as she was about to press her hand upon the horn Nathan's front door opened. As Nathan stepped out of his house, he turned around to catch and lock the front door. With his back to her, Angelica slammed the horn, startling Nathan. He threw his right hand behind his head offering her the same gesture that she had already offered several others that morning. He walked down the walkway leading from the front steps to the driveway, crossed the front of her red beast of a car and pulled heavily on the passenger door. Taking as much care as she had, he threw his things into the backseat and slumped down into the passenger seat taking three attempts to successfully latch the door closed. "Good morning, sunshine," he snidely remarked.

She looked over at him, lifting her sunglasses from her face focusing her eyes more, "what is that growing on your face?" she asked snottily referring to Nathan's light beard. His beard grew in a light red, which did not match the brown on his head. It annoyed him slightly, but all he really cared about was having the ability to grow facial hair.

"Funny, I could ask the same thing about those caterpillars on your forehead, Angel," he smiled curtly.

"God, I forgot how funny you are." She put the car in reverse and pulled out, heading onto their next destination. Cranking open her window, she lit another cigarette. "Call Nicholas, and tell him we're on our way."

"He's sick today. He's not coming to school."

Angelica — Angel — exhaled out a cloud of smoke, "of course." Her words solidified the tension in the car as they continued to school.

***

Monday – 13
Nicholas Peterson

Nicholas Peterson was easily one of the most gifted and paranoid minds I had ever had the pleasure of meeting. His parents, Guthrie and Evelyn Peterson were dear old friends of my father, and worked as two of the four head department advisors for the Blake Genetic Industry. That in itself may or may not have been the root of Nicholas's paranoia.

He, like my father, and unlike myself, could see patterns existing where few, if any, others could—his lens had been finely tuned to a wavelength that, unfortunately for him, marched on its own. For all intents and purposes, Nicholas graduated from Riverside Academy, our high school, about a year prior—a year early—but his parents urged him to stay enrolled in his adolescence for as long as he could. Nobody could have really suspected what was to come, after all.

His parents' research in disease control and the human immune system largely made Nicholas a hypochondriac, which in-turn also fueled the anxious fire that constantly burned within him. The work of Guthrie and Evelyn Peterson for the Blake Genetic Industry was invaluable, and often overshadowed their need to live a more fulfilling life. During the second semester of our senior year, Nicholas often found himself barricaded in his room, in his fear, in his anxiety, surrounded by innumerable patterns and buried in lines of meaninglessly meaningful research. He was searching for something—a something that he would never find in a scientific text—but he had no idea he was looking in all of the wrong places.

For such a calculating mind, it never ceased to amaze me what kind of company Nicholas often found himself in. Many of his acquaintances, my brother included, were not particularly of Nicholas's caliber—not to say that they weren't intelligent, although I cannot say much for Angelica Johnson, it was simply more that Nicholas was much less of an animated character than any of his cohorts. Their affinity for recklessness was contrary to his nature; however their connection was clandestinely cosmically defined centuries before. Nicholas would think that participating in reckless activities such as wasting his brain on mind-altering drugs, or petty theft would allow him a more inspired take on the human condition; ultimately to him, it was all an experiment. He was obtusely unaware however, how self-evident the experiment was.

7:35AM etched into Nicholas's dizzy mind and ripped him from sleep. The room swam around him as he snapped to reality. The roar of his alarm clock put him into a sudden panic, "I'm awake, I'm awake," he said frantically. The alarm clock ceased. He sighed, "God…" Massaging his forehead he groaned. As he labored to open and focus his eyes he could have sworn that there was yet another present in the room with him, however the glimmer of a pink light popped and he blinked. When he opened his eyes again, he looked around his dark room incredulously. "Shades?" His monotone voice cut into the silence. The black shades covering his windows responded to his request and began to wind up into the ceiling. As daylight poured into his room, he groaned again, his instincts for light having been wrong. "I lied—shades down!" the shades paused briefly during their ascension and obeyed his command; they reestablished darkness to his room.

He rubbed the sleep out of his eyes, cleared his throat and spoke, "Where are my parents?"

The wall opposite his bed jumped to life. A projection of the city appeared, a section densely populated with buildings highlighted and zoomed in. A "pin" appeared on the tallest building in the downtown district: the Blake Genetic Industry Complex – Blake Tower.

"They're at work already?"

The "pin" highlighted Blake Tower again, and hopped in animation signifying affirmation to his inquiry. A time stamp appeared next to the pins, informing Nicholas that his parents had arrived at work at 5:02AM, nearly 3 hours earlier than they would normally report to work.

Nicholas looked over at the clock display on his nightstand, which now read 7:53AM. He looked back at the "pin" hopping on the screen and stared at it incredulously. "Why would they go in so early?"

The "pin" responded by producing a speaking bubble with the words: MESSAGE RECIEVED. The heading expanded in detail explaining that his parents had received a message at 4:25AM from Vexandrees – The assistant to Joshua Blake, my father. His eyes traced over the contents of the message as he read them aloud: "PRIORITY ONE – DEADLINE IS WEDNESDAY."

***

Tuesday – 14

6:30AM came too early. The small LED screen protruding from my nightstand flashed the time, the red numbers were a blur to me, "I'm up." The numbers turned white, and the buzzing ceased. I rubbed my eyes and groped my bedside table for my glasses. Slipping them on, the world around me came to focus. The screen now read: TUESDAY 3.14 – 6:31AM. I ripped my covers off and flipped my feet off the left side of the bed, which was a deviation from my normal routine of stepping off the right side. The world was turning grey to me. Color was draining from it every single day. My alarm buzzed at 6:30AM every morning. And about ten minutes later, my mother would walk in to make sure that I was actually awake — *every morning.* The sun shown in the window to the left of my bed and painted my face. It was starting to get lighter out as the spring drew nearer. My foot touched the cold hard wood floor and recoiled. I firmly set my feet down, and stretched before taking a stand and proceeding two steps to the window.

Alexander Hamilton — my neighbor, not former President — was pulling out of his driveway and headed off to his dental practice. He was the lame neighbor growing up, who always had apples instead of chocolate for Halloween. Departing from home, he left behind his second wife, and two young boys, both of whom looked exactly like him. His neighbor, one house further down, Delores Kates pulled out seconds after him and followed suit. She was headed off to her job as a nurse at the Downtown Health Complex. She left behind neither a husband nor children; and with a personality like hers, I always maintained that it would stay that way. They all followed the monotony of this schedule to a dull point every day.

I woke up on the wrong side of the bed. That was the difference I had to contribute. "Forecast," the wall behind my bed ignited in activity as a 36-hour forecast was projected onto it. It had called for a high of 55, but it was to be mostly cloudy, so it was going to feel much colder. I picked out different components of my school uniform, choosing to wear a sweater vest over the top to keep me warm. I laid the clothes out on my bed, and proceeded down the small hallway, which led into my room and looked directly upon my bed. I turned to my left just before reaching my bedroom door, and found myself at the bathroom door to my personal bathroom. "Shower, 87

23

degrees," I closed the door and looked at myself in the full-sized mirror on the back of it. I looked tired, I hadn't slept well for days, perhaps even by this point, weeks. Nightmares. Taking off my shirt, I tossed it onto the toilet. I flexed each my right and left biceps. Trust me, it was nothing special. I was a simple, lanky, brown-haired boy. I wasn't fat, I wasn't skinny, I wasn't too tall, I thought I was just plain. Stripping the rest of the way down, I threw my clothes on the floor and placed my glasses on the sink counter.

I was dilly-dallying, I could barely make out the clock that was being projected in my shower stall. It was already 6:47, but luckily I was a good multi-tasker and therefore a fast shower taker. Minutes later, I jumped out and grabbed for my towel. The tile beneath my feet was heated, but the wood floor in my room was not, I was in for a shock. As I walked out, I wrung my wavy brown hair out; I looked up at the window next to my bed and was startled. Someone was standing at my window, from what I could make out of the person, they had white hair and were wearing a brown jacket and pants. Paralysis plagued me for a moment, I stood frozen; turning quickly, I rushed back into my bathroom to grab my glasses. As I walked back out into my room I spied the man again as he tranquilly stared out the window. He began to turn to face me, I put my glasses on quickly so as to catch a glimpse of his face, but as soon as everything came back to focus, he was gone. I looked around my room nearly frantic, removing my glasses to rub my eyes and replacing them...I was alone. "Sleep deprivation," I told myself.

I sat down on my bed still heavily dripping water from my hair and shivering, either from fright or chill. My left hand reached behind me to grab my comforter and I used it to cover up for a few minutes before dressing. *"And so it is..."*

"Sweetheart?" Her voice cut me open. I looked up puzzled, "is everything ok?" My mother asked.

I sat speechless for a moment, "Um, yeah," I slipped back into my body. "Daydreaming..." I looked at the clock on my nightstand, it read 7:17AM, "I gotta get dressed," I said looking back at my mother. She took the hint and pulled her head out of my doorway and headed back the hallway, proceeding down the stairs. I threw my clothes on haphazardly, threw a comb through my hair and ran out the door, grabbing my backpack on the way. I scurried down the hallway and descended the stairs. I bypassed the foyer, nice dining and living rooms and proceeded directly into the kitchen. My mother was standing at the kitchen sink looking out into our back yard peeling her orange. My father was sitting just beyond the island at the kitchen table sipping his coffee.

Without looking up, my father spoke: "What are the odds?"

"Not good, if I don't leave now!" that was not my normal response, but I did not have the luxury of answering him correctly. I was actually surprised to see him, to see either of my parents really. My father had dashed off early in the morning the previous day and returned late the previous night. There was something going on at work, but he was trying not to let it show. My mother was still standing in her pink bathrobe, staring off; she was normally half way to work. "Where is he?" I asked referring to my absent brother.

"Oddly, he made it out of the house before you. You feeling ok?" My father asked playfully.

"HA!" I shot sarcasm back at him. I slipped my shoes on by the backdoor and neglected to grab my jacket off the hook. I unlocked the door and walked out, but popped my head back in. "Seventeen to Three," I said to my father with a smile.

"I'd play those odds." He responded.

"I always do." I shut the door.

"Don't forget your coat!" My mother yelled after me, but her effort was futile, because I was already out of earshot. She shook her head, pursing her lips. After moments of silence, she finally spoke again, "What of the odds this time, Joshua?" My mother asked with watery eyes as she still stared blankly out the window.

"Let us not speak of such things, my love."

***

Tuesday – 14
Clecha Robinson

Tick-tock. Tick-tock. She stared at her watch – 7:27AM. "Where is he?" She looked into the mirror next to the door and stared at her reflection annoyed. I was seven minutes late after all. Her eyes wandered over her curled brown hair, and she ran her fingers through, making sure to put each curl carefully in its place. She licked her right pinky and smoothed out each of her eyebrows sitting arched over her dark brown eyes. She

26

resolved that I was not coming, and proceeded to put on her jacket and shoes.

Her parents, Norman and Areul Robinson were the colleagues of Evelyn and Guthrie Peterson. They had not returned in the night, as they were working endlessly to complete their work on my father's highest priority. It meant less to my father that they save face, so that he may save his own. Clecha, unlike Nicholas, and more like myself, did not much care for the affairs of our parents, so as not to presuppose any destiny of great achievement onto herself. We would be the type to simply, 'roll with the punches'.

She reached for the doorknob and ripped it from under my knuckles, startling both of us. "I didn't think you were going to show!" She said choking on her words as her heart beat returned to normal. "Why are you so late?" She pushed me out of the way, pulling the door closed behind her and securing it.

It took me a few moments to regain my own composure from startle, "sorry," it was all I could muster up.

She looked at me oddly, and then grabbed my arm, "C'mon," she dragged me down the walkway to the driveway and then to the sidewalk. The two of us walked together every morning that it wasn't snowing, and normally we were joined by my brother. She always managed to go on and on about this and that, and so on and so forth...Her voice carried on as I stared at her face. Her eyes lit up with excitement as she went on about, if I remember correctly, our history paper. The dimples in her cheeks always made me melt; I spent most of my time trying to make her laugh just to catch a glimpse of her beautiful smile. The wind blew her hair into her face; she used her hand to brush away the intruding hair and turned to me. "Are you okay?" she had caught me staring at her.

I shook my head, "uh, yeah." I looked away coyly.

"Are you sure?"

"I just haven't slept well lately."

"Doing your history paper?"

I laughed inside, "what else?" Truth be told, I hadn't even thought about the paper that was due in three days. I was already doing better than normal. Normally I wouldn't think about the paper that we had had assigned for six weeks for at least another two days. It was something I could blame my tiredness on, however, so I chose it as the scapegoat. I had to spend the rest of our walk from our gated community to Riverside Academy – which was just a block and a half away – drowning out her incessant ramblings about the paper and how she had spent three weeks on it.

She would have gotten a C+; I would have gotten an A. Not trying to brag—simple truth. As we walked out of the gates to Riverside Estates, Angelica Johnson's red beater came barreling down the street towards Riverside Academy. She flung her hand out the window offering each Clecha and myself the middle finger. Normally she'd stop and pick up my brother, offering colorful expressions as they sped off to make one more lap around the neighborhood enjoying their cigarettes and other such things. Seeing that Deavon was not in our company she simply sped by honking her horn obnoxiously with the hand that was not waving Clecha and I down.

I waved back with a gesture of my own and we continued down the street. "What a bitch," if there was anyone in the world that could not stand Angelica Johnson more than myself, it was Clecha. Clecha was the antithesis to everything that Angelica was. While Clecha often conformed to many social norms without taking a second glance, Angelica's nature made her rebel. They did not always abhor each other, there was a time – albeit, it was first grade – where the two of them were the best of friends. Something happened early in childhood, however, that set the two girls apart from each other. One day, Angelica simply hated Clecha. And that seemed to be that.

***

Tuesday – 14
Joycelyn Blake

"Where is that fucking tweed skirt?" My mother asked herself aloud as she sat rummaging through her clothes in her closet. My father had darted out the door soon behind my departure, and my mother had taken to pamper herself to a half day—really she was just trying to escape the inescapable.

"Lady Blake," his voice cut into my mother's solitude.

She gritted her teeth as her eyes began to water, "how dare you." She stared into the ether, not wanting to face the intruder. "Does my husband know that you are here?"

"I have not yet informed He that I am here." His voice was shaking.

My mother turned around to stare down the intruder. Standing in the doorway between my parent's closet and their bathroom was a tall, pale, dark-haired young man. "Why are you here?"

"Madam, present circumstance..."

"Do not patronize me..." she crossly interrupted the young man.

"Does He know?"

"I am sure of it. But he has enough to be worried about," my mother started very matter-of-factly, "do you understand me?"

"I understand Ma'lady, but you also must understand that I have a duty to fulfill, and *nothing* will get in the way of that." He stood firmly.

My mother stared blankly through him as she shed a few tears. "Go, my Shepherd. Tend to the flock," she chuckled to herself, "you will know when I will need you." The ring of the phone jarred her attention; when she turned back to the mysterious young man who was standing in the doorway, he was gone. "Identify incoming."

"Incoming – Loren Johnson."

My mother smiled ironically as a few more tears slipped from her tired, pale-hazel eyes. "Answer."

***

Tuesday – 14
The Shepherd

"How was first class?" Clecha asked as she approached her locker, which was just two down from mine. We had both skated into our first classes with seconds left before the final bell. As always, first class managed to be a complete and utter bore.

"Boring," I replied. "Have you seen Deavon yet?"

30

"Nope, why?"

"I have his lit book and he's going to need it for third class."

"Eh, his loss. You know how he is anyway. I'm sure he won't care." She closed her locker and headed off to second class.

I shrugged my shoulder and shoved his book back into the bottom of my locker. I gathered the rest of my things, the hallways were beginning to quiet down, I knew my passing time was waning. Hurriedly, I stood, firmly holding my books in hand, and turned directly into an oncoming passerby. "I'm so sorry," I offered shaking the blood rush from my head and my newly jumbled disposition. I studied him for a moment, I did not know his face immediately. "I'm sorry, I wasn't paying attention."

"No, I should have been watching where I was going," he said as he looked around. His deep blue eyes scanned the hallway as he studied his position, "I have to be honest; I have no idea where I am."

His statement struck me oddly, "Riversid…"

He did his best to hide his contempt, "No, I understand that I'm at school," he said slightly annoyed. "I can't find room 232," he turned back to me quickly startling me. I was staring at his thick, dark black hair, which contrasted against his pale skin.

I studied his face awkwardly for a moment, he had a familiar likeness to him. I'm not sure what it was, but something set off in my memory, I just couldn't pinpoint it. "Sorry, first day?" He answered my inquiry by nodding his head. I stood next to him and looked at his class schedule. 232 World History with Mr. Hansic was his next class. "Follow me, we're

31

going to the same place. But hurry!" The two of us navigated through the stragglers in the hallway hurriedly. We took a quick right into an intersecting hallway and swung into the fifth classroom on the left just as the bell rang.

"Thank you for joining us today, Mr. Blake," Mr. Hansic dryly remarked. "And your friend?" he asked grumpily. I never understood why Mr. Hansic continued to teach. He was 71 years old, more than old enough to retire, why wouldn't he just do it and put future generations out of their misery? Then again, I always postulated that it was the misery of his students that kept him alive.

"New kid?" I offered as I shuffled to my seat.

"Your name, son?"

The tall, pale, dark-haired young man scanned the crowd of students in attendance of the class. "Jack," he said turning his stare back to Mr. Hansic.

Mr. Hansic did his best to put a faint smile on his face, "well Jack, welcome. I suspect that you will be able to find us on time tomorrow. For now, why don't you sit wherever you like." Mr. Hansic said as he turned back to the board to continue his lecture on the Spanish Inquisition that he had started the day prior.

The young man took the vacant seat next to mine and leaned over, "you could have warned me what I was getting into..." he chuckled. I laughed at his remark, "what was your name?" he asked.

"Mr. Blake?" Mr. Hansic commanded my attention, of which I gave him quickly. "I do suggest you pay attention, after your last test score, I doubt you can afford not to." Mr. Hansic was good at making a student feel inches tall. I didn't speak the rest of the class. I fell into a haze, a daydream that commanded me.

———

"Written word shall come to pass. Veracity behind the Home of the One shall be revealed. Like the flow of water, the stream of time is endless. Her crying soul will bear anger unto the ground, whilst the fires will rage; breathing and taking life. The stars will shine down from the heavens and light the way for the most righteous. The four were borne to protect him. The ten were borne to deliver him. The Shepherds of Eternal Light will grace the child, and the Keeper of the Lighthouse will know the truth of Life and Death; paradox.

She, kissed with sight, will ignite the beacon and bring finality to deception. Without the Two, there cannot be the One. And so it is in the End as it was in the Beginning.

And so it is."

———

The bell brought the class back to attention; it jarred both Jack and myself from our deep slumbers we had achieved during lecture.

"Don't forget, your papers are due this week. No late papers, no exceptions!" Mr. Hansic yelled above the scrambling crowd of students as we hurriedly exited his room intermingled amongst our peers.

Jack followed closely behind me as we left. "So, he's like that...*everyday*?" he asked scared for my response.

"Painfully so," I explained. We walked down the hallway to the intersection again, and I turned for the direction of my locker leaving Jack awkwardly behind. I turned to him, "when I looked at your schedule earlier, I think I saw that you have first lunch. I do too, you are more than welcome to sit with me and my friends..."

"Thanks," Jack smiled.

I turned around to see my locker, and standing beside it was my brother, my carbon copy. "Finally, my brother!"

Jack's perception of the world around him came crashing down. Everything stood on end for a moment as he saw me hustle towards my locker to speak with my identical twin brother, Deavon. "Your brother?" he whispered incredulously. His grip on reality was slipping from beneath him. "Joshua, what have you done?"

***

Tuesday – 14
Joycelyn Blake

"You have tampered with destiny," his voice cut into my mother's trance. She ignored his intrusion and continued to wipe down the counter. She was dressed for work in her tweed skirt and a white blouse. She was just tidying up before the clock approached 11:30AM when she would have to depart for the office.

It currently read: 11:24AM.

"The things of which you are trying to accomplish by your ruse will all be in vain, Ma'lady."

34

"You speak with such absolution," my mother still did not pay his presence any attention. She threw the dishrag into the sink, and proceeded to the edge of the counter where her purse was perched. She buried her right hand into it to search for her lipstick. Groping every compartment, she finally found it at the bottom, near her keys.

"Destiny clearly dictates…"

"Do *not* speak to me about what destiny dictates," her tone was point blank. "You have not seen…"

"…that which you have seen, Ma'lady. I understand, and I do not dispute that." He interrupted her. He put his hand on her back to show her that he was not there to antagonize her.

My mother recoiled at his touch, "Then please do not try to patronize me with what you think you understand. What we have done here may provide a chance for the future." She was trying ever so desperately to hold back tears in her delivery.

"Ma'lady, He will be the End. What you have done cannot change that fact."

"No, I suppose, in that, you are correct. But what we have done can possibly make it better. Now, if you'll excuse me, I have a date…" my mother smacked her lips after having applied her lipstick and tossed it into her purse. Grabbing both her purse and her keys she proceeded out of the kitchen and toward the garage.

"A date? With?" He asked.

My mother stopped at the doorway leading into the foyer and formal dining and living rooms. Turning around, she finally dignified his presence with validation. She stared at him, at the tall, pale, dark haired boy. She stared at Jack; at The

Shepherd. An ironic smile curled onto her lips, "I think you know the answer to that question."

***

Tuesday − 14

Deavon Blake

"You smell like smoke," I coughed as my brother sat down next to me at our lunch table.

He responded to my anti-smoking demonstration by flashing me a curt smile. My own curt smile. Our own curt smile. He was, we were identical—he was identical to me. Nearly eighteen years prior, by a narrow window of 1.57 minutes I had beaten my brother out of the womb to be the eldest of the two of us.

Doctors had always marveled at our uncanny likeness. From our height, our weight to the way our hair crowned and even the way our eyes changed color when we were angry. In the deepest reaches of our brains, we knew how different we were from one another, but outwardly the difference was merely attitudinal. For whatever reason, Deavon craved rebellion, which I believed was simply just a ploy for more attention.

"You look like shit," Deavon finally retaliated.

"You're about ten minutes too late on that one," I sarcastically remarked dismissing his insult. Clecha sat down at the vacant seat next to me.

"How was Hansic today?"

I shot her a look, "How do you think?"

36

"I don't know why that guy doesn't like you so much…" she started.

"There he is!" I said scanning the crowd of students in the cafeteria. I had finally spotted the tall, pale, dark-haired boy, Jack. He was looking in every which way taking in the stimulus. I raised my hand and waved him down.

"Who's that?" Clecha perked up and started to adjust her curls.

I caught on, and sneered at her, "the reason Hansic didn't rip my head off earlier."

Jack saw me motioning for him, and happily started in our direction. As he walked to our table, his view became unobstructed, and he realized that the table contained both my brother and myself. His movement suddenly became more cautious, and he approached our table with haste, taking a seat staring back and forth between my brother and I.

I smiled and offered an introduction awkwardly, "Guys, this is…"

"Jack," He said extending his hand to each Clecha and my brother. "I'm a transfer student," his hand was clammy.

"Oh, a transfer student? From where?" Clecha asked flipping her hair off of her left shoulder.

I looked over at Clecha and tried to choke down my revulsion at her blatant display of flirtation with Jack. I chuckled to myself, apparently audibly enough for Clecha to shoot me a glance with scrunched up eyebrows. "Uhm, yeah, Jack, where did you transfer from?" I tried to legitimize her question.

He ignored the tension that Clecha and I were building, and stared at my brother who was unaware of Jack's gaze. "Oh

37

you know, out there…" little by little each sound echoed in Jack's ear, color rushed back into the world and finally he snapped back to reality. "Uhm, out there on the West Coast," he turned his attention away from my brother. "Yeah, my, uh, parents…my dad just got a new job here."

I chuckled again, "let me guess…The Blake Genetic Industry?"

"So you've heard of it?" He smiled acknowledging the fact that he understood the connection between my last name and the name of his "parent's" employer.

"Only a time or two…" I lifted my soda to my mouth to take a sip. Just as it reached my mouth, someone knocked into me from behind, causing me to spill the brown liquid down my sweater vest. I turned my annoyed attention at the perpetrator and watched as Angelica Johnson hurried away through the rows of tables. "Fucking Bitch," while I did not often indulge in such language, there were certain occasions that I always felt warranted it. Angelica Johnson was one of those occasions. I grabbed some napkins from the center of the table and began to pat the soda from my vest.

"Angel! Wait up!" My brother yelled after her.

She turned around and acknowledged my brother, "c'mon!" she screamed over the cafeteria buzz.

Deavon, Clecha and I turned back to the table, we were all astonished to see that Jack was no longer sitting at our table, "nice friend of yours," he said patting me on the shoulder. He got up taking his tray of leftover food with him.

"I'm telling mom and dad." I proclaimed annoyed.

"Do it," he shrugged walking away to join her and likely sneak a cigarette before next class.

"Damn delinquents."

"She really hates you," Clecha remarked of Angelica.

"No, she really hates *you*, she just hates me by association...I wonder where Jack went?" I said looking around the cafeteria trying to spot him to no avail.

Clecha shrugged her shoulders, "why was your brother in such a hurry after her?"

"He's been smoking."

"Ah. Well, I will be sure to keep my eyes peeled to see the explosion at your house when you tell your parents." She grabbed her tray and made her way from the table over to the trash. I stayed behind to continue wiping the soda from my clothing.

*

I was correct in assuming the motivation behind my brother's sudden departure with Angelica Johnson—of whom most knew as "Angel"—of whom I would never personally address as such. The two of them walked out of the front door to our school, and took a right out of the door, taking cover behind one of the six columns stretching down. "I only have one left, we're going to have to share," Angel said igniting the cigarette in her mouth.

He took a seat, back perched against the furthest column from the door. He stared off as a light gust of wind passed his face. Angel finally nudged him. My brother broke his trance and looked up, she was holding the cigarette down for him to take.

He grabbed it and took a soothing drag. "Sorry," he offered. He rubbed his eyes sleepily.

"Tired?"

He smiled staring blankly, "mmhmm," he hummed affirmation to her inquiry while taking another drag, and handing it back off to her. He wanted so badly to speak to an understanding soul. He hadn't slept. He had slept, but he hadn't dreamt. Not in weeks. He closed his eyes and instead of painting curiosity into his unconsciousness, he only experienced darkness. Angel was not the kind of friend he would confide that sort of information to. At least, she hadn't been, but recently Deavon saw her in a different light. His heart raced when she was around. She drew his attention almost immediately.

"*Here.*" She reiterated annoyed. Deavon looked up taking the cigarette again. He opened his mouth to speak, to reveal his suffering, when suddenly she interrupted him. "It's yours, I gotta go."

"Bye," Deavon said waving her off emptily as she scampered away.

Seconds passed, "Ahem, Mr. Blake," his voice caught my brother off guard. His eyes widened, but he did not really care for the gravity of the situation. He knew that standing behind him was the Dean of Students, Dr. Foreman. He could not be concerned with such trivial concepts as petty crime; something tribal was beating inside of him. The beat carried him away.

***

Tuesday – 14
Nathan S. Thomas

"I was beginning to think that you were actually staying for sixth and seventh class for once," he smugly remarked as Angel approached her ruby red car. Nathan was leaning against the passenger side door with his aviator sunglasses on shielding his eyes from the dimming sunlight. Clouds were beginning to roll in from the West.

She expelled a sigh of laughter, "right." She ripped open her car door, not having locked it, and reached over to pull the small tab locking the passenger door. Nathan climbed in as he did most days and the two of them sped off from campus to find a new adventure.

Angel reached into her middle console pulling from it a half empty pack of menthol cigarettes—her emergency pack. She pulled a single smoke from the pack and offered another to Nathan. He refused. He always refused. Rolling down his window, Nathan attempted to take in a full breath that wasn't tainted by the irritant second-hand smoke.

The two of them zipped through town uncaringly, ignoring the tension that still existed between them. Nathan still found himself longing to be a part of Angel's life; longing to be with her. Deep down, he had an unconscious understanding that things would likely never be the same. Something seemed different to him lately. Finality. Things seemed ending. Everything simply ending; he still continued to cling to that which seemed real to him, even when it wasn't.

He was born to Samuel and Sandra Thomas. They had had him late in life, not expecting to ever have children. He was a surprise, one that his parents did not understand they needed until he appeared in their lives. In their late 50's, they were at least ten years (if not fifteen) older than my own parents.

My father and Samuel Thomas were friends of sorts. Samuel never worked for my father, but he often worked *with* my father. He was the guy that everyone jokes about, the Aerospace Engineer—he was literally a rocket scientist.

Well, he *had* been. He had retired from his work in avionics years prior, and now worked as a flying instructor part time. He often took Nathan into the sky, using the experience to teach Nathan to understand the weight of risk, and the benefit of faith.

Nathan did indeed admire his father for the many lessons that he had taught him, but he also felt the distance of tradition that was so deeply engrained in his father. Samuel believed in the credence buried in tradition, while Nathan believed in the spontaneity of improvisation. Nothing that Nathan did had a rhyme or reason to it, other than his actions might possibly benefit him in the future. Samuel disapproved the view his son had taken on about the world. He had many plans for his son, but Nathan would have nothing to do with it.

Dreams of the father. Sins of the father. It was all the same to Nathan. Sandra had always kept the peace between the tensions instilled between the two of them, but she, as anyone else who knew them, understood that they had a deep respect and love for one another. As a stay at home mother, she fueled Nathan's craving to create, rather than conform and often reminded her husband that Nathan was destined for great things no matter his outlook on life. She was a dedicated woman. To her husband. To her child. To her family. To clarity.

In our childhood, Nathan and I did not click with one another. He, like my brother, had a more rebellious side, which is why I'm sure they grew to be such great friends. For years we had thrived on antagonizing one another, but now we understood as young adults that the conventions of which we were protesting as children no longer held validation. We simply existed alongside one another, and that was good enough.

"Where are we going?" Nathan asked as he watched the streets pass by paying them no attention.

"This adventure is already boring me," she took her sunglasses off, and threw them into a cup holder. The clouds had overcast the sky so quickly that she no longer needed them. Sprinkles of water fell sparsely upon her windshield as she pressed on. "I can take you home."

"HA!" Nathan laughed obnoxiously. "And face Samuel Thomas? No thanks. Just take me to Nick's." He slumped down in his seat as he watched the street turn darker shades of gray from the rain that was beginning to pick up.

"Nick's it is," she said mindlessly continuing on her path. She took a series of several rights in order to make a complete loop in order to head back in the direction of Riverside Estates. Passing the school again, she pulled up just a block or so away at the gates. "End of the line," she said coming to a stop and looking over at Nathan.

"You're not even going to take me to his house?" He asked.

"And how do you expect me to do that with the gates closed? I don't have all day to wait around for him to open them up, and you are the one that wanted to come here. You figure it out!"

"Look, he gave me the new gate code last week. Just wait here, and I'll go punch it in, and then you can drive me up to his house."

She looked at him annoyed, "fine," she reluctantly agreed.

He unstrapped his seatbelt, got out of the car, and slammed the door so it would shut. As he ran up to the gate code box, he heard Angel zipping away behind him. He turned around to confirm that she was gone, and saw as she sped off down the street. "Fucking Bitch," he exclaimed. Trudging back to the gate code box, he punched in: 2424-6425. The gates swung open, allowing him to enter. He stood at the mouth of the housing development to which Clecha, Nicholas and myself belonged. Standing in front of all of the grandiose houses always made him feel insignificant. Pressing along, he continued through the winding streets that constructed our development until he found himself upon an unsuspecting, and quite less threatening blue house. Now wet enough to make him annoyed, he approached the house surreptitiously and jumped over the fence enclosing the backyard.

Stomping up the few steps onto the wooden back patio, he approached the sliding glass doors. He placed his right hand on the handle, placing his thumb strategically at the top of the handle. For a moment a buzzing sound emitted from the door, and then with a click the door fell limp and unlocked. He slid the door opened and entered. "Honey? I'm home!" He proclaimed boisterously. He slid the door closed behind him, and heard another click as the door locked.

There was no response. There was never any response. It was always quiet in Nicholas's house. Nathan browsed about the kitchen looking for anything that might be enjoyable for him to eat. He treated this house as his own after having known Nicholas for so long. "I know you're here!" He yelled. Still no response.

He walked out of the kitchen and into the front living room looking out of the bay window. The rain was starting to pour harder. He persisted up the stairs following his instincts. He kicked open the door to the first room on the left only to find Nicholas buried in books at his desk as words projected on his walls swam about. Without a beat Nicholas turned around to stare at Nathan, the intruder. "I do not know how you keep managing to get in here..." He said raising his right eyebrow. He was wearing his reading goggles—which magnified his eyes so unfortunately.

"Are you ever going to give those things a rest?" Nathan asked laughing at Nicholas's magnified eyes.

"Are you ever going to start knocking?' Nicholas rebutted.

"I'm sure I have no idea what you are talking about," Nathan plopped down on Nicholas's bed. He *did* have an idea what Nicholas was talking about, but always managed to skate right passed it. He had learned new and trickier ways to reprogram the bioscan locks at the Peterson household. Their locks were based on previously recorded and stored details of their fingerprints. With the help of his father, Nathan had learned just enough about computers to be dangerous. He reprogrammed the computer to allow for four occupants, himself included among the Peterson's, thus giving him access to their house at his own free will. He never abused the power—almost never. "TV," he said. The projections of scrambled words swimming across the walls were replaced with a user guide detailing the lineup of shows, live or recorded, in the television library. He began to scroll through the options.

"Don't you have a TV at your own house to watch?" Nicholas asked having turned his attention back to his studies.

"There's nothing good ever on..." Nathan started.

There was a knock at the front door.

***

Tuesday – 14

Sixth class had, until recently, always been my least favorite of the day. It was gym, which in my earlier years was simply just an hour-long tribute to those who could do a pull-up. Now, thankfully, they had begun to diversify physical education programs and offered sports that more thoroughly catered to my abilities. The previous year as a Junior I had enrolled in Martial Arts and began to excel at it now in my fourth consecutive semester enrolled.

Standing in stances was meditative. I convened with the muscles in my body and begged more out of each of them. The

46

class brought me to center, and helped me focus my own anxieties. Low block, low block, high block, high block, punch and punch. Low spear, low spear, knife hand, knife hand, palm, palm, ridge-hand followed by ridge-hand. Over and over again, the feeling was operatic. It made me feel small, yet connected to something greater at the same time.

Piano played in the background, ballet moved through me. Movement, connection, separation, clarity. Each movement, with purpose. Each stance with commitment. "Hee-yah!" I channel and expel. Inhale, followed by exhale. Low block, low block, high block, high block, punch and punch.

Right in the face.

Disturbing reality.

Time slows down.

And in the silence, all that can be heard is that of her cry.

***

Tuesday – 14

Joycelyn Blake

My mother made her way into her tall stone office building. There were forty-seven floors, of which she worked at the top. After fifteen years in her career she had worked her way up the corporate ladder to become the Director of Affairs at the largest health insurance company in the country. With my father as an ally, the two companies prospered together in medical research. She straightened her white blouse, and brushed the pleats in her tweed skirt. "Good Afternoon Amanda," my mother addressed the brunette at the front desk in the marble filled entrance at the welcome center.

"Joycelyn, it's a pleasure to see you today," Amanda greeted my mother warmly.

My mother smiled and continued by the welcome center and onto the large elevators. Her pulse began to jump slightly in her veins, and she could feel the anxiety pitting in her stomach. As her elevator arrived to deliver her, she let out a lonely tear. With haste she entered and selected her floor. "I do not have much more time," she said these words out loud matter-of-factly, but did not wholeheartedly embrace them. The bounds of her own mortality crept up upon her for the first time in some time. She smiled as she began to finally understand, *"Veracity behind the Home of the One shall be revealed..."* the doors opened, arriving at the top floor.

The office was a flurry of activity. She peered out the wall comprised of floor to ceiling windows just opposite the elevator. Looking out she admired the view of downtown that her office had to offer her. The cubicles were all filled with eager agents, hell-bent on carrying out the slightest whim of my mother. However, instead of radiating discipline and determination today, my mother simply radiated with life.

Each step off of the elevator was even heavier than the last. The ringing phones pounded through her head, the rustling of papers etched into her skin, and the incessant ramblings of her employees made her nauseous. "Joycelyn, I was worried about you!" A rather large woman approached my mother as she tried to dash for her office.

"Just a busy morning," my mother uneasily laughed off the interaction. She pushed passed the woman and down the walkway to her private corner office. Resting her hand on the doorknob, her heart skipped a beat. She pushed through with all of her might, closed the door behind her and leaned against it for support as her legs buckled beneath her. She balled her fists and then stretched them back out, continuing on by wiping the sweat that was dripping from her forehead. Her head began to pound. She had not felt a tension quite like this in nearly a lifetime. There was something quite different about this circumstance—about this day.

"Written word shall come to pass," the voice came from my mother's desk chair. The back of the chair was facing my mother, obscuring the vision of who it was taunting her. "Those are the words she spoke, were they not?" My mother took note of the familiarity in the voice of the stranger; something was so strikingly familiar about it.

"What do you want?" My mother pleaded. Her chest heaved with every breath she tried to muster. Her vision began to blur slightly as her head pounded ever so heavily against itself.

"I think we both know what I want, Joycelyn. Where is he?"

A drop of blood trickled from my mother's nose and landed on her hand glowing an ever-beautiful light. "I'll never tell," she gritted between her teeth.

"Oh, I think you will." The chair turned around slowly, and sinisterly. My mother coughed in the corner, trying to take a complete breath; she summoned her strength to focus her eyes enough to identify the intruder. She gasped when her eyes caught glimpse of herself sitting in her seat; a complete carbon copy of my mother. The vision of my mother was wearing a white flowing dress, while her long curly brown hair surrounded her face. The vision, the ghost, the reflection of my mother stared back with an ominous glare.

"How dare you take my image," my mother cried.

"How dare you try to defy me," my mother's twin stood from the chair and crossed in front of the desk, making its way to my mother. She knelt down, so they were face to face with one another. "You have seen that which I desire. You, and you alone know how it will end. And I simply cannot have that."

Mortal terror filled my mother in this moment.

Sitting as an unsuspecting audience were dozens of interns and agents in the mass of cubicles outside of my mother's office. Among the many soulless drones scurrying about the floor was the calm and collected Loren Johnson. She sat at her desk, fielding a phone call from the Central Health Complex to dispute an improperly filed charge. As terror struck throughout my mother, through the spread of a sick sense of empathy, the same terror filled Loren Johnson. She froze in her seat, ignoring the rant of the accounting executive on the line opposite her. Loren carefully reached up to take off her headset and set it down on her desk, failing to disconnect the line. The executive on the other end was unaware of her sudden retreat from the conversation and continued to lament on about hospital standards and practices when it came to accounting. He was completely unaware of the events about ready to transpire.

My mother continued to struggle against her imposter in her office. The sinister twin of hers had her pinned by the shoulders against her door and attempting to peer deep within my mother's eyes. She could barely feel anything other than the sting of pain reverberating throughout her body.

Desperately flailing, my mother reached into her purse, clawing for her contingency plan. Upon grasping the handle with as much force as she could stand, my mother withdrew one of our kitchen knives from the bag with her left hand.

Her twin looked at the instrument, and laughed with a sigh of futility, "you cannot harm me with such conventional methods. You should know that by now..." her twin screamed.

My mother did in fact know what her twin was insinuating. The knife would never hurt this apparition, but the knife was not meant for her likeness, it was meant for her self. "I'm sorry, Joshua," she whispered. She whipped the knife across the air and sliced off much of the palm of her right hand. She screamed in horror and pain as the blood gushed from her self-inflicted wound.

Screaming, beautiful, white light illuminated from the pouring life force of my mother. It filled her office, crashing through the windows, and igniting the downtown skyline.

Her sinister twin recoiled at the display of light and screeched as the flesh of her reflection began to melt away. The color drained from my mother's eyes and the light flowing from her own blood began to intensify. Her twin had evaporated in a smoke-like effect, but she was too far-gone to stop now.

She stood, having gained her strength. Others had begun to gather outside of her office as they heard the struggle ensue inside. They peered at the threshold of the door as light poured out of it. Loren Johnson finally stood from her desk, and turned to face my mother's office. She stood calm, cool, collected, behind her scurrying officemates. She knew better.

The door exploded in front of them, and blew them all back away from my mother. Light continued to pour from her veins as she walked slowly from the office understanding her part in this farce.

"Written word shall come to pass..." My mother's voice was deeper than normal. It commanded silence, respect and wisdom. "Veracity behind the Home of the One shall be revealed. Like the flow of water, the stream of time is endless..."

Loren stood there, tears streaming from her stoic face, "Her crying soul will bear anger unto the ground, whilst the fires will rage; breathing and taking..."

"Life." My mother continued. "The stars will shine down from the heavens and light the way for the most righteous." All words they had heard before, but had yet to fully understand. All words my mother now fully knew.

"And so it is." Loren cried. She raised her hands as those around her gathered to watch. With great reluctance lightning struck from Loren's hands, lashing my mother brutally. The top floor of the office building exploded outward spewing debris and bodies for blocks. Loren dropped her hands, ending the stream of lightning. She fell to her knees in horror, asking for forgiveness.

My mother reached her hand upwards toward the sky, and as she did so, the light flowed from her body and into the darkness. It was as if her essence was being given to the storm-filled skies. Dark clouds began to converge on my mother's office building, and as the light poured from her mortal body, everything ignited in rage. Lightning struck down from the clouds furiously onto the grounds below dispersing panic and reigning destruction amongst the growing crowds.

"I vowed I would try," Loren said staring at my mother, and regaining her stance.

"And so it is. I hope you know what you are doing, Loren," my mother's voice tenderly remarked.

"Me too." Lightning exploded from Loren's hands striking my mother yet again.

The top of the building illuminated beautifully against the backdrop of black clouds that had taken residence in the sky. My mother's white essence flowed into the sky, cascading violently through the many thick layers of clouds that descended upon the region.

Loren let out a final whimper as her body was consumed by lightning. The top of the building exploded, sending either woman in the opposite direction. As they graced the concrete

with force their bodies lay miraculously unbeaten, but severely changed.

The rain picked up.

***

Tuesday – 14
Joshua Blake

My father sat at his desk, on the other side of downtown, when a sudden wave of emotion overcame him. It was unlike any he had felt in some time. He turned his chair around to face the window, looked passed the storm clouds gathering, and peered across the skyline at my mother's office building. He pressed his hands against the glass, and as he did, he saw the top of the building explode in white light. His body tensed, "written word shall come to pass," his eyes widened.

"Sir Blake," Jack said standing behind my father.

My father jumped, "very few people have the capacity to sneak up on me like you." They stood awkwardly for a moment, my father trying to regain his composure before facing Jack. "I did not expect this for some time."

"I know, I hope that I am not out of line, sir."

"No," my father finally faced him, "of course not."

"Sir, I am afraid that the time has come."

My father stared passed Jack, passed reality and simply replied with: "it has always been here." He sat down at his desk and looked around at the contents of his office with tear-filled eyes. "You understand that I will continue to do everything in my power to stop this, correct?" My father nearly scolded him.

"Of course, Sir. But I can almost guarantee that it will not be enough."

"No," my father loosened his tie a touch, "I don't suppose so." He stood and walked towards his office door, passing Jack. He put his hand on the knob, "but I at least have to try." He ripped the door open and ran out of his office. He was off to retrieve his most precious possessions.

"Of course, Sir…" Jack replied to the emptiness.

***

Tuesday – 14
Deavon Blake

"Are you still with me, Mr. Blake?" Dr. Foreman was interrogating my brother whom he had just caught with a cigarette on school grounds. This act was of course forbidden for anyone, especially someone who was just shy of the age eighteen. Deavon did not stir from his empty stare. "You're not even listening to me!" Dr. Foreman exclaimed in anger.

For once in my brother's life, he was legitimately an accessory—a pawn in Angel's scheme. And while his accessory status may have been truth, language escaped my brother in this moment, leaving him defenseless. Many things failed both he and I in this moment. His eyes moved from Dr. Foreman's desk and shifted to the clock above his bald head, it read: 1:01pm. "Sixth Class. It's going to rain." He unconsciously whispered.

The sound of lightning cracked behind Dr. Foreman, causing him to startle. Thunder followed, rumbling the ground; it had stricken closely. Dr. Foreman turned around in his desk chair to peer out the window. Rain dumped from the sky above suddenly which caused him to recoil in fear. He turned back to face my brother and studied his empty features. Scrunching his eyes in worry, he changed his tone and addressed my brother again, "astute." Dr. Foreman's secretary walked in moments later cutting the tension. She handed him a piece of paper with writing on it, and whispered into his ear. He turned to look at her incredulously for a split-second, and then brought his attention back to my brother, "if you'll excuse us, Mr. Blake, please take a seat out in reception." He said dismissing my brother.

Deavon sat there lifeless for another moment, as he regained the ability to move, he stood to leave. Before exiting, he turned back to Dr. Foreman and his secretary, "my brother, he's in gym with Instructor Lynnadon. I'm sure you will be needing him as well."

Dr. Foreman turned his head from his secretary to confront my brother. He bore the same incredulous look onto my brother's shocked face, "of course." My brother did as he was instructed and exited the office to take a seat in reception.

Lightning cracked in the background.

***

Tuesday – 14
Angelica Johnson

Angel zoomed away from Riverside Estates and set course for home after leaving Nathan high and dry. As she progressed home, she noticed that the clouds were growing darker and darker, sprinkles of rain turned into pellets of rain quickly. She pulled her red car up to her house and turned off the ignition bringing an end to the roar of the car. She slammed the car door and scampered up the walkway to her front door. As she approached the door she entered the code on the security pad: 1016. She placed her hand on the doorknob, allowing it to secretly read her finger prints; the door unlocked.

As she pushed the door open, she looked over at her elderly neighbor's house next to her. She noticed the senile woman sticking out of her door waving to her. Angel did not take her waves to be anything more than a welcome rather than a warning. "Hi Mrs. Kelloway!" Angel yelled trying to offer appeasement to the woman. She walked into her house and slammed the door behind her. "Mom?" She asked just trying to verify her solitude. When there was no response she ran to her room and lit a cigarette, bringing it back out to the kitchen. She rifled through the previous day's mail, and realized that her coffee from the morning prior was still sitting in the thermos on the counter she had left it in. She picked up the thermos and walked over to the sink to dump it out.

A knock at the front door startled her, and she dropped the thermos in the sink. She grabbed the lit cigarette from her mouth taking a drag just prior. Exhaling, she spoke, "be right there!" she stowed her lit cigarette in her left hand, and opened the door with her right just enough to stick her head out. "Mrs. Kelloway, I don't have..." she stopped immediately realizing that the knock did not belong to her senile next-door neighbor. Instead there was an ominous middle-aged man standing at her door. "Oh," she said taken aback, "I'm sorry. What can I help you with?"

He stood there for a moment silently and smiled, "may I borrow a moment of your time?"

She smiled at him, "I believe you already have." She was trying to discern where she had seen his face before.

"Then may I borrow a few more?" he shoved his way into her home knocking her down onto the cold laminate floor. He shut the door behind him, and she shuddered in terror as her vision began to blur. Her cigarette had whipped out of her hand in the commotion, and lay lit in the distance. She looked up at the man horrified.

"Whhh...wha...who are you?" she shuddered.

"You don't recognize me?" he made several steps closer to her.

"Should I?" she asked, scooting herself back on the floor, trying to make her way to the kitchen. There she could possibly grab a chicken tenderizer, or a butcher's knife, anything to beat the menacing man with.

"That hurts, sweetheart," he said bending down to her and looking at her closely. His eyes were black as night. He reached out in front of him and snatched her neck. Bringing her terrified face close to his he growled, "Where is your mother?"

She looked at him through the side of her left eye as he pushed his face against hers, "woor..." she tried to whistle the word out but was terrified. She swallowed, and repeated, "work."

The man sighed heavily, "tell me, child...what is thy name?" He asked poetically.

"What?" Her face was turning red.

"*For the bastard child will bear the name of the messenger.* Now, what is your name?" He hissed again.

"Don't," his courageous voice barked into the tension.

Angel diverted her glare from her left periphery to that of her right. There was another, she tried to make out his likeness. "Who...?" she quivered; the sinister man grabbed her and stood her up. He was using her to shield him, putting her in a headlock to face the new intruder standing at the door. Her eyes rested upon him, and a flash of memory exploded through her mind.

Standing before them was the tall, pale, dark-haired boy, Jack. "You," the menacing man started, "do not belong here," he finished between his teeth.

"Funny, I could say the same of you," in a flash of light a sword appeared in Jack's hands. "Do you know this man?" Jack asked Angel.

She shook her head trembling in fear. "Of course you do," he turned his mouth to her ear and ever softly whispered, "I'm your father."

"You are *not* her father," Jack said drawing closer.

The prospect of this man being her father fascinated her. He let go of her face, and she turned around to face him. She stared him in the eyes, trying to decipher his truth, all the while getting lost in abyss.

"You…?" She asked.

"Now, what is your name my child?" He asked caressing her face familiarly. She had felt such a touch before, and suddenly trusted this man.

"She is not your child," Jack screamed raising his sword in fury.

"Angel," she whispered.

The man claiming to be her father smiled in glory. His black eyes ignited in rage as they pulsated red. Angel began to feel chaos and terror. Jack plunged his sword through the intruder's head. "What I thought…" the man smiled and exploded.

***

Tuesday – 14
Nathan Thomas & Nicholas Peterson

"Expecting visitors?" Nathan asked in response to the knock at the front door.

Nicholas turned from his studies again and looked first at Nathan and then at the door to his room. "No," he said confused.

There was not another knock, not another warning, the door simply came down. "The fuck?" Nathan proclaimed. The two of them ran out to the hallway and looked down the stairs at the two men standing in the living room.

"Dad?" Nicholas asked.

"Dad?!" Nathan exploded in defense, "what are you doing here? I mean to say…what are you doing here? Wait no, what am I doing here? I'm supposed to be at school! I uhhh…uhm…what are you doing here?" Nathan was terrified and confused.

"No time!" Nathan's father retaliated.

"What's going on?" Nicholas asked amidst the commotion.

Both Nicholas and Nathan resembled their own fathers. Guthrie Peterson was just as tall, skinny and nerdy looking as his son, and Nathan was just a younger, handsome, less heavy version of his short father.

"Nicholas, we're leaving!"

"Where are we going?" Nick asked as both he and Nathan made their way down the stairs to their fathers.

"Nowhere, if I have anything to say about it," the four of them turned to the open doorway. As soon as he stepped into the house his face came into focus. The man standing before them was my father...or at least someone claiming to be. Lightning cracked behind them.

"Joshua?" Samuel Thomas asked.

"That's not Joshua," Guthrie Peterson responded.

"Astute," my father's emanation said raising his left brow casually.

"Get behind me son," Nicholas's father commanded as he crowded both he and Nathan behind Samuel and himself.

"Now, Guthrie...don't you trust me?" My father's impersonator asked Guthrie Peterson mocking the situation.

"I think we both know the answer to that."

"And you, Samuel?" he asked turning to Nathan's father.

Samuel smiled and let out a little laugh, "you should have just given up."

"If that's not Mr. Blake, who is it?" Nicholas whispered behind his father.

A pink light exploded in front of Guthrie Peterson and Samuel Thomas, separating the ground between them and my father's imposter. The light blinded both Nicholas and Nathan temporarily, but Guthrie and Samuel had seen this light before. As things came back to focus, a woman stood before them. Her skin was tanned and her hair was pulled back in a wide ponytail of pink dreadlocks. She donned a white skin-tight suit and stood awkwardly between the two factions.

"Amalya, how nice of you to join us." My father's evil twin snidely remarked.

She turned her face away from him and back to Guthrie and Samuel. Her red eyes glared back at them. They burned not with anger and rage, but rather with compassion. "Grab your sons," She exclaimed.

"Who..." Nathan could not even complete his inquiry. He was startled by the firm grasp from his father as everything came crashing down around him.

Guthrie and Samuel offered their free hands out, and the woman with pink hair grabbed them. "Sorry to leave so soon," she remarked. The five of them exploded in light.

"No!" my father's apparition jumped for them to no avail. He landed on the bare floor and picked himself back up. He looked around, his face cracking, his eyes firey with rage. "NO!" He screeched as loud as he could. All of the glass in the house shattered, and he disappeared in a smoke like effect.

***

Tuesday — 14
Joshua Blake

The three of us did not speak many words. My father did not speak many words to Dr. Foreman. I remember that I was standing in back stance. I think I had my hands up around my head, in some sort of block. I saw Dr. Foreman's secretary make her way into the studio. I smiled, for I knew she was after me. Something inside of my being yearned for her to find me, like a needle in a haystack.

We walked down the hallway back to the offices in silence. She knew as much as I did. Which was not much, simply tragedy. When we convened with my brother in the office, I could sense his despair. We did not console each other. We did not hold each other. We simply existed in the same space; he in mortal terror, me in quiet revelation. When our father arrived, instead of running to him for answers or for comfort, we simply stood and joined him.

He looked at Dr. Foreman and his secretary through worn eyes, and simply said to them, "I'm taking my sons." He grabbed each of our shoulders, trying to hold on to his own sense of reality.

"Of course," Dr. Foreman did not even put up a fight.

The three of us walked in out silence, and headed to my father's car, which was parked haphazardly in the fire lane at the front of the school. He laughed uneasily at the prospect of a ticket for parking in the wrong spot. He understood the truth.

The rain had picked up considerably. While I understood the gravity of the situation, it was almost as though my brother and father had exchanged information without words and left me out. Both of their blank stares weighed them down heavily. The silence was deafening, and while I had no true idea of what was going on, I knew somehow that it concerned my mother.

"It wasn't supposed to rain today." I simply said aloud as my father put the car in drive and sped away.

His driving was erratic; it did not match his stoic exterior. It was as if some other force was guiding us to where we needed to be. Weaving in and out of the cars, we raced toward the heart of downtown, the Central Health Complex. I turned my attention from the road in front of us to the unsuspecting passersby in the cars around us. A woman speaking to herself with such passion, I surmised that she was instead singing.

I never had really paid much attention to others as they drove in this manner. The act was fluid, built in, inherent. The foot pressed on the accelerator, which throttled up or down, allowing either more or less gas into the chamber, a spark, combustion, cylinder revolutions. Such a mechanism at the tip of our fingers. Another car merged onto the interstate next to us. An older and younger woman; I could tell they were fighting. My father sped passed their assaults on one another and merged into their lane taking the next exit. We had arrived, exit 10, Central Health.

It was chaos inside the hospital, more so than normal. Something had happened, something terribly grave. How had I not known? The silence of the car did not help quell my fears for what we were about to perceive. Walking in, I immediately felt a chill run down my spine.

I hate hospitals. I don't know many people who don't, other than doctors and nurses of course, but even then I have to ponder as to whether they truly enjoy them over time. You can only watch people die so many times, before it becomes a loathsome duty. The sterility of the complex left me uneasy—unfeeling. I had spent many days in my infancy and early childhood in the hospital. I was born with a defect in my immune system, which made it very easy for me to contract the simplest of sicknesses. Imagine being born out of the womb defective. Not yet able to understand the full weight of being broken, and having to triumph passed conventions such as defect.

I did triumph, narrowly. Those nights were the longest nights of my life, the nights in the hospital cribs. Every now and then, I'll get a flash of memory, which will jar me awake in slumber. That was all behind us now, with every flash, I tried harder at burying the latent memories.

We pushed passed scurrying hospital patrons, and through the screams of pain and agony. My father did not stop to speak with a doctor or nurse, or information clerk. He knew where he was going. We made our way through the crowds and to a set of ominous elevators.

The doors opened slowly, and the three of us entered the crowded machine that was to deliver us to our final destination in the sinister building. "What number?" she spoke to us.

There was an awkward silence, I nudged my father, who had been silent until this point, "Hm?" he inquired coming to attention.

"What floor number?" She asked again holding her hand over the buttons.

He sat there staring at the numbers for yet another split second, "take us to the top." My father looked at each my brother and I, putting his hands on our shoulders, "everything is going to be ok." It sounded as if he was trying to reassure himself more than us.

One by one, the elevator emptied, leaving only the three of us to exit on the top floor once it arrived at our destination. The doors opened with a whoosh, and yet another chill went down my spine. They always had the air conditioner on.

Deavon and I followed my father off of the elevator and walked closely behind him as we made our way down the hallway, to the last door of the hall. As we approached I noticed that the door was closed tightly, and standing outside of the room were two men dressed in black attire, with bulletproof vests protecting their lives. In their hands, they each displayed a firearm, ready to fire at any intruders. As we approached, the two men stood at attention, and blocked our entry.

"I'm sorry, sir. But we have been instructed to not let anyone passed this point," said one of them looking straight ahead, right through the three of us standing before him.

Off to the right in the near distance, a doctor took notice of the three of us, and hurried to our position in front of the door. "Can I be of assistance?"

My father turned his glare to the male doctor, "I am Dr. Joshua Eason Blake of the Blake Genetic Industry. I believe that you have my wife Joycelyn."

The elderly doctors eyes widened, "yes. Dr. Blake, if I may have a word with you," the doctor pressed upon my father.

"First, tell your men to stand down. My sons need to see their mother."

"I do believe that to be unwise..."

"I will be the one to dictate that which would be unwise. My sons need to see their mother," he pressed harder this time. I had never observed such an assertiveness in my father before.

The doctor peered back through his glasses uneasy. He realized that my father would not back down. "Of course." He motioned for another man off to the right in the distance to come to him. Another man dressed in black, and suited for combat approached them. "Sergeant of the Guard, please tell your men to stand down." The man did as he was told reluctantly and the two armed men standing at the door stepped aside to allow my brother and I entrance.

None of it made any sense at all.

"Dr. Blake, if you will come with me," the elderly doctor inquired after my father.

"Of course," he looked at each my brother and I and then nodded his head toward the door indicating he wanted to us to see our mother. Staying behind, he knew he was going to be interrogated about my mother's condition.

The beeps. I can't forget the beeps. They still haunt me now. Beep...followed by silence and then another dull beep. They echo through my dormant mind, bouncing off each other and beeping every more. My mother looked like an angel, still as night. I didn't cry, I was close, but I was strong enough to hold emotion back. There was a machine: inhale, followed by exhale.

She had a few scrapes, bumps and bruises and her right hand was bandaged tightly. She however, looked no more worse for the wear than someone who had maybe taken a tumble down the stairs. She certainly did not look like she had pulsated light from her mortal body, and then exploded in catastrophe striking the ground with such force.

None of that could have possibly been possible anyway.

But somehow it was.

"Mom?" I choked. Clearing my throat, I addressed her comatose body again, "mom?"

Deavon broke his vow of silence, "she can't hear you."

67

Shooting him a look that could kill, he turned away from me. I proceeded deeper into the room, so I could take a better look at my mother. Deavon stayed just in the doorway, sitting in the lone chair behind the curtain. He did not have the strength, or the will to continue further into the room.

I pulled up a chair to my mother's bedside and held her left hand as the machine continued to breathe life into her. I put my head down on our clasped hands, and let the sound of the machine carry me away into dreams.

***

Tuesday – 14
Angelica Johnson & The Shepherd, Jack

As Jack's sword dug into the man's skull, the man's menacing eyes widened with joy and fury all the same. "*What I thought,*" he whispered disturbing Angel deeply. He exploded sending Angel and Jack flying through the house in opposite directions. Angel struck the wall above the couch, and conveniently landed upon it. Jack, however sailed through the wall separating the entryway from Loren's room, and crashed on the other side of her bed.

He laid there on the floor for several minutes, allowing himself time to recover from the shock of what had just happened. This was not the first time he had crashed through a wall in such a manner. He pushed himself up on all fours and gathered his strength to push him to his feet. "Angel?" He asked rummaging through the debris. His mission sank back into his skin. "Angel?" He asked again. Making his way out of Loren's room and into the living room, he looked for her. She was not on the couch. "Angel, where are you?" He was starting to turn frantic.

"Who are you?" She surprised him standing up behind the counter separating the kitchen from the living room. She cradled a butcher's knife in her trembling hands, much the same way that Jack had moments ago clutched his unsheathed sword.

Jack lifted his hands to calm her, "Angel..."

"Don't use my fucking name like you know who I am!" She screamed shaking the knife in his direction.

"Angel, listen to me," he took another step closer to her, slowly. She was in shock, and unable to largely process what was going on. "Angel, there are things working here that are larger than either you or I. But I need you trust me."

"Why should I?" She gritted between her teeth.

"Because Angelica, you will never know what you mean to me," he spoke with such tenderness.

She stared at him for a moment, trying to examine his face more closely. "I do not know who you are, but you have such a likeness to you." Her guard was beginning to come down, and her breath was returning to her.

"Listen to me," he lowered his hands, and she did the same, setting the knife down on the counter. He approached her slowly still, and gazed warmly into her eyes.

"Where is my mother," tears were welling in her eyes.

He let out a sigh, "there's been an accident...I guess you could say."

"An accident?" She asked scrunching her eyebrows.

Jack offered out his left hand. Angel peered at it, debating its worthiness. He watched her silent discourse, "you have to trust me," he whispered.

She shook her head, and put her hand into his. And just like that the two of them evaporated out of existence, leaving behind a faint popping noise and a gust of wind forceful enough to extinguish Angel's still lit cigarette rolling on the kitchen floor.

When the two of them exploded back into existence, they found themselves standing in the entryway to a patient's room in the hospital—one that was not my mother's. Angel immediately began to sob into Jack's arms at the prospect of what was happening to her. Jack shoved her head into his chest, and placed his head atop hers, stroking the back of her head. "Shhhhh," he shushed her as he rocked back and forth. Staring out of the small curtained window, Jack could see the silhouette of people standing immediately outside the door. A commotion began to stir, and he understood that they had been detected. "I want you to know that I've been here; every step of the way. Bad things are coming, my dear, and I'm going to fight just as hard as I always have..."

Angel ceased crying and pulled her head away from his chest to peer at his face again. Her eyes tried to focus through the smog of her tears, "Who are you?" she asked.

"Just a shepherd tending to his flock," he smiled. The door began to open, and with the blink of an eye, he exploded out from her arms, disappearing into the air.

"Hold it!" the soldier exclaimed charging the room with his firearm raised. Upon entering, he stopped startled at the appearance of a Angel's limp body on the ground. He could not fathom how she could have possibly entered the room undetected. It was as if she had appeared out of thin air. "I need a doctor in here!" He screamed as he bent down to her to check her pulse.

Several medical personnel sprinted into the room, knocking the armed guard to the side and proceeding to tend to Angel who was more and more unresponsive by the minute. "How did she get in here?" the blonde-haired doctor screamed at the guard.

He sat there stunned, and shook his head. "I...I don't know, ma'am. I don't know. I don't know..." he repeated the words over and over again. They filled the room with confusion and chaos. The doctors worked tirelessly to breathe life into Angel, just feet away from where her own mother lay in a comatose state following an incident that should have definitely killed her.

In those few moments of tension, Angel lingered there in the limbo between life and death. She felt the weight of damnation and salvation tugging her back and forth. However, as she had been in living, she was also in dying; and she fought back. She chose life.

Whether or not that was the damnable act, or the act of salvation, she was not quite one hundred percent sure.

***

Tuesday – 14
The Blake Family

"Sweetheart," her voice roused me from sleep. I pulled my head up from our clasped hands and looked at my mother laying on the bed so innocently. The dull beeps of the machines had rocked my tired body to sleep. I looked up at the small clock perched upon the wall across from where I was sitting. It read: 8:17PM. There was no possible way that I had taken to slumber for that long without being disturbed. I felt as if I had just awoken from a five minute nap, not a nearly five and a half hour sleep. The clock had to've been wrong.

I shook my head, and looked back at my mother. The light above her bed shone on her. The machine: breathe in...breathe out. Breathe in...breathe out. The pattern was so artificial. She had become so artificial.

"Such fragile things," her kind and gentle voice said from next to me.

I looked again to my left, at the wall opposite, and standing there was an angelic body radiating the most beautiful white light. "Mom?" Goosebumps ran throughout my entire body.

The apparition of my mother bent down to the physical body of my mother, the one of which I was holding onto so tightly now. She caressed her own cheek, and I could feel my mother's hand tense in my own. "Such fragile things," she repeated.

I gulped looking at my mother's twin, still glowing with light. "I...I don't uhm...I don't understand." My stomach was in knots.

Her heavenly twin smirked at me, and turned her attention from her own body to my face, "you're looking in all of the wrong places. Prophecy, legacy, oracle...premonition...damnation...all right out of a heroes' fantasy." Her voice had a distracted skepticism to it. "You can never understand my gracious divinity..." Peering deep into my eyes she drew me into terror, "time can just stop," the 'p' popped out of her mouth like a bubble in the wind. "It really is such a shame," she slowly made her way over to my side of the bed, taking perch just to the side of me.

"Mom, I don't understand?" I started confused.

She grabbed my face, and leaned in so our faces were directly in front of one another. "I knew I'd find you sooner or later," she smiled. "Be scared."

I coughed, choking for life. Sitting up, I realized that I had merely dreamt the interaction with my mother's celestial twin. I labored to breathe, as I felt my heart catch up to itself. I looked at the clock on the wall opposite where I was sitting, and was stricken with fright as I read the time: 8:17PM. "Deavon?" I cried, hoping that my brother was still in the room with me. I got up from my seat hurriedly and jaunted around the curtain to see my brother curled up on the chair, just as passed out as I had been. "Deavon, wake up," I said nudging him.

He took a swing at me, but I was ready for such. He woke up startled and looked around, "what time is it?"

I stood awkwardly silent for a moment, "'bout 8:20."

73

He looked at me incredulously, "what time is it?" he asked again, pressing more seriously upon me.

"Go find dad," I said ordering him, indicating to him that I was not going to repeat the time I had just recited. I was not lying. We had been laying unconscious in the hospital room for five and a half hours, without the single intervention of another, doctor, nurse or even our father.

Deavon scrambled to his feet, and gathered himself before walking out of the door. I turned back to take the few steps back to my mother. She was still laying in the bed where I had left her. I noticed a drip or two of blood dripping down from her nose. I walked over to the bedside table which had tissues, and began to dab at her nostril. I heard the door open and close again, "did you find him?" I asked.

"Excuse me?" Her voice startled me.

I turned around to see that it was not my brother who had joined me in the room, but rather a nurse who was to check on my mother. "Oh, I uhm...I'm sorry. I thought you were my brother..."

"Your brother?" She asked intrigued.

"Yeah, you see, we've been in here with our mother for about five and a half hours now, and haven't seen or spoken to another soul..." she continued to stare at me. "I'm glad you're here though, her nose has begun to bleed," I said referring to my mother.

"Yes, I can see that," she grabbed me by the back of the head and shirt, and whipped me away from my mother, throwing me against the wall. "Hm, I had no idea it would be this easy," she cackled in my ear. "What a disappointment," her breath was hot and her skin cold.

"Who are you?" My breath quivered delivering this inquiry. I could feel my pulse racing, and my blood was beginning to boil in fright. Nothing in life could truly prepare you for something like that. I was caught completely off guard and in a very vulnerable state. None of my training could come to me, only panic.

"You need not be concerned with such matters. He that seeks you will be so pleased..." her voice hissed in my ear. The ground rumbled below us. The entire complex trembled, she sniffed at the air and grumbled. "Damnit. So close..."

The door and doorframe were ripped from the entry. The nurse peeled me from the wall, and walked over to the wreckage, dragging me along firmly. A woman stood in the new makeshift doorway, a woman of whom I had never encountered in my life. She was lightly tanned, and had pink dreaded hair. "Put him down," she commanded. Her voice was deep, yet soothing.

"Or?" the nurse asked maniacally.

"Else," the pink haired woman proclaimed. She kneeled down, paving view to my father who was sprinting down the hallway. He leapfrogged over the knelt woman, and lunged directly into the nurse knocking me out of her grip and flying back to my mother's side. My father landed on top of the woman, taking hold of her collar and punching her face repeatedly. There was so much passion in each punch, so much anger and frustration. I sat horrified. The pink haired woman came to my father's side, "Joshua, your sons!" She exclaimed.

She threw my father from the nurse, and instead took her own turn at abusing the woman.

The pink-haired woman, Amalya, as my father's imposter had called her earlier, was much more of a match for the woman nurse. The two of them struggled to take the upper hand. My father did not allow me to be a spectator for much longer. He grabbed me by the collar and yanked me out of the room and through the rubble. He turned around staring at the two women fighting, and my mother laying lifeless in the bed next to them. "Come back to me, my love."

The two of us continued to run down the hallway, through the mass of doctors, nurses, patients and soldiers, all of whom had been injured in an altercation that I had been unaware of until that very moment. "What about Deavon?" I yelled as we ran the length of the hallway for the elevator. I heard a cry coming from behind us followed by the sound of a large explosion. Seconds later, my heart skipped a beat as Amalya crashed through the ceiling, and stopped us dead in our tracks as she landed among the rubble in front of us. I stood shocked, mouth wide, heart racing, and thoughts rushing through my head uncontrollably.

Miraculously, Amalya jumped to her feet, and threw both my father and myself over the pile of rubble and launched herself back at the woman nurse. My father grabbed my arm again, and we proceeded further down the corridor. Sitting in the corner, cowering with fear was my brother, whom my father had left to gather myself. He pulled Deavon up onto his feet, and the elevator door dinged open. We entered, and my father pressed the button for the first floor. As the doors closed my father watched the battle between women and hung his head in shame. "Too soon," he whispered. The door closed, but not before I could catch the glimpse of another light, and what I swore to be the new kid in school, Jack.

The ride home was trivial. I couldn't even describe the events that unfolded ever so casually around me at that very moment; simply as if the elevator ride down, and the trip through the hospital to our car just did not happen. It was only the lightning that roused me from my daze in the car, and even then I'm still not sure I could comprehend what was going on. Deavon sat listless in the backseat, unable to communicate. I looked over at my father. His hands clenched the steering wheel making his knuckles white. I could tell that he was clenching his jaw trying to hold back his tears, but it was not working. They were streaming freely down his face. I dared not speak. I simply closed my eyes and tried to force myself to sleep. If I were to wake up, it would have to be from this nightmare. None of it made sense, none of it could possibly be real.

Seconds later, I opened my eyes. No one was in the car with me. It was parked neatly in the garage, all by itself. My brother and father were nowhere to be found. "Time?" I whispered. The clock in my father's car displayed the time: 11:39pm. Time had displaced itself yet again without any sense of passing. I felt groggy, and my head pounded. Opening the door engaged the door-ajar alarm. The 'dings' etched into my head and with each ding, agonizing pain piled on. I slammed the door; my sudden hypersensitivity was getting to me.

Walking into the mudroom, I removed my shoes and proceeded through the formal dining, living room, and finally into the kitchen. The house was pin-drop silent. Entering the kitchen, I peered into the darkness and noticed that I was not alone. I had finally regained the courage to form words, "Dad?"

"You cannot possibly begin to understand that which I am trying to do for you, my child." Lightning cracked, and I looked over at the window-filled back wall to our kitchen looking out into our large backyard. He was leaning against the table, peering into the darkness and storm.

"You're right," I whole-heartedly agreed with him. My face began to tingle, and I rubbed my eyes, "I don't understand a single Goddamn thing that is going on around here!" I gritted my teeth, mostly to ward off tears.

"I do not expect you to understand. You must simply know that what I am trying to do will change your destiny, it will give you a chance..."

"For what?" I screamed into the silence. I was tired of this charade.

"It's time for bed."

"Answer me!" I screamed again. I could feel a rage building within me.

"Go," he paused, "to bed." His remark was concrete.

I stood defeated for a moment; I turned and began to walk towards the stairs. "What is happening to you?" I asked him over my shoulder. Turning out of the kitchen, I walked to the stairs and ascended heading to my bedroom.

"I wish you wouldn't find out," lighting struck again revealing the tears in his eyes. He scanned his home in the darkness, and smiled. Heading out of the kitchen, he took for the formal living room, of which harbored his piano. He hadn't played it in some time, but when I was younger he had used to play it all the time. He said the music helped him to focus, to see patterns where none existed, to find clarity. Sitting down, he brushed the key cover, and lifted it. He placed his hands on the ivory keys, finding their right places. Music flowed from his hands quietly, in the form of Beethoven's *Moonlight Sonata*. It was his favorite piece and knew it by heart.

"It is time, Joshua," her voice cut through the music.

My father did not open his eyes; he continued to let himself drown in the beauty of the music. "This is not their war," he whispered.

"You cannot prevent this. What is written is written," her tone was matter-of-fact.

He finally opened his eyes and stared at the beautiful apparition of my mother. "Joycelyn, how can we condemn the ones we love, when we ourselves could not fully carry the burden of this task?" He stared at her heavenly vision, much like the one I had witnessed in the hospital room. She wore a gorgeous white dress, her hair flowing onto her shoulders, and a light shining all around her.

"This life is not of fairness, Joshua. You, of all people, should know that."

"Please, do not remind me," he continued to play. He smiled as his fingers moved, each with purpose, "Shining Corona Joycelyn Miracula Blake," he addressed her royally. "I just wish that there was something more that I could do. Something more than what we have already done."

"I, too, fear that what has been done is not enough. Destiny dictates that there is *nothing* we can do. No, I fear there is nothing that we can do to stop this, short of murder," she simply responded.

My father was rustled by her words. He chuckled, "right. We all know how that played out last time."

"I, unlike you, was not speaking of the creatures..." my mother began to laugh to herself. Her nose began to bleed.

My father ceased playing again. He was suddenly troubled by their interaction. "The blood," he said looking at my mother's heavenly embodiment more closely. He slammed the cover closed over the keys and stood. "I should have known. Get out."

"Or?" She asked looking at him maniacally and approaching him slowly.

"I will banish thee," my father proclaimed. His fists were clenched and ready to fight.

"HA!" She laughed in his face. "You cannot idly banish *me*. I am everywhere," she replied.

"*He* will be the end of you," my father stated firmly.

"He *cannot* be," she contested. "You were all wrong...all mortally wrong," she smiled. Approaching him, she held her hand out to caress his face. She did so while staring him directly in the eyes.

Like a zombie, Deavon walked down the stairs leading directly to the confrontation. He looked back and forth between my father and the vision of my mother. "What's going on?" He asked.

She looked over at my brother and then back at my father. She smiled, "Be Scared." She disappeared in a smoke-like effect from our living room. The house shuddered on its foundation, but I was again too far into sleep to be disturbed.

My father shielded himself from the explosion of light, and quickly diverted his attention back to my brother, who was now lying unconscious on the floor. Taking a seat on the piano bench, my father wept.

II: The Deamons

Wednesday – 15
Joshua Blake

My father looked at the clock, it was midnight, officially Wednesday. He sighed and turned to look out the windows lining the back wall of our kitchen. Rain continued to pour down, as if quenching a thirst that could not be satisfied.

"And on the third day..." Jack began, startling my father.

"Don't. Know your place."

"Of course, Sir Blake."

Turning around to face Jack, who was standing in the doorway to our kitchen, my father looked at him solemnly. Jack entered the room and stopped short once he realized that my brother's unconscious body was lying sprawled out on the table. "I still do not quite fully understand what it is that you are trying to accomplish here sir."

"It is of no importance for you to understand, my trusted Shepherd."

"The storm, sir. I can feel its intensity growing," Jack remarked. The two of them turned their attention to the wall of windows in our kitchen and watched the rain come down silently.

"I'm afraid there is nothing I can do to avert this from happening," my father pleaded quietly.

"There never was, sir. I will do what I can for a time, but it is up to you to finish your task." Jack assured my father. He walked over to my brother and studied his face. "They look so much alike," he smiled.

My father stared at my brother's face and admired Jack's comment. He wiped a final tear from his eyes, "of course." It was already 12:12AM. "Time seems to be just slipping out from under us," he stared blankly for a moment. Turning to Jack sharply, he patted his colleague on the shoulder, "take care of them."

Jack looked at my father, who was gazing at his youngest child. He turned back to look at Deavon, "I will sir, within my power." When he turned to address my father again, he was gone.

***

Tuesday – 14
The Thomas & Peterson families

Nathan Thomas felt as though his insides were exploding: his stomach in terror, his heart in anticipation, and his lungs in sheer panic. His brain ripped apart lobe by lobe and he simply ceased to exist for mere milliseconds. When he, Nicholas, their fathers, and the beautiful pink-haired angel exploded back into existence, his stomach regurgitated its terror and he expelled the food he had just eaten. In this very rare instance, Nicholas too felt the exact same sensations running through his body, and pulsating to the beat of his heart.

Both he and Nicholas fell to their knees clutching their throats as their lungs found breath yet again. Their fathers turned around to comfort each of their sons, helping them find strength to regain focus; to come back to center. After moments of tension, calm began to return to them, and vision came back from blur.

As Nicholas recovered air to his begging lungs, he stared all around him, and nearly passed out at the prospect of where he was. He was in some sort of box, a glass box, a crystal box surrounded by fire, intense fire. Buried deeply within the burning blaze was the silhouette of a grand, pyramidal machine encasing them. In his company were Nathan and his father and mother who rushed to their side, his own father and mother who had done the same, the pink-haired woman, and another man, who was kneeling in the far distance of the translucent cube.

The pink-haired woman, named Amalya kneeled down on her left knee immediately as they reappeared into existence. She cupped her hands in front of her face and bowed her head at the other man of whom neither Nicholas nor Nathan had ever been acquainted. "Keeper, I have retrieved that to which I was entrusted." She waited for his response before moving from her knelt position.

The man in the distance was kneeling down, with his bottom perched upon his calves. He too had his hands cupped in front of his head with his face turned into his palms and his eyes closed in deep meditation. He wore an orange dress, which traced down his thin and aged body, and upon his head sat an orange open-topped hat as a sort of crown. Silence followed Amalya's offering. He was not ignoring her words, but was lost in translation. Inside of him, he felt a fire ignite unlike any he had felt in a lifetime. Starting with the opening of his eyes, light spilled out of his stare into the bowl of his palms. The light radiating from him ignited the glass room in blinding white light, bright enough to cause discomfort for anyone willing to stare at it.

Like a shade covering a light-filled window, he closed his eyes and the light disappeared. Both Nicholas and Nathan's heads began to pound uncontrollably as they fought to regain focus of their blinded eyes. Nathan's vision came into focus first; he could see the man standing from his knelt position and turning to face them. He was smiling, his eyes a very dull shade of brown. He walked to them, and bowed to each family. He knelt down again on his knees and placed his hands on each Nicholas and Nathan. "Written word shall come to pass..." his voice was delicate but wise. "And so it is in the End as it was in the Beginning." He closed his eyes and continued to smile as he turned his head upward to face the fires burning all around them.

"And so it is." Guthrie and Evelyn Peterson chorused woefully.

"And so it is." Samuel and Sandra Thomas recited.

"And so it is," the man joyfully exclaimed.

"And so it is." Nicholas and Nathan both repeated, now starting to somehow understand their parts in this fantasy.

Both of their eyes fell closed, and the vision of their parents faded away from view—unknown to them—for the last time.

Evelyn Peterson burst into tears as her son slipped into unconsciousness; her husband, Guthrie, tried to comfort her, while also trying to keep grasp upon reality himself. Two crystal tables formed from nowhere, as if sprouting like a fountain from the existing crystal around them. Both Samuel Thomas and Guthrie Peterson hoisted their sons onto the tables, and stared at them tenderly as their wives joined their sides.

The four of them stood there, emotionally shocked, and mentally drained. They understood, for they had prepared their entire lives for this moment tirelessly. Amalya's touch startled Evelyn Peterson, as she placed her hand on each Guthrie and her. "I share your grief, my flock. But you know where we must go."

Evelyn, unable to speak through her sobs nodded her head in understanding, and placed one more gentle kiss upon her son's forehead. Guthrie managed to keep his tears welled in his eyes, and choked down his fear as he turned to face the Thomas family. Samuel looked up, and stared directly into Guthrie's eyes, "take care of him for me, Sam."

Sam looked down at his own unconscious son, and felt the weight of his wife, as she pressed her face into his shoulder. He returned his gaze back to Guthrie, "of course, Guth. Keep out of trouble," he half smiled holding back his own tears.

Guthrie nodded his head, "And so it is." Amalya laid her hands upon Guthrie and Evelyn Peterson and in a flash of light and a puff of smoke; they had exploded out of existence, off to a place far, far away.

"And so it is," Samuel hung his head.

***

Wednesday − 15
Joycelyn Blake

My mother continued to lay in her coma under heavy lock, key, and guard. In many years, she had orchestrated safety. Angelica Johnson, along with her mother and my own were safe, deep within the hospital, buried in a secret bunker built for research, which had been funded by my father. After our sudden exit from the hospital complex and the miracle that followed, including the appearance of Angelica Johnson, my mother and the Johnsons were moved into secure seclusion by predetermined order of my mother. The beeps of monitors echoed back and forth, like a tennis match keeping time with my mother's heartbeat.

To the layman, she was dying, all three were. However, in the presence of a truly trained mind, they would see that none of the three of them had ever been more alive. Her eyes raced back and forth underneath her eyelids tracing an impossible past, and looking for a promised future.

The beeps of my mother's heart monitor began to slow, which alarmed several doctors who were monitoring all of their heart rhythms closely. A single tear traced down her closed eyes as a smile found its way painted onto her unconscious face. The doctors scurried into the heavily guarded room where their three most mysterious patients lay.

Rushing to the side of Joycelyn Blake, the team of suited doctors analyzed her vitals. The six doctors stood dumbfounded in the dark chamber, within a small section surrounded by clear flaps, encasing the area in sterility. Standing at guard just on the other side of the clear, thick rubber curtains, were several marines ready to destroy any unauthorized intruders.

"This doesn't make any sense!" One of the panicked doctors exclaimed. Her vitals betrayed her, defied the laws of science. Dead, that's how they read, but the doctors could clearly see that she was still alive. "Get a shock cart in here!" the same panicked doctor screamed. He put his hand on my mother's head feeling her warm forehead. He shook his head, "I don't understand," he pleaded.

"You cannot."

The words, two simple words, left the room standing frozen in time. They had been spoken with such absolute certainty, and with such precious care. The doctors stood, astonished, scared. The words had spilled from my own mother's mouth. Inexplicably, she reached her hand above her head and placed it upon the hand of the doctor who still had his hand precariously perched upon her forehead. As her fingertips grazed the top of his palm, his flesh began to melt away. He opened his mouth to scream in horror, but instead, it opened to silence. He could not speak, could not scream, could not cry.

My mother's eyes ripped open, they were completely colorless, "*She, kissed with sight, will ignite the beacon and bring finality to deception. Without the Two, there cannot be the One. And so it is in the End as it was in the Beginning.*"

88

The marines were apprised to the situation by this point, and were standing with their firearms raised, cocked and aimed at my mother. She easily broke free of the restraints keeping her tied to the bed. Sitting up, she looked at
each of the marines, and doctors and at the lifeless bodies lying next to her. She raised her left index finger to the mouth of the doctor who was trying to scream in pain. As she touched his face, his body disintegrated into nothing but ash.

A woman doctor screamed in terror, as bullets began to shower the small sterile enclosure. My mother stood to her feet, amidst the barrage of ordnance, and simply waved her hand off. The bullets withered away to ash just as the doctor had moments before. She looked at the, so far, unharmed remainder of doctors. They sat huddled, underneath the tables of which Loren Johnson and her daughter Angelica were still contained.

"I *am* sorry." Her voice was different. She exploded in a beautiful white light, immediately incinerating anyone within her vicinity, except for that of Loren and Angelica Johnson.

***

Wednesday – 15
Joshua Blake

My father trudged through the dark, silent streets of our city alone, stomping through the puddles as the rain beat down upon him. The streetlights flickered as he walked by, each one exploding as he stepped passed them. With each step, his heart broke more completely. He was fighting a war with inevitability, and he was going to lose.

He approached an ominous tower and closed his eyes, feeling the rain descend upon him. With each drop, he felt a small bit of guilt wash away. Opening his eyes, he peered upon the stone building. Lights illuminated the name of the building, which most could not ignore against the backdrop of the night sky: 'Blake Tower'. It was the centerpiece to the Blake Genetic Industrial Complex, the heart, where his most dangerous work took place. Rage began to pile up through my father's body. Burning anger pulsated through his veins, and swelled with each beat of his heart. He yelled out onto the silent street, which echoed throughout the entire assembly of skyscrapers.

He fell to his knees sobbing.

———

"Tell me, my child, what do you know of destiny?"

"Why have you brought me here, father?"

When my father opened his eyes again, the landscape of skyscrapers and silent night was replaced with the furor of life in a serenely green pasture. He was not my father, not yet anyway, he was younger, a child, perhaps my age. "Always so many questions, my young Joshua."

He turned his head to his right and noticed a man, but not just any man, sitting beside him, the two of them meditating. My father closed his eyes again, several tears slipping from them, "father please," he pleaded.

"Look beyond your sadness, my child."

"I'm scared."

"Look beyond your fears."

"I'm angry."

"Look beyond anger. Take in the air around you, and let it fill your lungs. As you exhale, feel it join one with the world around you. Feel the earth beneath you, and feel it calling to you."

My father's breaths were more labored as he listened to the words from the faceless man in front of him. His heart slowed, and his body shuddered, "I can feel it."

"Let go of the emotion," the man's voice was very stern in this command. "Look passed the conventions of meager mortality. Feel life."

The sounds echoed through my father's head as they bounced around in beautiful chorus. The sunlight bathed his body, and the crisp air burned his lungs. He was at peace, one with the earth. "Something is wrong, my father."

"They're coming. The Deamons."

____

The hiss of the 's' ripped my father from trance. He opened his eyes and peered into the darkness around him, as the water continued to pour from above. He gathered, again to his feet and searched his surroundings. "The Deamons," my father replied to silence. With a whip of lightning and a clap of thunder, my father exploded from his place on the street, leaving behind a small crater in the concrete.

***

Wednesday – 15
The Shepherd, Jack

Jack sat perched on the ground with his legs crossed, at our front door. His hands were pressed together, and his were eyes closed in meditation. He had carefully placed my brother back in the safety of his own bed, where he would continue to sleep, just a hallway away from myself, where I also continued to sleep deeply into the night.

After my father disappeared, Jack took it upon himself to venture throughout our home, trying to piece together the narrative of our lives. He found pictures spread throughout the house containing memories of our childhood, and the life my parents had shared together. At each picture, he gave out a subtle sigh, not fully understanding the mockery that my parents had fabricated so far.

Her voice penetrated his concentration, and startled him, "Tell me, my Grand Shepherd, what do you know of Destiny?"

He opened his eyes, and took in a deep breath. Standing slowly, he straightened out his shirt and turned around to face my mother. He knew her likeness to be true, and it was. Unlike the apparitions prior, this was truly Joycelyn Blake standing before him. She was glowing with beautiful white light, and was standing in a long, flowing white dress. Her brown hair was in delicate curls, flowing and laying ever so gracefully upon her shoulders. Her eyes were not their normal, pale shade of hazel, but rather glowed ominously white.

Jack knelt down on one knee before my mother, "my Lady, Shining Corona."

She hastily smiled, "Stand before me."

As Jack stood, his clothes singed away into dust, and were replaced with skin-tight, black body armor. He wasn't nearly as lanky as I had originally credited him to be. Strapped around his back, a sheath holding the cunning sword he had donned earlier when encountering Angelica Johnson and her intruder. Upon realizing, he nodded his head at my mother.

"Tell me, what do you know of the written word?" she asked.

"I know almost every passage of the Scripture."

"Then tell me, what do you know of the Book of Destiny?"

"I simply know that it gives us Life, therefore it concurrently gives us Death."

"In the Beginning..." she was fishing for something.

He looked at her furrowing his eyebrows, "In the Beginning, there was nothing but chaos; beautiful and utter chaos. Life forged from energy, energy forged from life, it was a complete and infinite cycle..."

She shook her head, "and soon..."

"And soon, chaos ceded to order. The struggle between darkness and light prevailed over the Pivotals and would so continue for punishment over the Cataclysm. The Universe as it is Known."

Again, she shook her head. "The Writer of Whom is Most High wrote water into existence, driving life to the creatures born unto the Known Universe. As the Records passed into Ages, fire was given to man to fuel purpose. It burns with rage; however it not only takes life, but breathes it. Her embodiment will cry, and so it was written the Natural Element, to give expression to that which surrounds us. The countless lights upon which life was based will reign upon the skies. The cosmos will ignite the path of which the Chosen are to follow. The stars will guide life and essence Home."

"And then, he is born," Jack begins.

"The Savior of Man," my mother finishes.

"It will be up to the Savior to protect the Known Universe from the persistence of Chaos; to follow the path of time and bring humanity back to the path of righteousness. And it will be the Seventeenth Savior of Man that will unite the Universe as it is Known and save all that is worth saving...that's more or less the gist." Jack finishes.

"But that is where you are wrong, my Shepherd."

"My lady?" he inquired incredulously.

"You are correct, it does speak of the Seventeenth Savior of Man. Joshua Eason Blake is in fact the Seventeenth Savior of Man. However, it will not be his destiny to complete the cycle, he will but merely play a part." Her eyes slowly traced up the stairs, and then turned to look at the ground. "And so it is in the End as it was in the Beginning."

Jack gasped, "a second coming?"

"For the bastard child will bear the name of the messenger. The messenger will be revealed to be the Harbinger, the Harbinger will mark the second rising of the DarkestHeart."

He traced his eyes up from the ground and stared directly into my mother's eyes, "And so it is." Jack stood there crying silently.

"Tell me, Shepherd, what do you know of the Deamons?"

***

Wednesday – 15

Joshua Blake

"Vexandrees," my father said aloud. He was standing alone in his office, dripping wet against the backdrop of the storm bearing down upon the ground outside.

The door to his office opened, injecting little light into the darkness-filled room. She did not flinch, "aye?"

"Report." He stared at her stoic, slightly shaking to the chill running throughout his body.

She swallowed heavily as she stared at him, ceasing to break eye contact. "It *is* ready sir; however I must caution you that it has not been properly tested yet."

My father nodded his head ever so slightly, "then that will have to do."

"What are your final orders, sir?" her voice was heavy.

"Lock down the building." He clenched his fists, and let out a deep exhale, before giving his next and final order. "Deploy Operation: Legacy."

She stood straight and recited aloud as if the words had been burned into her eyes: "Joshua Eason Blake, it has been spoken by you, to deploy Operation: Legacy."

He finally broke eye contact with her, and turned his back so he could take one more look upon the city outside. After moments of silence, he spoke: "Aye."

"Then let it be heard." She lifted her right hand to cover her right ear, there was a loud tone over every floor of my father's building. Her voice echoed eerily over all of the hallways, "Deployment of Operation: Legacy has commenced. Lock-down procedures have been initiated."

"Thank you, Vexandrees," my father turned around and smiled, nodding his head at her gratefully.

She stepped out of automation, and looked at my father dearly, "is there anything further I can do, Sir?" My father looked at the floor for a moment and chuckled to himself. She furrowed her eyebrows, "Sir?"

"Just pray." My father said turning his eyes back to hers.

"Of course, sir." She broke their trance, and looked at the floor. She disappeared in a flash; she was a hologram.

"Thanks, pal." He turned around again to spy the city as thick metal blast doors came down over all of the windows and portals into the complex. A few emergency lights flashed on as the last of the blast doors came down and sealed the light from the outside world out. One of the bookcases lining the wall to the left of my father retracted, sliding into the wall, revealing a secret elevator. He stepped forward slowly, each step weighing down on him until he stepped foot in the elevator.

"Destination?" An eerie woman's voice asked above my father.

"Fountain," he replied.

The door slid closed in front of him, locking him in the chamber alone. The transport gave a jerk and began to descend very slowly. "Biometric scans initiated," the voice announced again. As he lowered ever so slowly, a green grid of lights filled the elevator. The light measured my father's density, took his fingerprints, registered a scan of his retinal patterns and checked his bodily vitals. "Biometric scans complete, and confirmed: Occupant Joshua E. Blake." Railings extended out from the walls of the elevator, my father grabbed hold, while his shoes were magnetically sealed to the floor. "Rapid descent commencing," her voice rang as the elevator plummeted far into the crust of the Earth. He hadn't taken this trip in some time, and his stomach turned slightly as he continued to freefall. My father closed his eyes to keep his concentration on the task at hand. It wasn't long before he noticed the descent beginning to slow; he was approaching the end of his ride. There was a ding, "Destination achieved: Fountain." My father let go of the railings, and they ceased to exist as the pad beneath his feet continued to descend down into a long clear tube. Encased in the darkness of the cavern, was an ominous white sphere. The pad slowed almost completely, and finally clicked into place. My father's feet were let go from their hold.

A set of glass doors opened in front of him, and he stepped out of the tube. As he did so, the doors shut behind him, and the lights illuminating the long tube turned to menacing darkness. He began to step forward into the sound of deafening waterfall filling the background. The narrow glass path that he was standing on suddenly illuminated as he took one step further forward. Lights traced down the walkway, and finally rested once again upon the grand white sphere. Under the glass he was walking upon was a body of dark flowing water, which poured over a drop of unknown depth, causing the waterfall to roar in his ear. My father walked forward grudgingly, with each step the lights behind him dissipating ominously.

He began to speak aloud, "The King of Nights bound of DarkestHeart, could not foresee the ends from start, so he spoke to darkness kind, none be found, fore none to find..." he finally approached the forty foot tall sphere of beauty, his voice acted as key and a doorway cracked open for him. He stood still at the threshold for a moment, and finally stepped in.

The room was blindingly naked. As my father stepped in, the crack, which had formed for him to enter, mended itself. He looked around the white room; it was completely desolate except for the small cluster of people in the near distance. There were no consoles, no computers, no doorways, no desks, no cubicles, no projections; solely the humans. Stepping further into the sphere, my father finally spoke to those who were in his company, "you were to evacuate."

A man stepped forward from the huddled group; it was Norman Robinson, Clecha's father. "We could not leave you sir," he did not look my father in the eyes. While Norman was much taller than my own father, Joshua Blake had the capacity to intimidate him beyond words.

Behind the two of them stood four other individuals: Areul Robinson—who was simply just an older version of her daughter—Guthrie and Evelyn Peterson, and the Shepherd Amalya. The pink-haired woman stepped forward, and instead of addressing my father, she knelt down on one knee, "we are merely trying to preserve your life, my Savior."

My father laughed, nearly inaudibly, "You know that to be a futile effort. Stand Shepherd," my father commanded. As she did, her white suit melted away, and much like Jack, she donned a beautiful skin-tight white body suit of armor. "Now where is it?" He asked Amalya specifically.

"It is untested, Joshua," Areul Robinson called, still huddled with Evelyn and Guthrie Peterson. Guthrie put his hand on Areul's shoulder, trying to bring her thoughts back to focus.

"I am completely aware, Areul; however I am sure that *you* are aware of the present circumstance. We do not have the luxury of tests; it will simply have to do."

She was visibly upset, but she touched Guthrie's hand still perched upon her shoulder, "of course, sir." The three of them looked collectively distressed for my father.

"Shepherd, where is it?" my father asked.

Amalya bit her cheek pondering what to do; she looked at each member standing behind her, and at Norman Robinson whom was standing next to her. After moments of tense silence, she finally spoke, "Command Directive." There was a loud tone above them and the lights in the room went dark. The white tiles making up the floor began to illuminate slightly to compensate for the darkening. Turning around, she grabbed Norman Robinson, and stepped back to join the group standing behind them, my father also followed. "Eternity deployment for final stage of Operation: Legacy."

The six of them stood in a circle around one tile at the center of the sphere. The tile itself lifted up out of the ground exposing a column of command console that stood ten feet tall. My father turned to look at the other five individuals around him. With a heavy breath, he spoke, "let's finish."

The six of them collectively began to recall the poem that my father had begun to recite earlier to allow him entrance to the ominous white sphere. "*...the fountain of eternal youth bore the start for finding sooth. The light abound could naught be sought, for truth be hid for none to thought.*" As each word flowed from their mouths, the sounds bounced off of the grand sphere, collecting around them in a beautiful array of lights. As they finished, the column standing in front of them illuminated an increasingly intensifying white light. When the final 't' left my father's mouth, the column shifted to blue, and began to sink back into the ground, halting at just four feet. The tile atop the column was glowing a dark shade of navy blue. The tile split into four, and opened carefully to reveal a syringe placed in its safekeeping.

My father looked at the syringe with a hunger in his eyes, "it's beautiful." He was speechless.

There was a buildup of static energy several feet from the group. The hair on my father's neck stood on end, and light gathered in a small cloud before it finally exploded revealing another. She stood tall, in a white dress with her brown hair a mess in her face. She brushed the hair from her face revealing that it was my mother. Kneeling behind her was the Shepherd Jack in his black body armor.

"Joycelyn," Evelyn Peterson gasped. She looked relieved at my mother's sudden appearance.

"Ma'lady," Amalya said now kneeling down to her.

My mother bowed her head in their direction; she looked at my father, and then at the column, "it's..."

"Untested," Norman Robinson cut in.

My mother's colorless eyes darted to Norman, "while I would normally agree with you Norman, circumstance precedes us," she finally finished the matter.

My father looked at her oddly, and also at Jack kneeling just behind her, "Joycelyn, our sons..."

"Are safe, my love." She approached my father, and rested her hands upon his shoulder, as the two of them peered at the blue syringe.

"The Cerulean Combine," my father whispered.

My father cautiously brushed the syringe with his left hand, and swooped in with his right to take it from its pedestal. The tile recombined from its four separate pieces, and the column retracted fully into the ground. The lights of the room began to come back to life. He looked at the distress painted on the faces of the Petersons and the Robinsons. Lifting the syringe, and his eyebrows he spoke, "cheers to the future..." he plunged the syringe into his left bicep. The irises of his eyes exploded, then contracted and nearly escaped into nothingness. The empty syringe fell from his grasp and dropped to the ground, shattering. His breathing turned labored.

"Sir Blake!" Jack exclaimed in the background.

"There's no way of knowing what may happen now..." Areul Robinson spoke up.

My mother put her hands on my father's face, and turned to look at him tenderly. His face was filled with insanity and pain. She caressed his cheeks and forehead, and drew him close to her. "My love," she whispered as she pressed her lips upon his. A violent gust of wind exploded from my parents, and knocked the other occupants of the sphere to their bottoms.

The sphere shuddered, and several tiles fell from the interior, crashing to the ground.

The two of them shared the passionate kiss, and opened their eyes to survey each other. My mother's eyes had returned to their normal blue, albeit perhaps a shade duller, and my father's face turned from certain insanity and pain to a quiet slight suffering. "They will undoubtedly be upon us soon," my father said.

"We will stay and fight," Guthrie said standing forward.

"No, Guthrie," my mother started, "you know that you cannot." She turned her attention to Jack, "take them; keep them safe."

"No," my father interrupted Jack from being able to carry out his order. "Take Norman and Areul to their daughter. Let them spend their last with her." He pleaded.

"I shall be the one to stay and fight, Ma'Lady," Amalya said, turning her red glaring eyes to my mother.

My mother nodded, "how sincerely noble of you, my dear Shepherd. Jack, you heard my husband, now go." Jack nodded in understanding, and grabbed the free hands of each Guthrie Peterson and Areul Robinson, whose other hands were in their spouses. The five of them disappeared in a flash of light, and a boom. The sphere shook around them, "They're here."

There was a deep boom from outside the grand sphere, and it shook again. "Go, Ma'Lady. Cherish them." Amalya commanded.

"Of course, my Shepherd...we shall meet again," my mother assured her. Grasping my father's hand tightly, she closed her eyes, and the two of them exploded into nothingness, leaving Amalya to face the oncoming alone.

****

Tuesday – 14

Samuel & Sandra Thomas

As the Shepherd Amalya disappeared taking with her the Petersons, Samuel and Sandra Thomas stood alone with their child and Nicholas—both of whom lay unconscious before them.

"I was so hard on him," Samuel said staring at his son; the crystal box was vibrating. "I even hit him a time or two," it was as if he was trying to apologize for something. "I bruised him once," he coughed to hold back his tears, "my own flesh and blood…I don't even know why I did it. I knew that his life was going to be hard enough as it was."

"Do not beat yourself up," Sandra tried to comfort her husband. Her gentle hands slid up his back, and perched upon his shoulders, trying to remove the tension from him. She had always been the voice of reason to Samuel.

The narrative of their lives had been told as such: Sandra Carmine was a simple teen of her generation. She, like her peers, heeded the words of her father, and fiercely obeyed her mother. She, too, attended Riverside Academy; fifty years prior—the first year the Academy was open. She did not get the chance to go on further and learn any trade; that was not her place. Her place was at home with her child. At seventeen years old, Sandra Carmine crossed paths with Samuel Thomas, who back then was the star quarterback of Riverside Academy. In his

103

day, Samuel was quite the looker, he was lean, well built and what he lacked in height, he made up for in his fierce determination. By the time the two of them graduated from the Academy, they each had eyes for the other. At eighteen years old, they married and planned their future together.

Samuel continued on with his education, graduating with honors, in the field of Aerospace Engineering with a specific focus in avionics. He devoted his twenties to study and the construction of more efficient flying vehicles. It was his firm that produced designs for the first most feasible, cost-effective, and fundamentally safe passenger space vessel. There had been other models before his. There had also been roughly thirty-six open cases of families seeking grievances over lost loved ones during the maiden voyage of the most recent attempt of a company trying their hand at the commercial space scene.

Sandra, on the other hand, stayed behind at home, not needing to pursue a career to lead them on their journey through life together. She often talked of having a child, but Samuel never quite seemed ready to start a family. After fifteen years of marriage, and quite accidentally, Sandra became pregnant with their one and only son, Nathan. Sandra was elated at the idea of finally having a friend to join her in her daily adventures, but Samuel found himself deeply reluctant to celebrate. Sandra planned her son's life: when he would marry, how many grandchildren he would provide for her, and what his career might possibly be. Samuel did not indulge himself in such, he constantly kept his eyes on the prize, fore he knew the destiny laid out before his son.

"I see that look upon your face, child," his voice was calm, but intrusive enough to disturb Samuel's gaze.

Samuel diverted his attention from his son, to that of the strange man standing before them—the only other occupant in the crystalline box; the man wearing the orange dress, and crown. "And what face is that?" Samuel asked.

The dark-skinned man smiled, showing his pearly white teeth, "the face that knows you cannot stop what is to come."

Samuel slammed his clenched fist down upon the crystal table, on which his son lay, in a fit of rage. "And why can't I?" Samuel screamed at the man, enraged.

The man closed his mouth, but left his lips in the shape of a smile. He blinked slowly. Then motioned for Samuel to follow him. He turned his back to the crystal tables and proceeded a few steps away then perched himself upon his knees. Samuel stood there reluctantly, following the man to the far corner to his seat. He took in a deep breath, swallowing his anger, and proceeded around the crystalline tables to meet the man. Samuel sat down with his legs crossed just next to the now meditating man.

"I am sorry, Keeper," Samuel whispered to the man.

There was an audible chuckle from the man that Samuel called 'Keeper'. "No need, child." He took a few deep breaths before speaking again, "close your eyes." Without further question, Samuel obeyed. "I'm going to tell you a story."

"A story?" Samuel's eyebrows furrowed over his closed eyelids.

"The Tale of the Deamons," the Keeper whispered.

***

Tuesday — 14
The Shepherd, Amalya

She had taken the trip so many times before. Exploding out of existence for fractions of a second, and then rearranging matter to exist impossibly somewhere else. It had become a reflex, like the blink of an eye, or the shudder of a chill. When her scrambled molecules recombined to take form, she breathed in deeply. Her red eyes focused quickly, she had built resistance to the upheaval. The room was as blindingly white as she had remembered it nearly a quarter century ago.

The distant sound of circulating air filled her heightened sense of sound. She turned around to see that Guthrie and Evelyn Peterson had also safely traversed the trip. Her eyes wandered just behind Guthrie and Evelyn and rested upon two others in the room who seemed to be undisturbed by their sudden intrusion. "Norman, Areul," Amalya said bowing her head in the direction of each of Clecha's parents. "It has been some time since we have convened here," Amalya said studying the spherical construction of the room around them. "I wish it could have been longer," she bit the inside of her cheek and looked down at the white tiles below her feet. She picked her face back up and looked at each of the four members in the room with her. Hastily, she finally spoke again, "Command Directive."

The white tiles of the room dimmed slightly, and a tile near the center of the spherical structure began to glow dark blue. It lifted out of the ground, and stopped after ten feet of computer console, built within the column, was exposed. She turned her look to Guthrie and Evelyn who were both still standing next to her, "I believe the rest is up to you..."

Guthrie and Evelyn reluctantly accepted their duty, and walked away from Amalya to join the Robinson's who now stood at the computer tower. "Initiate terminal phase of pre-operation deployment finalization," a bunch of long words exploded from Norman Robinson's mouth. The lights in the room completely faded to darkness and the only light left was from computer screens housed within the column. Guthrie, Evelyn, Aruel and Norman each took a side on the rectangular computer column, and placed their feet firmly. The three tiles immediately in front of each of them illuminated and lifted off the ground, setting to a hover at their fingertips. Gently placing their hands on the tiles, the computer screens ignited with life. Each of them had a piece of the puzzle that would complete their life's work—my father's life's work.

The Cerulean Combine.

"Time continues to move, my flock." Amalya whispered watching their work from afar. She blinked her eyes and exploded from existence yet again. She knew that she had set each of them on the right course, and could feel that she was more desperately needed elsewhere.

*

She spied the clock curiously, 7:42PM. Bullet. Bullet. Scream. Blood. It all happened in slow motion. Like ballet, her body flowed through the air, dodging each strike ever so gracefully. Each bullet meant for her, but never lucky enough to find her. Grab, grip, pull, punch, kick, strike and strike.

Screams, flashing lights, klaxons, it all filled her ears. "None of this is real," she assured herself closing her eyes. She was hiding—peek-a-boo—no one could find her. The scent of smoking barrels, sweat, and blood filled her nose. The scent was sweet, sweeter than she had remembered. It had been some time since she had last gotten a taste of it all, really. She lived for this moment; the ecstasy filled her with an abundance of excitement.

Exhaling, she let go of the glory of endless time. Sparks flew, and she opened her eyes. Amalya had reappeared on the top floor of the Central Health Complex. Surrounding her, were unconscious bodies, some dead, some dying, some simply sleeping by the will of an unknown, perhaps higher power. At her feet, the bodies of two, armed marines lay motionless. She bent down, and closed each of their eyes, "it didn't have to come to that." She looked up, and stared at the room number, she knew it to be my mother's, but this was not where she was to start her curious little adventure. She turned to her left, and walked down the long hallway to the final door on the right.

Touching the door in front of her, it exploded out from under her fingertips. She entered the poorly lit small room, and noticed it's only occupant, my father. She stared at him, and bowed, kneeling down to one knee, "Sir Blake."

"You sure know how to make an entrance," my father smiled. He sat chained to a chair, which was bolted to the floor. His face showed the fatigue of having been beaten at least once, if not twice. He was anchored to the floor with thick chains and shackles, which wrapped all the way around his body to the bottom of the chair. "You could have taken perhaps a bit longer," he winked.

"I am terribly sorry, sir," my father's twisted humor had always escaped her.

"Do not, fair Shepherd," my father alleviated her guilt. "Were you well-received?"

"No sir, however, I did as you had instructed: I invalidated the confines of their existence."

"Such an ugly way of putting it," my father chuckled to himself.

She thought for a moment before she finally offered, "I unmade them from this reality which you have bestowed upon such desolation." Amalya stood facing my father, she placed her hand on the thick chains gently, and with a curious glow of light, the chains around my father began to fall away to nothing but dust and soot.

"Thank you, young Shepherd," my father said stretching his body back into use.

"My gracious duty," she bowed her head.

My father stood, using his legs for the first time in hours. "Amalya," he said directly addressing her. She furrowed her eyebrows, for she knew not what my father could possibly have to tell her. "Have you yet been able to validate the presence of the Deamons?"

She hesitated for a moment, "No. Sir, what is going on? What is this about?"

My father stood for a second weighing his words carefully, "we're in dire straits my dear," his voice quivered as he tried to force out a chuckle, "the fractures are reuniting..."

He paused and hung his head, delivering the final blow, "a second coming."

"But what of your destiny?" She asked.

"It was never mine, it was always theirs. And now, somehow, the Deamons are here…"

"Dad?" his inquiry shot directly into the intimacy of the situation.

Amalya was ripped from the tight grip that she commanded of reality. Things began to move back in regular motion. She gasped, and turned her startled face to the doorway to see my brother standing there, uneasy, scared and in shock. "Your sons," she whispered exploding out of existence. The displacement of her body caused a small sonic boom, the shock of which knocked my brother to his bottom. My father leapt from the room and lunged for my stunned double. As his fingertips brushed the collar of Deavon's shirt, the two of them exploded in a puff of smoke and reappeared at the end of the corridor leading to my mother's room. My brother sat wide-eyed and unable to speak as my father moved him to the corner.

Turning to look down the hallway, my father spied Amalya who had reappeared just feet from my mother's doorway. She bent down, and forced all of her energies toward focusing on the immense power buried within her. One jarring tone filled her ears as her red eyes ripped open in rage. She lifted her closed fists in front of her, and concentrated as the foundation of the building began to tremble. Inhale. Her lungs filled with fire. Exhale. She let out of a blood-curdling scream. The door, and frame were ripped from the wall, and tossed to the side. Many of the lights on the floor exploded in excitement. Amalya fought to catch her breath, and knelt down onto her right knee.

Bending down, my father launched himself from the end of the hallway, and lunged just as passionately at me as he had at my brother just moments ago. His fists rammed into the nurse's face—the woman who had been holding me ominously in her sinister company.

The sound of klaxons filled the hospital corridors. Everything was a blur. Amalya, the pink-haired shepherd jumped in and threw my father from the woman, commanding him to take me from the living nightmare. My father obeyed and grabbed me, dragging my limply stunned body from the hospital room toward the elevator, where my brother was still as equally stunned and waiting for us.

Her fists beat into the woman's face repeatedly and relentlessly. The nurse pulled her knees to her chest, and placed her feet upon Amalya's stomach. The nurse, pinned down on the ground, launched her feet upward, and with them, Amalya sailed through the ceiling and high into the air. She was growing annoyed as she flew twenty or so feet above the building, and then arced downward. She curled up into a ball and stretched back out, now diving toward the building. She crashed through the ceiling, and landed just a foot in front of my father and I. Grabbing the both of us by our lapels; Amalya launched us behind her, and jumped for the crazed woman nurse.

Landing firmly, Amalya stood to face the nurse. In the background she could hear the closing elevator doors, letting her know that we were safely on our way. "I should have smelled you sooner," Amalya growled.

"You must be losing your edge," each word was carefully articulated from the nurse's mouth. She whipped her left hand in front of her and screamed as a dark purple light briefly ignited between them.

Amalya knocked the nurse's arm to the side, and quickly thrust her clenched fists into her chest. The nurse flew back, and landed with a thud. "Not quite," the Shepherd approached the nurse cautiously. Upon reaching the weakened woman, she placed her foot firmly on the woman's sternum. "What are you doing here?"

"The same as you," the nurse labored to breathe, "trying to find the answers…"

"You are *not* the same as me," Amalya grit her teeth and dug her heel into the intruder's chest more firmly.

"You hardly know what you speak of. You are far too young to understand the tale unfolding before you," the nurse calmly replied. "Simply, we are different sides of the same coin," she smiled. Amalya curiously lifted the weight from her foot, and offered her hand to the woman. She stood and the two of them stood uncomfortably staring at each other. "I am but a mirror…"

"You are no such thing," Amalya whispered back tersely.

The woman nurse stared into Amalya's red eyes, and as she did the color faded from her own and filled in with a curious shade of yellow. Her skin began to darken as she stood there, and her hands were cold as they slid across Amalya's face resting at her jaw line. "You have no idea."

Amalya blinked her eyes, and jerked her body waking her. She stared around herself frantically, but realized that she was safely resting in the comfort of the chair observing my mother. Scrambling to her feet, she continued to scan her surroundings furiously. My mother lay unharmed in her hospital bed, still as night. Amalya stared around at the destruction around her, and shook her head in shame. She turned her look to my mother, "the Deamons have returned, M'lady. Please, do hurry back to us." Amalya looked around at her surroundings before she finally closed her eyes and brought her hands together in front of her torso, as if she stood in prayer. The rubble around her feet began to tremble, the building began to tremble below her feet. "All of the pieces are still here…" The air rushed around her in a whirlwind, and suddenly, she exploded out of existence, leaving behind a shockwave of light. As the light spread across the hospital complex, the lights were replaced, the walls were resurrected, and the rubble was cleaned away. Those left dead or dying were replaced, as if they could possibly be. The memory of events having really just transpired were completely erased from time.

Absent were three: my brother, my father, and myself. And our absence did not go long unnoticed. The mysterious force that Amalya had imparted on the hospital complex was unable to rectify the destruction waged on the room in which my father had been held. The chains still lay on the ground in a pile of soot and dust, and miniscule bits of debris from the door spread across the floor. Klaxons filled the hallways again, this time to alert of our "escape".

****

Wednesday — 15

The Shepherd, Amalya

"I shall be the one to stay and fight, Ma'Lady," Amalya said turning her red glaring eyes to my mother.

My mother nodded, "how sincerely noble of you, my dear Shepherd..." The sphere shook around them, "They're here."

There was a deep boom from outside the grand sphere, and it shook again. "Go, Ma'Lady. Cherish them." Amalya commanded.

"Of course, my Shepherd...we shall meet again," my mother assured her. Grasping my father's hand tightly, she closed her eyes, and the two of them exploded into nothingness, leaving Amalya to face the oncoming alone.

What my mother was unaware of, however, was the growing curiosity flooding all of Amalya's senses. The encounter with the woman nurse, the deamon in disguise, troubled her deeply; she had a score to settle. Another shock to the exterior of the sphere caused her to fumble slightly. Dust and rock fell from the top of the sphere, crashing onto the ground below. A final blow to the outside exploded a crack in the sphere large enough to allow entrance. Amalya scrambled to her feet, and stood with her fists clenched in front of her, ready to fight.

The commotion ceased, and the dust began to settle. From behind the thick cloud of dust now collecting on the ground, a single cloaked individual entered from the newly worn crack. "I've been expecting you." Amalya's words were concrete and fearless.

114

"Have you? That does seem quite impossible." Its sinister voice echoed back and forth throughout the sphere. The words were followed by maniacal laughter, which etched into Amalya's calm. "You know not who I am, do you child?"

"It does not matter," Amalya confidently proclaimed.

"You are foolish to have come here alone."

"And you are foolish if you stand to fight me."

"All of you Deamons…you're all the same; speaking so highly of yourselves…" Amalya remarked disgusted with the cloaked individual.

A snicker came from under the cloak, "I'm no Deamon…"

Amalya raised her clenched fists and pointed them in the direction of the one cloaked in darkness. A spark of radiant white light surged from her hands, and rushed for the intruder. With a whip of its hand, the cloaked figure slapped the trajectory of the light away, and raised its free hand, which emitted its own flash of light. Amalya was struck off guard by the flash of dark purple light, which surged passed her, grazing her right arm. She recoiled, grabbing the wound and cried in pain. The cloaked figure planted its feet, and raised its left, clenched fist. With its free right hand, black strands of tentacle-like ribbons slithered from its fingers, wrapping themselves around the wounded Shepherd. Clenching its left fist tighter and tighter, the tentacles strengthened their grip, cracking Amalya's ribs. She cried out in pain, and struggled to gather one breath after the next.

The cloaked figure brought its right hand closer to its covered face, the ribbons shortened, bringing Amalya sinisterly closer. Each breath was harder and harder to take. The world

115

around her began to blur, and the color from her burning red eyes began to dim. The creature unclenched its left fist, revealing talon-like claws. Grazing Amalya's face, it lightly sliced at her chin, "you should not have meddled, young one."

Amalya's drunken eyes raced back and forth, trying to fixate on the dark creature, "what are you?" Amalya choked, a trail of blood dripping down her mouth.

"I have a message for an old friend, and I need you to deliver it...I need you to tell your Keeper that Oblivion is on the horizon...understood?" Its voice hissed creepily. Amalya coughed, which it took for affirmation. Loosening its tight grip on her, the creature set Amalya down, and retracted its tentacle fingers. She barely stood on her own feet, bleeding out. The creature turned to leave her battered, but whipped around suddenly to take a final swing; thrusting its rock-like fists into Amalya's chest, the force sent her across the sphere, crashing into it. The shock caused an unsettling in the foundation of the cavern excavated around it. Rocks began to tumble down, and the sphere began to cave in. "I should have based that message's delivery upon the contingency of your survival..." The cloaked individual grabbed at its dark robe, swinging it around which was followed by a flash of light and the disappearance of the creature. The cavern partially collapsed, crushing the sphere, burying the chamber which held the deepest of my father's secrets.

****

116

The Keeper & Samuel Thomas

"The Deamons?" Samuel inquired carefully.

"Yes, child, the Deamons," the quiet man responded as he sat perched upon his knees, in meditative state.

"But Keeper…" Samuel tried to press further understanding.

"Please," he softly interjected, "no more formality."

Samuel shook his head and reluctantly proceeded, "Do'Shon, I have already heard the Tale of the Deamons. Many times over in fact…"

The Keeper—Do'Shon, as Samuel had addressed him—smiled, ignoring Smauel. "The Writer of Whom is Most High began the story…

Into nothingness, came light. And from light, were borne the *Primordials.* The six original; the *Suns of Solaria.* Three were known as Keepers, two were known as Watchers, and the vacant final was known as the Embodiment.

Following the endlessness of creation, infinity spiraled into forever, creating the counterpart—*The Darkest Heart.* Our destinies were impossibly intertwined.

The Keepers were charged with keeping balance between Solaria and the DarkestHeart. *I* am a Keeper, *I* am a *Primordial. I* am one of the *Six Suns of Solaria…*" Do'Shon's eyes opened, and darted to make clear contact with Samuel's. Samuel could detect that the story he was hearing was in some way fundamentally different from the story he had grown up with.

The pain, the passion, the truth that Do'Shon spoke was with immense consequence and beautiful articulation. His eyes broke from their stare, and fell into blank gaze. "We were given the original Gates," Do'Shon looked around them to the silhouetted machine encasing them, "and from the Gates poured the contained shadow of the DarkestHeart. And so it was ordered for inconceivable time.

However, as every great storyteller must come to understand: order will cede to chaos, and chaos to order..." the smile painted on Do'Shon's face was not one of happiness or gratitude, but rather of mania. Performing the same task endlessly, expecting a potentially different outcome: insanity. Do'Shon had driven himself nearly insane. He had pursued his past many times, in hopes to change that which was arbitrarily unchangeable. A man aware of his insanity makes him that much more dangerous. Same is true for any living being. Simple fact. "My sister, Daxum, had come to sympathize with that of the DarkestHeart; a metaphorical road to perdition. I was a naïve child, then.

The disharmony that she potentiated was treasonous to the covenant of existence; the covenant of which we were sworn to protect. Convention brought us together," Do'shon's eyes raced back and forth as he recounted the memory. His four brothers and sisters convened in a ribbon of darkness illuminated by a single light so that each of their distinct characteristics were hidden from view, allowing only their eyes to be seen. "I accused her of insubordination, and in haste I demanded the resignation of her rite. When she refused, chaos ensued..." Flashes of light exploded across the darkness, illuminating the five robed figures caught in struggle. "In the end, I was successful in denying her rite. I deprived her of that which she had been bestowed, and imposed the miraculous Gate unto my brother, one of the twin Watchers. I banished Daxum..." he paused, clearing his throat. "I banished her to the farthest reaches of existence for her treachery. And in the interim, I was undermined by my eldest sister. In pursuit of Daxum, I had unknowingly turned a blind eye to the sympathies, which were also radiating from Oracle. Truthfully, I was no match for her. She was the progenitor; the one through which all things came. She, and she alone knew what it was to exist as one before there were many; she was the only one to *truly* know the Beginning. Perhaps that is what drove her to such madness..." tears welled in Do'Shon's eyes. "Oracle turned on my brother, the one of which I had bestowed Daxum's gate," he paused, "she killed him. Then she turned to his twin, our brother, and as I had done to Daxum, she banished him to the farthest reaches. This left only the two of us opposed, so wary, so lost.

She berated me for my actions. She insisted that her response was the only possible course; she insisted further that I be punished for my hasty actions. I knew her to be incorrect. In the conflagration that followed, we unleashed what we could of the cataclysmic energy built within us. The impact of the two forces being unleashed convulsed across the Universe, and devastated existence as we had come to know it.

The upheaval resulted in the fracturing of the *DarkestHeart*, and my eventual settling of this now, which I call home.

And so it is.

The Writer of Whom is Most High pushed the pen, and with it, created the child kissed with light. At the dawn, she is born; and as such she brings fire back to the heart of the smoldering star looking down upon her home the vacant and final Sun of Solaria. Her heart is of purity, her blood is of life, her essence is of light: Solaris.

Like a Phoenix, she was destined to lead existence out from the ashes.

With the flick of a pen, The Writer of Whom is Most High gave unto Solaris purpose. It was she, Solaris, that embodied the elements of nature, the one of whom gave unto the Universe as it Known the Guardians.

And for Ages, there was peace. Until..."

————

"The Age of Darkness," Samuel interrupted.

————

"The Age of Darkness. And as Ages passed into Pivitols, Solaris grew weary evermore. With a heaviness, she journeyed to the heart of the Embodiment, and took from it a shard. With the shard, she fashioned man. Together, they bore unto existence a child: the First Savior.

The Age of Darkness was perpetuated by the extrication of the *DarkestHeart* from its containment. The breach led to the fracture, and from each piece, bitter rivals rose from the shadows. Mighty clerics from within each fracture harnessed the ever-expanding reach of darkness and the creatures took form: The Deamons. Each fracture launched a campaign to destroy Solaris and the newly established order of mankind.

When their disjointed efforts failed, the fractures were led to reunification to guarantee certain doom; revenge.

As the shadow descended upon man, Solaris's child was able to produce the most pure of lights, sending the Deamons to the Darkest Reaches of Space, bringing an end to the tyranny of the DarkestHeart."

_____

Samuel was right in his previous proclamation. He had heard the story over and over again. He had never heard it with as much care and detail as what Do'Shon had to offer him, however. The account had moved him, changed him; but he was unaware that it was not over. "Do'Shon, I *have* heard the story..."

_____

"Written word shall come to pass. Veracity behind the Home of the One shall be revealed. The four were borne to protect him. The ten were borne to deliver him. The Shepherds of Eternal Light will grace the child," he choked on his words, "and the Keeper of the Lighthouse will know the truth of Life and Death; paradox..." he delivered the lines that were more or less necessary. "Without the Two, there cannot be the One. And so it is in the End as it was in the Beginning.

The bastard child will bear the name of the messenger. In time, the messenger will be revealed to be the Harbinger. The Harbinger will reunite the fractures, and mark the second rising of the DarkestHeart."

_____

"But Do'Shon, the Seventeenth Savior of Man is born.
The Seventeenth Savior of Man will be borne for this Universe

as the child blessed with the capacity to move existence back to the path of righteousness..."

"No child," Do'Shon sighed. "Perhaps it should have been recounted as such: Veracity behind the *Homes* of the One shall be revealed..." Samuel still did not understand what Do'Shon was getting at. "Joshua Eason Blake is in fact the Seventeenth Savior of Man, but his role in all of this was mere deliverance. It will be the Son of the Seventeenth Savior of Man who will know the End."

Samuel sat heavily, laboring to breathe; tears welled in his eyes. He looked back at his son, and at Nicholas, both of whom still lay on the crystal tables, unconscious. "But..." he still had so many questions. However, when he opened his mouth again, instead of finding the power to articulate his burning inquiries, he simply remarked, "and so it is?"

"And so it is, child."

****

Wednesday – 15
The Shepherd, Jack

Like being turned inside out, and then sucked through a straw. That's the only way that Jack could ever explain the trips. When he exploded back into existence, he did so in the middle of the Robinson's living room. Evelyn and Guthrie Peterson rematerialized on top of Areul and Norman's couch, while Norman and Areul ended up on their coffee table; which collapsed beneath them.

Jack jumped, startled as he stood between the two groups of them on the floor. He looked up at Guthrie and

Evelyn and down at Areul and Norman, "I am sorry. I'm normally much more precise than that..." Jack said helping the Robinson's to their feet and the Peterson's down from the couch.

"It's fine Shepherd, it must be your age getting the better..." Guthrie started with a smile.

"What's going on here?" Clecha interjected into the darkness of the living room. She was standing in the front room, near the door, and peering through the archway into the living room. Her silhouette indicated that she had some sort of blunt object in her possession intending to bludgeon whoever had dared disturb the sanctity of her home. She groped the wall behind her with her left hand looking desperately for a switch to turn on a light. Her trembling fingers finally reached their destination.

"Honey, it's fine," Areul Robinson finally spoke breaking the tension.

Clecha's hand sat rested on the light switch for a moment, debating whether to trust her mother or not. Lightning cracked in the background, and startled her, knocking the light switch on. Her eyebrows scrunched as she fell against the door, and laid eyes upon the Peterson's and Jack standing next to her parents in the next room. She dropped the umbrella in her right hand, and gasped, "you?" directing the question to Jack.

Out of automation, Jack reached for the Peterson's, and the three of them exploded from existence, leaving behind a faint pop, and a flash of blinding light. Clecha blinked her eyes over and over, her knees gave way, and she fell to the ground.

Her parents were quick to respond, rushing to her side. As she dipped between consciousness and not, she forced a series of words from her tingling mouth: "what's going on?" over and over again.

*

Jack hastily exploded back into existence in the crystalline box with the company of the Peterson's. He gasped for a breath, as he stumbled to his feet, and Guthrie was quick to grab firm hold of him. "Just breathe," he implored with Jack as he continued to convulse.

"What happened?" Sandra Thomas asked rushing to their sides.

"Just caught...off...guard," Jack managed to stumble out in between coughs and gasps.

"You are not one to normally scare so easily, Shepherd. What was it?" Samuel persisted, taking leave from his son's side. "Deamons?"

Jack laughed, "not quite..."

Samuel turned to look at Guthrie, he could not understand Jack's sudden levity, "a child," Guthrie offered.

"She recognized me." Jack said finally having gathered his breath.

"I think it will be fin..." Samuel Thomas began as he approached Jack.

"No!" Jack exclaimed. "It won't be. None of this has been fine. I was under strict order to keep the children safe and as unaware of present circumstance for as long as possible. And now I have tainted that promise..."

"Shepherd," Samuel raised his hands as he approached Jack, "I do sympathize with you. And I am not dismissing that which you have confessed. However, I think we have larger things to worry about here." Samuel then turned his attention to the opposite corner of the crystalline cube.

"Do'Shon?" Jack asked scrambling to his feet. He could suddenly sense the tension in the room and dropped formality. He rushed to the Keeper's side, and knelt next to him, trying to study his face. "Do'Shon what is it? What has happened?" Do'Shon did not stir from his meditative state, and after several inquiries, Jack grew weary. "What has happened?" He turned back to Samuel.

Samuel shrugged his shoulders, "The Tale of the Deamons," he simply said.

"So you know, then? You know about the second coming?" Samuel and Sandra nodded their heads in agreement. Jack shook his head, "and so it is," he hastily responded.

Do'Shon broke the solidarity of his meditation, and turned his completely blank face to Jack. Cocking his head to the side, his mouth curled into an odd smile. His pale eyes traced over Jack's face. "You..." his voice escaped from his mouth, "you must find Solaris..." He brought Jack's forehead down to his mouth, and placed a kiss upon it. In doing so, a beautiful white light surged throughout Jack's body. Jack squirmed, winced, and screamed in pain. In the blink of an eye, his body exploded with a screeching pop.

"Do'Shon, what have you done?" Samuel screamed approaching him.

"Joshua Eason Blake is not the only one with the deftness to tamper with destiny."

***

Wednesday – 15
The Blake Family

The island in the kitchen exploded apart as my mother and father crashed violently back into existence in our house. My mother filled the kitchen with inappropriate laughter, as she crawled out from the debris pile, and to my father who lay stunned. "I'm sorry, my love," my mother said touching my father's face, still giggling. She brushed the dust from his face, and stroked his hair off of his forehead.

"For?" He asked laboring for breath.

"The landing...it's been a while," she smiled and exhaled a chuckle.

He smirked, "I'll say," followed by a deep cough.

"What is it?" her voice asked him so tenderly.

"I am fighting the urge to depart from this moment my Shining Lady..." my father's eyelids drooped to cover his deep blue eyes. "I want to keep this forever," he fought the sudden atrophy of his muscles and slid his hand closer to hers to take hold.

"Do not fight, not yet my love. Reserve what you can, for what is to come," tears welled in my mother's eyes as she fought to keep the smile on her face. Her lips quivered as she exerted what effort she could. My father's eyes drooped completely shut and he fell into a deep slumber. My mother sat in catatonia for moments as she embraced what was to come.

126

Her eyes stared blankly at the tile on the floor as it ignited with light as lightning struck in the background. Her mouth began to move, and without thought her angelic voice sang into the night,

"Star of Wonder, Star of Night, Star with royal beauty bright, Homeward leading, still proceeding, guide us to thy Perfect Light..."

A lifetime Ago

Joycelyn Blake

"Tell me, beautiful child," her voice was soft, careful, gracious, "what has brought you here?"

The sound of trickling water rushed in the background, the universe spun in wonder around my mother, as she tried to comprehend marvel. "Who...who are you?" her eyes continued to betray her, deceiving perception of existence.

"I am one. I have been of many, but stand now in solidarity."

"To whom do you stand against?" My mother's voice quivered as she dared to inquire.

"Imbalance."

My mother gasped, "It cannot be...could it be thou? Thy word, which ever so gracefully moves the story of creation, and details existence...The Writer of Whom is Most High?"

There was a slight chuckle, "I cannot claim such stature, no. I am but also a mechanism in a labyrinth larger than myself.

127

In neither convention can I be considered good, nor evil. I exist to protect that with which I have been burdened to accept."

"And what is it that you accept?" My mother continued to probe.

"The fundamental truth of hope."

"Please remove the veil from my eyes so that I may look upon your face and take from it the wisdom of which you have to offer," my mother pleaded.

"You cannot possibly conceive an existence which you do not understand. To lift that veil, would transcend the linear notions of time, space, and the Universe as you have come to understand them."

However, as my mother blinked her eyes, the marvel that surrounded her in a chorus of lights was replaced with a scene of which she could comprehend. She found herself dizzily perched upon a plate glass disk floating in the dark of space. Creation swam around her, as galaxies continued to spin to the beat of the universal pulse. Standing before her, was a being radiating a beautiful luminescence.

Behind the creature of light, stood a short podium, also constructed of glass, containing an ominous glowing box atop it. The box was beautifully crafted with ancient etchings, marking a larger story. My mother's curiosity peaked as she spied the box behind the being of light. "What's in the box?" My mother was very straightforward.

The creature of light stood in silent observation for moments judging my mother's worthiness. "This Universe was born out of struggle and turmoil. There is but one who exists, as you know the word; one who truly can account for the Beginning. There is also but one who exists of whom can truly account for the End. It is not my destiny to know my own, my objective is merely to have seen the conclusion to what you have branded as 'life'. On this eve, one shall become two, and you shall evermore be known as the child 'kissed with sight'."

"Why me?" My mother choked on her words staring blankly into the cosmos. "I am not worthy."

"You are Shining Lady Joycelyn Miracula, are you not?"

"I am."

"Then, as the last in the lineage of the Solarian Kin, you know that you are the **most** worthy." The being of light moved ever so carefully closer to my mother. The box atop the crystalline glass table began to glow a beautiful light, a color of which my mother had never before perceived. Her eyes began to burn again in convulsing radiance. My mother could feel the warmth of the light singeing her skin as the being turned to move toward her. As the creature finally reached my mother, it opened its beautiful eyes, made of crystal, radiating a color of which my mother had never experienced. Existence faded away from my mother; she felt the kiss from the being of light, the kiss, which blessed her with sight.

Sight of what is to come; the End.

A blessing, a curse.

———
***

Wednesday – 15
The Robinson Family

Clecha was so impossibly entangled in dream, that she could not navigate her way out of the maze of her unconsciousness. Her feet moved like water across the smooth, cold floor...step sideways to the right. Bring the left foot next to the right foot. Step backward with the right foot...Violins began to play beautiful harmonies in the background. But, then suddenly, there it was...the rhythmic beating.

It was tribal, primal, soothing. She felt it beat against her own heart; in it she felt likeness. But that was all for a different time. The music faded, the beating faded, and as it did, the world as she knew it began to crash in around her...

"Clecha...sweetheart, can you hear me?"

Clecha's eyes wandered erratically, finally opening to settle upon the sight of her mother, Areul Robinson. "Mom?" Clecha asked, trembling as each sound out of her mouth caused her a great deal of intense pain.

"Clecha?" Norman asked approaching both his wife and daughter, of whom were crowded on the couch in the living room.

Clecha's eyes drunkenly scanned the room, and finally settled upon the sight of her parents. "What...what happened?" The total of their interests pooled together and focused when the television in the background began to stir with news of current world circumstances:

"Please excuse our disturbance to your current programming schedule: WGBL – World Global News, Angela Kither reporting. Hour 41 of continued rain without stop, and more dangerously, no end in sight. Satellite reports are flooding in with images indicating that the storm is rapidly growing, and spreading globally. The unprecedented event has forced the grounding of most air-traffic, and a significant amount of flash flooding throughout the entire continent. Scientists are measuring tectonic shifts of unprecedented proportions, spreading across the entire Northern Hemisphere. The President has joined in conference with other major world leaders in trying to devise a disaster plan, hoping for an eventual end to this tireless storm. Reporting live from our nation's capitol, we now turn to Lane Ava..."

A screeching dissonance filled Clecha's ears and she winced in pain, pulling her attention from the TV. "What's going on?" She asked again confused.

Areul looked down at the broken coffee table laying in pieces on the ground and then turned her gaze to that of her husband. Finally she turned her head back to Clecha, "you just had a startle, and a stumble," Areul winked.

"My head is vibrating," Clecha whispered shutting her eyes, trying to focus the spinning room.

Areul smiled and leaned in, whispering as well, "mine too, baby." She stood to leave, motioning for Norman to clear out as well but Clecha's hand reached out and stopped her mother, "what is it?" Areul whispered carefully.

131

Without opening her eyes, Clecha responded, "tell me a story."

Areul perched herself next to her daughter again and looked at her queerly, "what kind of story?"

Clecha smiled, "a good kind."

Areul contemplated for a moment, and stole a glance at Norman, hoping he could offer her help. When she realized he could offer her nothing, she waved him off. He proceeded to the kitchen, to retrieve a glass of water, leaving Areul to appease their daughter. She seated herself comfortably and cleared her throat, laying her hand upon Clecha's sweating forehead. "Once upon a time, there was a child born of the stars. And as she lived, she traveled the cosmos, visiting each of her other cosmic brothers and sisters. She splintered across existence, connecting the beat of the primal heart to that of the stars surrounding her. A cyclic web of connection and utopia…" her voice trailed off. As Areul shared the story with her daughter, the one in which Clecha believed to be completely fabricated by her mother in that instance, she was closer to Clecha than she could ever know. She rested her hand upon Clecha's warm forehead, and stroked the hair from her face.

"How does it end?" Clecha asked smiling, keeping her eyes closed; she was close again to dizzying sleep.

Areul sat in quiet contemplation before she finally offered her daughter an answer, "with a beginning."

***

Wednesday – 15

The Keeper, Do'Shon

    Silence. Samuel, Sandra, Guthrie and Evelyn sat in complete silence as they watched over their sons, and Do'Shon whom sat in solitude in the corner of the crystal cube. Collectively, the four of them still stood in relative shock over the events they had earlier witnessed. Do'Shon had not moved, nor spoken another word after his brief exchange with Samuel; and the only words exchanged between the four conscious adults were in the silence of their stares.

    A chill ran down Sandra's spine, a spark flicked, and the hairs on Guthrie's neck stood on end, a popping sound startled Evelyn, and a wind tickled Samuel's ear drum. In a miraculous explosion of pink light, Amalya exploded back into existence; blood splattered the floor, she fell to her knees, and finally her head smacked the ground of the crystalline cube. It was only this moment that caused Do'Shon to stir from his trance.

    He jumped to his feet, as Evelyn screamed in the background, and rushed to Amalya's side. The elderly man quivered as he lowered himself down to the gruesome sight. Slowly and tenderly he reached his hand out to caress her. Once his fingers touched her forearm, he felt the beat of her heart begin to slow. He grabbed her arm and turned her over quickly, to face him. Tears were welling in his eyes, "Child," he cried, "what has happened?"

    She labored to breathe, and stared drunkenly at Do'Shon through a thick veil of blood, "O…" she coughed, "Oblivion…is on…the horiz…" her eyes began to roll into the back of her head.

Do'Shon's face took to one of utter horror. He knew what she was trying to tell him. Those simple words drove his blood to course through his veins at a terrifying pace. Closing his eyes, he drew Amalya's hand to his forehead, and whispered, "Dear Writer, please give me the strength…" He thrust his hands down placing them upon her chest and screaming as a beautifully blinding white light filled the crystalline cube. Strikes of lightning lashed out of Do'Shon's body, and in the snap of an instance, he was gone. Left behind were the unconscious bodies of the four adults and Amalya, whom now lay recovered to the *edge* of death; with Do'Shon's intervention, she would survive.

*

The Keeper, Do'Shon, took no measure to mask his apparition within the confines of the Earth. Appearing on wobbly feet upon the rubble that was now our kitchen island, Do'Shon stumbled to where he finally rested his hands upon the tile counter. The cool, slick surfaces sent chills radiating down his fingers, into his gums, tickling his teeth. His entire body shook as his heart raced, beating out of his chest.

Tears rolled down his cheeks; he knew he had only moments, but sensation overrode even his most basic instincts to survive. He turned his head behind him, and looked upon the pile of rubble, which lay on the floor before him. He studied the debris closely, "all the pieces are still here." He smiled and lifted his hands, curling his fingers as he felt a surge of energy flowing through his being. He closed his eyes, and concentrated, clenching his raised hands to fists and taking in the air around him. Upon opening his eyes, he smiled again and bowed his head at the kitchen island, which had been completely restored as if it had been untouched.

He slowly, and silently proceeded out of the kitchen, and walked up the stairs carefully to reach my mother and father. Lightning exploded loudly and violently behind him, the light of which ignited the entire house, but disturbed neither my brother nor I. Pressing even further, Do'Shon reached the top of the stairs, and stared at the doorway in front of him. He continued to walk, and as he pressed the door, it exploded into a million little pieces. Do'Shon brushed the pieces aside, and stepped through; as he stepped safely into my parents' bedroom, the pieces realigned, reforming the door.

My mother stood in vigil, at my father's side, whom still lay unconscious. She startled at the presence of another, she turned, and stared wide-eyed. "Keeper..." she gasped.

"Child, we haven't much time," his voice quivered into the silence.

"What has happened? Why are you here?" My mother's voice was filled with terror as she tried to control herself from convulsing into a fit of screams.

"The time has come, child. The one, who has truly seen the *Beginning*, shall seek the *End*. Oblivion is on the horizon."

And just like that; just as Do'Shon had proclaimed, a bolt of ferocious lightning surged through the roof of our house, crashing through and materializing as a being shrouded in darkness within my parents' room. The cloaked individual turned its cowl to stare both at Do'Shon, then my mother.

135

"You…" its voice was deep, dark, "…are quite elusive, Joycelyn Miracula."

"Who are you?" My mother asked standing her ground.

"Sister, do not do this," Do'Shon pled from behind.

The cloaked individual turned its cowl to stare at Do'Shon, hissing with rage, "how dare you?" it screeched.

"Oracle, I cannot allow you to tempt fate in such a way…" Do'Shon pled. The cloaked being raised its hands screaming in rage, as light surged in Do'Shon's direction. The Keeper stood firm at the doorway, and swung his hands, clapping them together, exerting a force upon both the lightning surging for him, and the being cloaked in darkness; the one of whom Do'Shon accused of being his sister. In a whirlwind the being inched ever closer to Do'Shon, and a battle of wills ensued.

My mother turned from the quarrel, to retrieve my father in hopes to escape. Her hopes were immediately dashed as she turned into a cold, rock-like wall. Looking up, she stood horrified at the sight she beheld, a Deamon. With no time to think, she plunged both of her fists into the black crystal of the creature's abdomen. The strike left no mark, but the force was enough to propel the rock-like creature to the other side of the room. She knelt down, and twisted to face the doorway. She held out each of her fists in front of her, and closed her eyes concentrating. She gripped reality in such a way, that a ripple scattered through the walls of my house, hiding any trace of my brother or myself.

"What are you trying to hide?" The creature screamed, recovering to its crystalline feet. It lunged over my mother, jumped past Do'Shon's struggle with the cloaked figure, and crashed through the wall, landing in the hallway. By the massive force that my mother exerted upon existence in that very moment, a wave of energy began to consume our house. The wave had safely safeguarded my existence, and concealed me from sight, however, it was not quick enough to intervene on my brother's behalf. The Deamon crashed through the wall, just as his doorway was beginning to fade from existence, but the creature was quicker than my mother's attempt at salvation.

Snickering, the Deamon approached the disappearing doorway, and violently struck his way through, finding my brother, lying peacefully unconscious in his bed. "In one fell swoop, the Savior *and* the Son..." the creature's clunky rock-like, crystalline hands reached out, and grabbed my brother's limp body.

My mother still knelt down, holding onto reality with what might she could. Her eyes burned as the struggle between Do'Shon and the cloaked figure reached a peak. "*I seek the End!*" The line caused the hairs on the back of my mother's neck to stand on end. A beautiful light emerged from between the two warring individuals, and in a brilliant flash, the two of them were gone. Tears streamed down my mother's face, her heart ached for the atrocity that was being committed unto her home. The Deamon filed back into the room with my brother in its hands, "You have failed," its voice bickered.

"You will pay for what you are about to do, I promise you that," my mother growled between gritted teeth.

"Then, even you know that trying to fight me would be futile." The deamon bit.

"Futile or not, I will fight to the end."

"Then you are foolish," the Deamon retorted. Whipping its empty left hand, a surge of black lightning smacked my mother across the room. Approaching my father's unconscious body, the Deamon shuddered in excitement.

My mother shrieked in horror as she looked up to spy the Deamon clutch my father, and disappear in an explosion of violent black lightning, which tore a hole in my house, and rendered my mother unconscious. Her grip on reality slipped from her, and all of the artifacts she had worked to conceal, including the doorway leading to my bedroom, rippled back into existence. A tear slipped from her eyes, as her mind faded off to a dream that was more beautiful than the life she was given.

***

Friday – 17

Every muscle in my body tensed. I suddenly woke, and jumped from bed. A nauseating chill ran down my body, and left me uneasy. I tried to stand, but the movement made me sick. I leaned over the side of my bed and convulsed as I puked onto the floor. I wiped the excess saliva from my mouth onto my shirt. I reached for my nightstand, grabbing for my glasses and finally placed them on my face bringing clarity to my room. I blinked several times, trying to adjust my eyes to read the clock. Finally rubbing the sleep out of my eyes, and perking them enough to interpret my surroundings, I read the time as 9:35AM; further, to my horror, I read the date: Friday, March 17.

The doorbell rang. My head was still spinning, which had to have been the explanation for my misreading of the clock. I blinked several times, but it was of no use, each time, I still read the same time on the same day. I was dreaming. The doorbell rang again; it jarred my attention. "You're going to wake up when you open the door," I said aloud. That's how it always worked.

Fighting every urge I had to vomit further, I managed to my feet, and used the walls to guide my way to my bedroom door. The doorbell rang twice quickly. I tried to control my breathing, as I felt my heart beating in my ears. My hand touched the cool doorknob, which chilled me. I opened the door, and continued to crawl out of my room. Looking at the opposite end of the hallway, I stared for a moment carefully studying the pile of debris sitting in his doorway. There were dark marks trailed on the carpet from my parents' doorway to my brother's room. The entire house was bathed in darkness, so I could not fully discern the amount of damage that had been mysteriously incurred upon my house. The doorbell rang again.

I glacially moved down the stairs, and stepped slowly to the front door. Without even peering outside first, I unlocked the door, and opened it. Lightning cracked in the background, startling me. "Clecha…" I gasped. She stood on my front porch, soaking wet and in disarray.

"What day is it?" Her eyes were sunken and distressed.

I stared back at her just as confused, "slap me."

"What?" She asked trying to hold back her tears.

"Slap me." I commanded her again. She did not hold back this time. She raised her right hand, and slapped me across the face. Her wet hand left a sting and a red mark across my cheek. A tear welled immediately in my left eye.

"I'm so sorry," she apologized profusely.

I cupped my left cheek, "it's really Friday..." Clecha's bottom lip quivered at my proclamation.

"Where is everyone?" Clecha asked looking around our dark house.

"I...I haven't checked." I turned around and looked up the staircase leading to my parents' doorway. Leaving the door open, and Clecha on the front porch, I proceeded upstairs, slowly. As I continued on, Clecha stood at the doorway still. Her eyes were fixed dead ahead of her. Slowly peeling her eyes away, she looked up at me, nearing the top step. Swallowing hard, she pushed herself to follow.

I reached the doorway, and upon closer investigation, I noticed that half of their left door had been ripped off, and part of the doorframe had been damaged. I approached cautiously, motioning for Clecha to keep quiet and at a safe distance. Step by step, I inched closer to the doors with every muscle trembling in fear. I reached my shaking right hand out, and groped for the doorknob. Turning it carefully, silently, I whipped the door open, in hopes to surprise whomever, or whatever was on the other side waiting for me.

Instead, the air rushed out of my lungs, as I stood in complete astonishment. "What the...fuck." I wasn't quite sure if it was a statement or a question.

Clecha rushed to my side, and stared in horror. My parents' bedroom lay in thousands of pieces, mostly scattered between our first floor, and backyard. The sound of water rushed into my ears, I had somehow misplaced it until that moment. "What's going on?" Clecha asked, immediately tearing up.

"I'm losing my damn mind," I whispered, staring at the hole in my house, wide-eyed.

III: The Legacy

77 Years Ago
Joshua Blake

"I don't...I," he sighed. "I don't get this, dad." My father was at one time also a very impatient child. He sat in a field filled of tall grasses, flowers, and shrubbery. Meditation, my grandfather would have maintained, was the only way one could peer through the arbitrary illusions of reality, to find the coherent string of harmony. My father kept his eyes closed, as he was commanded, and did his best to follow along.

"Just breathe," the voice belonged to another, to my grandfather, a voice that I, unfortunately, never had the pleasure of hearing in person. His voice was filled with rasp, age, but most of all a deep sense of heart.

The air rushed into my father's lungs, stinging his nostrils as it entered. Exhaling, he opened his mouth, and felt the air rush from his body until he had nothing left to push. "Why have you brought me here?"

"Just breathe," the man's voice commanded again.

"Damnit father! I asked you a question." My father, my young father yelled in anger. He pounded his fist onto the ground and opened his eyes, breathing heavily now. He stared across from him, at the man he had just cursed, his father, my grandfather. The man, he sat with his legs crossed, his fists resting on his knees, his eyes closed, his heart beating, and his mind in meditation. "Well?" My father asked expectantly.

Without opening his eyes, his father chuckled softly, "my young Joshua, you are always seeking the answer, before you have the correct question."

"What is the correct question, father?" My young father tried to close his eyes, and focus as my grandfather had been leading him to do.

"That, is not the correct question."

My father took a deep breath, and opened his right eye to stare at his father grudgingly. Closing his eye again and returning his focus to his breathing, he finally spoke, "my patience is waning..."

"I am but trying your patience, my son." He was very matter of fact.

"For?" my father's eyebrows furrowed indicating his inquiry.

The two of them sat in the silence, as my grandfather ignored my father's persistent impatience. The sound of rushing water filled my grandfather's ears and carried his mind to peace. Just beyond the field, in which the two of them were perched, there was a large lake with several smaller streams feeding into it. Each breath was filled with life, and as he exhaled he spoke, "Why are we here, Joshua?"

My father breathed deeply, trying to keep his breath in sync with my grandfather. There was a sudden ache building in his chest, and could be visibly seen on his face. Trying to conceal emotion, my father finally spoke, "so I may seek the answers to the questions of which I must ask."

"The creation that surrounds you is a part of you. The miracle of life permeates your being. Take in the air around you, as it has been given to you, let it fill your lungs. As you exhale, feel it join one again with existence. Feel the earth beneath you, feel it calling to you..."

My father unclenched his fists, which were resting upon his knees, and began to slide them down his legs carefully. Exhaling, he moved his hands to the ground, and brushed the ground slowly, before he dug his fingers into the earth, burying his fingertips under the dirt. He inhaled again, and quivered as he felt an explosion erupt in his chest, and travel throughout his entire body, leaving him trembling. "I...I can..." he shuddered in fear.

"Let go of the emotion," my grandfather was very stern in this command. "Look passed convention, and truly *feel*. My sweet child, in time you will leave me, but before you do, I have brought you here for a very beautiful reason..."

"I will never leave you father," my father's eyes were still closed.

"Do not speak in such absolutes, my young Joshua, it is unbecoming of you. I have foreseen a great many things, and who am I...who are we to contest?"

His voice echoed around my father's head, and bounced around in beautiful chorus. The sunlight bathed his body, the

144

air burned his lungs; he was at peace. "I can feel it, father." A sudden jolt surged through his body, and ripped his eyes open. "Everything…" he stuttered, "is happening…"

My grandfather finally opened his sunken blue eyes, and looked back, studying my father's face carefully. He grinded his molars, clenching his jaw as he did; and after moments of deafening tension, he cleared his throat to speak. "I have brought you here to feel…"

"…the heartbeat." My father cut in.

Nodding his head lightly, he acknowledged my father's words, "You see, my young Joshua, you are very special to this Universe, and in time, you will come to know that a heartbeat is a very powerful thing…"

***

52 Years Ago

"This is Scout-12, 3rd hour past morningrise, First-Class Ranking Officer Joshua E. Blake reporting. Our second pass through the nebular regions on the outer edge of Tier Three Territory, near the Klondaessian Empire has shown to be as tedious as the first.

All spectral analyses using GRID have shown negative correlation for weapon's signature of any type. The, so-called, nebular flares reported by Klondaessia III cannot be confirmed at this time to be of a ballistic nature. Other causes point to be of natural spatial occurrence. The Specialist on the survey team will report with further detail on those grounds…End Log."

My father stared at the computer screen in front of him, reading over the log to make sure that his dictation had not been lost in translation. His tired blue eyes looked carefully over each word to make sure that the computer had in fact correctly dotted all of the i's, and crossed all of the t's— knowing full-well that the computer had no other way to possibly complete the task. Nearly insane, the computers performed the same task time and again, with the same care and detail as before, but they did not beg for a different outcome. Nor did they hope for one.

"That looks good," he said accepting the authenticity of the message. "Encrypt and transmit to the Tier Three Central Dispatch. Request recall orders. Command." He exhaled as the screen went dark, rubbing the sleepiness from his eyes and pushed himself out from the computer station at which he was docked. Turning around, he walked across the cramped, dark cabin and approached a small metal-plated door preceded by two stairs. Climbing the stairs, he pulled the lever, disengaging the locking mechanism on the door, and pulled the door open. As he stepped through the portal, he stared out at the amazing sight laid out before him. The small cockpit he stepped into was lined with windows, which gazed out into the beautiful expanse of space.

Standing confidently, "helmsman, bring us about," my father said crawling into the small chamber, and taking his seat above two others, each to either his left or right. He took his seat strapping in, and began to scroll through the survey readings for the last few hours.   Without turning his attention from the reports, he spoke again, flatly, "begin heading to the nebula's rim."

"Have we received recall orders, sir?"

146

Annoyed at being questioned, my father barked back, "I'm drowning in anticipation." Without further exchange, the helmsman—the man to my father's right—obliged the order. The beautiful gasses surrounding the craft as it swam through space began to cascade as an illusory dust cloud as the small ship moved through it. The stars began to shine through the silky veil of the nebular gasses as the ship pushed closer to the nebular rim.

There was a warning from beside my father. It was the kind of sound that indicates something is wrong; a grating noise, a klaxon. "What is it, Specialist?" My father asked, quickly coming to attention.

The woman sitting to his left was furiously working over her computer console while trying to discern what she was reading. "Sir, I'm...I'm not sure. I'm reading something..."

"Can you be a bit more specific?" My father begged annoyed further.

She continued to labor over the readings, trembling, "no sir, I'm afraid I cannot. I've never tracked an anomaly quite like this before. I cannot correlate it to anything in the GRID databases!"

"Relay," my father interrupted impatiently. He began to study the readings, scrunching his eyebrows as he confirmed what the Specialist was telling him. Suddenly, before he could speak, there was an explosion of light before their eyes. My father's breathing betrayed him, as his pulse began to race. A surge of ballistic and technical data was overwhelming my father's eyes, as the information continued to relay to his computer station. "Po...Polarize the hull!" He scrambled watching the disbursal pattern of the energy wave cascading their way.

"Sir?" The helmsman to his right cried.

"Do it!" the Specialist yelled back staring at the ballistic detail of the concussive force that was exerting itself their way.

"Course?" The helmsman asked, this time, reacting just as frantically as my father and other crewman.

As my father looked out the window at the shockwave that was quickly heading for them, he gasped, "anywhere but here."

"Hull polarized. I'm pushing Scout out of the nebula..."

"There's no time!" The Specialist cried in horror.

"Sir, if we..."

"Just do it," my father said between gritted teeth.

"Aye," The helmsman responded.

The small craft jerked from its held position, and began to move in a beeline for the rim of the nebula. Just as the shockwave began to descend upon the small ship, which would likely be torn apart in the wake, the ship exploded in a flash of green light, disappearing from harm's way.

"The SAFE portal enveloped some of the nebular gas, it's reacting with the Event! Attempting to compensate!" The helmsman yelled.

The hull of the small craft shuddered violently. My father worked to keep his eyes closed, and his fists clenched, holding on as the turbulence shook them. "I'm trusting you, Samuel," sparks flew from a computer console above my father, startling him. "Keep it together."

"Brace yourselves..." the helmsman, Samuel commanded, keeping the course. "3," he started counting, "2," my father inhaled through his nose, "1."

Exhaling, my father's stomach lunged out of its place, and flew into his throat as the small scout ship exploded back into existence in the dead of space. Pieces of the hull detached, and splintered across the weightless star field. The ship spiraled out of control into the infinite abyss of space, and the three of them began to fade to unconsciousness, the blood rushing from their brains against gravitational force. When my father came to, some-time later, he was disturbed to behold that both of his officers lay in their posts, still unconscious, possibly wounded, and that the forward cabin glass plating was cracked in several locations.

Clearing his throat, the vibrations radiated up his neck and erupted his senses into vertigo. Taking a deep breath, he closed his eyes, as he tried to focus, "status?" my father asked into the ether. The cracked computer screen in front of him came back to life, flickering intermittently. Becoming mildly preoccupied with a gash in his head, and the resulting blood dripping from it, my father turned his attention back to the detail the computer was trying to deliver. Running through the list of damaged items, my father fell into a depressed sulk.

"Engine plating, major structural stress, running on partial auxiliary power reserves, leaking oxygen levels...What are the chances I can repair the Scout to make another SAFE jump?" My father asked.

Without even needing to calculate the odds, the computer responded stoically: "0." The screen made a hissing noise, before a set of sparks flew from it, leaving it dark. My father fell back into his seat, defeated.

It took my father three hours to drag his two other crewmen from the cramped cabin into the aft chamber to assess their vitals. They had lived, however they had sustained injuries that my father could not repair. He shuddered at the thought, as if they were pieces of machinery that required 'repair'. He moved quickly to the back computer station to determine whether it had been damaged or not. To his relief, it was still functional. Using what little finesse he had with computers, he did his best to sustain control over the lifeless craft.

Oxygen levels were falling from 87%. The reactions from the nebular gas as the helmsman, Samuel, had stated, interacted with their faster than light event with great volatility. When the ship had crashed back into existence, several pieces of the hull and the engine casing had been ripped violently off, leading to major structural damage, and now a punctured oxygen tank.

The repairs necessary to the craft were, like the repairs to his crewmen, beyond his capability. He peeked his eyes to the left to spy the stasis units embedded into the wall, thankful that they looked intact. When he queried the computer station to their status, he was unhappy to find them disabled due to power preservation. Crunching the numbers, he did his best to devise a plan that could keep his crew alive for as long as possible. He was the highest-ranking official on the ship. If it came down to it, he would go down with it.

Taking a labored breath, my father rose from the computer station, and began to prep two stasis chambers for occupation. Moving each the helmsman, and the Specialist to the stasis units, my father tethered them to the computer to monitor their vitals. Before sealing the tubes, my father turned back to the computer and began to input a script of computer code. Upon finishing the string of code, he proceeded back to the stasis tubes, and sealed them carefully. "Stay safe…" he whispered. Pressing the final command button on the computer console, the computer began to process the commands my father had input. The lights began to dim throughout the aft chamber, the heating system shut down, oxygen output slowed and the magnetic field being generated by the centrifugal motorizors ceased. Anything that wasn't nailed down, including my father, lost their gravitational tie to the surfaces beneath them. The stasis tubes erupted in life. My father had sacrificed pleasantries in order to hopefully save his crewmen.

At the new current state of oxygen output throughout the small craft, and the reduction in ambient temperature not only for the stasis pods but also for my father, the ship would not run out of oxygen for what my father estimated to be five days. Floating weightless, my father made his way to his bunk, through the field of debris now surrounding him. He needed to gather his thoughts.

Days one and two in solitude, my father devoted much of his time and effort into sustaining energy reserves, and reestablishing a basic sense of direction by focusing his limited knowledge of computer subsystems into the navigation controls. When that failed, my father turned to simple observation, and compiling what he could to analyze against star charts, hearkening to men before him. By day three, however, my father's resolve had begun to wane. His calculations had been highly marginal and the oxygen reserve was depleting much faster than he could come up with a solution for.

In flagrant disregard for his life, my father decided he would have his last few hours, day, however long, spending it watching the stars spin infinitely before him. Sitting at his command station at the front cabin of the small craft, he huddled to conserve what body heat he had left; draped in a thermal blanket and wrapped in several jackets and scarves my father tapped at the computer screens in front of him. To his delight, with a final flick, he was given fractured sight. Slowly typing in his final request, he smiled as he pressed enter.

The screen went black momentarily, and when it came back, it was simply blank, with a blinking cursor. Inhaling, and exhaling, my father watched the cold air as it billowed out of his mouth. Licking his lips, he began, "Joshua Eason Blake, rrrre...reporting." He shivered. The cursor moved, scribing each word that my father managed to quiver out:

"Scout-12 encountered a spatial...spatial gravity well, of um, made of uhh...of some kind. Inter...um...mix between gasses, and SAFE portal...and gravity distor...Scout-12 was heavily damaged..."

Each gap in my father's speech reflected his inability to keep his composure, often falling off to a small two to three minute nap, sometimes even coming to an hour or so later to find himself in the middle of a sentence. He wanted so badly to convey everything that was racing through his mind, but his mortal body was keeping him from being able to get it all out in time. Frustrated, tears began to stream from his eyes, and freeze on his cheeks as he came to the realization that he was running out of time, and there was nothing that he could do to stop it. He sat quietly in contemplation, knowing that his next few words could likely be his last.

"Fath...Dad, I, I don't have much time left. It's been what, 18...? As it sit here in the silence...alone, I think back to your words...I'm sorry that I let you down. I'm sorry I left you. I thought...I thought that I could make a bigger difference out here. Now, in facing...Death, I stare wide-eyed...out into the expanse of beautiful stars. The Pioneers before us; and the Ones to come after. The Children. I, I cannot be the One to save all that is worth saving. For this life...I have only you to thank..."

The screen went black after that. My father could not be certain as to whether it was keeping a record any further. But he had said all that he had wanted to say, more or less. He would spend these, the last few moments that he breathed, staring in glory, as his heartbeat slowed further more.

"I have not the power to create where there is none. I merely have but the power to grant you understanding. Do as you were told. Breathe. Feel the Universe. Feel its heart beat within your own. Feel its fire..."

"Who...who are you?" My father's eyes were growing heavy. The voice he did not recognize, as it intruded into his thoughts through his ears. A gorgeous light exploded before him, blinding what sight he had left. Laboring to breathe as his heart worked to push his crystallizing blood through his veins, his world caved in around him and darkness crept from the edges of his mind, taking over his body.

*

A magnificent and terrifying bolt of lightning surged through the darkness. In quiet solitude, my father's senses roared to life. Unable to command most of his motor functions, my father turned his head sorely to his left and right. Simultaneously trying to open his eyes and speak, when he failed, he resulted that he was dead. Death was cloaked in darkness, a darkness where no scream could escape. No light, no beat, no life could exist.

A murmur crept into his ear, and traveled down into his heart. His heart. His heart, it was all that could fill his thoughts. It raced through his mind, as his blood raced through his veins. His heart was beating. A delicate touch wiped across his eyes, removing from them blindness. Emerging from the murkiness, my father was saved.

When sight was restored to his tired eyes, my father was graced with a vibrantly beautiful portrait come to life. Standing before him, was a beautiful angel, halo made of light and all.

*Perhaps he **was** dead*, he thought. Opening his mouth to speak, he was shushed by the touch of its hand. Moving closer, his pupils dilated, trying to encapsulate her beauty. Gasping for air, pain inundated my father's senses. He *had* lived, and for now, he would again find comfort in unconsciousness.

Some time later, after my father's resolve had returned to him, he again found the strength to open his eyes. As the blurry world around him came back into focus, sound vibrated through my father's ears and traveled to his brain. Feeling the beat of his heart, my father heard a faint beeping noise in the background echoing his vitals. Inhaling and exhaling, my father turned his neck to the right, to spy two other beds, filled with his crewmembers. Carefully turning his neck to the left, he noticed his other company, a woman sitting at a computer console just feet away from him.

"You're an angel..." my father's raspy voice managed.

Startled, the woman looked up, from her station. "Not quite," she laughed, "but I am a doctor." Moving to her feet, she stepped around the computer station, and proceeded to my father. As she came closer, my father could make out her features more fully. Her black hair was pulled back tightly in a long ponytail, which rested upon her back, and she wore a long white lab coat. The coat was form fitting, and reached down to her ankles, she wore it as though it were a dress. Her yellow eyes peered into my father's, "how are you feeling?"

It was he, who smiled this time, "like death."

"I hate to disappoint, but there will be none of that today, least not in my infirmary."

"Where am I?" my father inquired.

155

"I should best leave that up to my Lady to explain. I will fetch after her," she said departing from my father's side, and back to her computer station. The room sat in relative silence, only recounting the beats of each of their hearts. My father did not speak again, nor did the woman.

After minutes, perhaps even hours of tense silence, there was a hissing noise. My father watched as two white panels in the wall came to life, and finally split open, revealing a doorway. Slowly, the 'click-clack' of shoes bounced off of the empty walls. Finally coming into focus, the air rushed from my father's lungs. "You..." he said breaking the tension. "You, are an angel," he corrected himself.

She smiled queerly, "I am Lady Joycelyn Miracula..."

My father's eyes widened, his blood slowed, "the last of the Solarian Kin."

My young mother stood before him, radiating beauty and exuberance. Her eyes were locked with his, and for moments the world around them dissolved away leaving only the two of them in existence. Time stopped, leaving only their pulses to intrude. She brushed her soft, gentle right hand over his forehead carefully, and leaned in to kiss him. Pressing her lips against his, she fulfilled her primal desires. Opening her eyes, and slowly parting her lips from his, she spoke, "we must get you Home."

"For?" My father asked wearily.

She smiled in response.

****

Thursday – 16
Joshua Blake

Water splashed onto my father's face, stinging the open lacerations, and bringing him screaming back to life. With each roar of pain, his body ached even further. Unable to completely open his left eye, he opened his right as wide as he could. He was surrounded in darkness, not able to discern any detail. His hands were bound in cold hard shackles, and chained up, leaving him dangling from his arms in his unconsciousness. Struggling to use his feet, he finally planted them down on the ground, trying to ignore the pain radiating up his shins, and alleviated some of the tension on his wrists.

Focusing what energy he had left, my father did his best to reconstruct the events that had led him to current circumstance. Having been deep within hibernation, however, my father was unable to recollect how he had negotiated his way into this dark, dank place. "Hello?" he finally commanded enough to speak.

No response humored him immediately.

Leaning his head back, my father rested his head upon what felt like a rock wall behind him. His chest heaved as he breathed; tears welling in his eyes. "Joycelyn..." there was nothing but silence. "Father...?" there was nothing but silence. "Keeper...?" there was nothing but silence.

He wept.

There was a stir in the darkness. My father picked up his gaze to peer into the abyss. A tiny glimmer of light sparked in the distance. Squinting his eyes, he tried to discern who, or what was approaching him. Adrenaline sped through his body, his heart raced; there was nothing he could do. Coming into view, the image that stood before my father, filled him with rage, terror, and fear. "My child?" he whispered.

It was not I, nor was it my brother. The sinister impersonator used my face, our face, fixing its eyes, not ours, on my father. Curls appeared at the end of its mouth, flashing a brilliantly evil smirk. As if the apparition were made of smoke, its essence began to billow away into a cloud of unrecognizable matter. Chills shuttered down my father's spine. The fire died down, the smoke cleared away, leaving my father with a new, more disturbing visitor. The creature, the spirit, whatever it was, now stood as a sinister twin to my father.

After moments of tense silence; staring in stalemate at one another, my father spoke, "What are you doing here?"

A sinister chuckle giggled out of my father's mouth, although the sound did not belong to him. His twin smirked, glaring at him in mania. "I could ask you the same question, young Joshua. I have yet to fully understand what it is you have attempted to do here. You have made things very difficult for me. I will say, however, you are much more clever than I remember. It must be your wise age catching up with you," it winked at my father.

"What I have done, will change the very fabric of existence as we know it. It will change the future…"

There came a snicker from the surrounding darkness. The snicker did not belong to my father, nor did it belong to his sinister twin. "You arrogant fool." Footsteps rustled in the shadows, each one heavier than the next. A single, rock-like, crystalline foot stepped into the shadow being cast off by the light from the apparition of my father's sinister twin. The steps ceased, and there was a thud, followed by a groan. There was now a body stirring on the ground next to my father's evil copy.

Trying to focus his eyes, my father squinted to discern any identifying features. His breath ran shallow, and his bottom lip quivered as his head tilted to the side. The color drained from his eyes, and tears welled. "My son," he whispered.

The evil apparition of my father kneeled down to the ground, casting more light for my father to make for certain. Grabbing the limp body by the back of the collar, my father's twin lifted it, facing it to my father, confirming his worst fears. "What was it that you always used to say, young Joshua?" His twin smiled looking at the body, "your job was to deliver Him unto us?" The creature laughed.

The air rushed out of my father's lungs. "Deavon...no..." he pled.

My brother's limp body began to stir. His head bounced back and forth, and finally, his eyes began to break open. A dizzying array of lights surged into my brother's eyes, blinding him. His body ached, and with each breath, his heart palpitated.

"Son," my father's sweet voice quivered.

"Da...dad?" Deavon barely scrambled out through his agonizing pain.

"De...Deavon, son, listen to me. We don't have much time,"

"Indeed," my father's sinister twin hissed.

My father continued, "Deavon, look for the light. Listen for the beat. And everything will be..."

159

"Just fine," the evil apparition growled placing not my father's hand, but rather a claw-like talon on my brother's chest. A terrifying scream filled the cavern, and tore through my father's heart. He could feel my brother's pain radiating throughout his body, filling his stomach with helpless rage. His chest heaved with sorrow as tears poured out of each of his eyes. When it was done, the sinister copy of my father removed his hand from my brother's chest, letting go of his neck simultaneously. My brother hit the ground without resistance; smoke billowing out from under his chest. My father's knees gave out from under him, and an eruption of bile and acid exploded from my father's mouth onto the cold ground. He hung from his wrists, in pain, in shame.

A maniacal smile crept onto my father's twin's face as it turned its glare back to my father. When my father did not stir, emptily staring into the darkness, his twin approached him, kneeling down to him. In the darkness my father could hear the sound of my brother's body being dragged away by the rock-like creature. "You have put together quite the ruse here, young Joshua..." his twin remarked. Again, my father showed no interest. Kneeling down further, the sinister apparition moved into my father's line of sight. "I simply do not know what it is that you think you are trying to accomplish..."

Shaking, my father turned his face to his double's, "you..." he heaved. "You fucking monster!" He screamed ripping his shackles from the rock walls, and lunging through the incorporeal being. Flying through the apparition, it disappeared, billowing away in a cloud of smoke. My father struck his head violently against the rock wall opposing him in the cavern. Falling to the ground, my father felt the warmth from the blood pouring out of the gash in his forehead; slipping, he let go to unconsciousness.

****

47 Years Ago

The sound of water filled my father's ears. The cold stone on his neck, hands and along his back slowed his racing heart. "My son," the sound intruded into my father's concentration, but he did not stir. Inhaling, his racing thoughts collected into one, exhaling he shuddered. "What is bothering you?" My father finally opened his eyes to peer at his father, who was sitting across from him, cross legged and studying his son.

Eyes darting back and forth, my father did not know where to begin, "I have many emotions, father." He looked down at the ground, at the artificial grass upon which he sat, and began to run his fingers through it. "You look tired, father."

"Pay it no mind, my son. Continue."

"There is unrest."

"There is *always* unrest, my child."

"There are injustices."

"There is always injustice."

The two of them sat in quiet contemplation and meditation, hoping to come back to some sort of center amongst the chaos reverberating between their beings.

"The water brings me peace." He finally picked his gaze up to look at his father again. "I have asked Lady Joycelyn

Miracula for her hand in marriage, and she has accepted," my father was very matter-of-fact in his proclamation.

"Then this is a joyous occasion, is it not?" My grandfather implored.

My father sat in quiet contemplation for moments, deliberating his response. "Such celebration among such chaos. So much turmoil and tumult."

"My Joshua," his father sighed, "you must draw lines. You must learn when to let go of these grievances, lest you let them consume you whole. This news of wedding Lady Joycelyn Miracula is of the grandest celebratory nature. Dear child, you must live."

My father chuckled at my grandfather's advice. "But father, how can I? How can I possibly, when I know what I know?"

"Destiny is not something you can contest, my child. What has been written has been written in proverbial stone. And it is your destiny that is so precious, my son."

At this, my father darted his eyes to meet his father's again, "Of course, father...my destiny."

****

40 Years Ago

The dull beeps, coupled with the mechanical sounds of breathing had cooed my father to sleep. When he opened his eyes again, he was startled to see that he was not alone, not in the sense that he had catered to understand. He was sitting in a circular room, the walls most of which were covered in computer screens displaying models of a human body and correlating a series of vitals to the model. Lying on the table in front of him was his ailing, aging father—my grandfather. It was not his father's presence that startled him, but the presence of yet another, in the darkness across the examination table.

Turning his attention back to his unconscious father, who continued to lay on the table, my father took his father's hand, and began to caress it softly. He had cried enough leading up to this point, that he no longer had any sorrow left to share. With a simple point, and without turning his attention away from my grandfather, my father spoke: "You are quite brave to disturb my peace."

"I am. But that was never my intent."

"Which?" my father inquired to the still shrouded intruder.

"Either. To come off as brave, or to disturb your peace."

"You cannot harm me," my father confided.

"Of this, you are quite correct, young Joshua."

My father was not threatened by the voice. In all actuality, he was comforted by the intruder, and the soothing way in which he addressed him. My father leaned forward, closer to his father, under the only light in the room. He tenderly stared at his ailing father, whom slipped further and further from life with every second that passed. Tears welled in his eyes as he tried carefully to hold his emotions back. Emotions of rage, sorrow, fear and trepidation filled his body. Trembling, he licked his lips, "he," his voice cracked, "he was the first one to call me 'young Joshua'. It was always 'my young Joshua' this, or 'my young Joshua' that. It drove me nuts," he laughed uncomfortably. "It made me feel small, weak. It filled me with resentment. When my mother was still alive, she always assured me that it was not a diminutive remark, it was meant to be endearing. I never understood what she was trying to get at—I never trusted her words. I regret that I didn't try harder now. But I suppose hindsight is 20/20." It was as if, in this moment, my father had suddenly felt a deep call from within to confess his worldly transgressions to the stranger in the darkness. He had no reasonable reason, he merely sought absolution.

"She was a diamond in the rough—my mother, that is. She believed so passionately in the independence and democracy of our government and had such a beautiful faith in our existence. She taught me such a kind sense of humility...and she was taken too soon. Now my father is on the verge of death, and I am at the precipice of venturing into a life where I have neither of them to turn to. And I'm supposed to be this great leader, to fulfill some destiny that some monk, or some Author, put on paper Pivotals ago words that said that one day I might make a difference." Each sentence flowed into the next as if there were no punctuation whatsoever; he did so in order to shield his pain. "I spent too much time hating him for things that were out of his control. We're all just puppets; I merely wish I would have stopped fighting that truth a long time ago." Staring at his hand, which was still clasped to his father's, my father chuckled once under his breath. "The Alliance is falling apart. We're at the brink of civil war, built upon mountains of misconceptions and Ages of preconceived prejudice. Yet here I am, this child...this man, lost in the void." He chewed on his tongue for a moment, and then lifted his eyes to stare at the stranger in the darkness. "I can't...I can't guarantee that I won't try to kill you for disturbing me today. I simply do not have the patience."

"You may save your effort, child. I am not of a malevolent nature. Nor am I truly here..." Stepping closer the cloaked being came closer into the light. Slowly raising his hands, he reached for the hood, which shrouded his face in darkness. Carefully, he peeled the hood back, revealing his face. "You, child, are not alone," his words were gentle, sweet. "I am but an echo; a light in the darkness. I burn at the center of a star at the center of a galaxy far from here. I keep balance, and beauty, and love in harmony. My name is Do'Shon..."

"*Joshua*?" Her voice infringed upon my father's quiet meditation.

When my father opened his eyes again, he still found himself in the circular room, where his father still lay upon the bed in front of him. Instead of being in the company of the stranger, however, my father was now in the company of my mother, my young mother. Taking his free left hand, my father grabbed my mother's hand, which was perched upon his right shoulder. He closed his eyes, and felt still in the moment, taking in the finality all he could. Opening his saddened eyes, my father gazed upon hers, "Be still."

Letting go of his father's hand, my father stood and joined my mother. The two of them moved to the foot of the examination bed, taking each other's hands. Standing before them was a woman, wearing a long white cloak that extended well beyond her feet. Her head was completely covered in a skin-tight white bonnet, which revealed only her worn, wrinkled face. Her delicate hands extended out of the sides of the white garment, and were the only other parts of her exposed flesh besides her uncovered face. "These are grave circumstances that we are gathered under today, young Joshua. Are you sure you wish to proceed?" Her voice was dry, and pointed, but somehow carried a tone of care. Her yellow eyes turned to my father addressing him.

He tried to fight off a sick smile, "there's no time like the present." He turned his face from my mother to that of his dying father. "He should be here for this."

The woman bowed her head honoring my father's request, "And so it is."

"Are you okay?" My mother asked as my father turned his eyes back to her face. Taking a moment to look at her glowing face, my father smiled and nodded his head. She squeezed his hands more tightly, and turned her attention to the robed woman.

"He shall bear witness to this occasion: for in grieving, we will find new meaning; and in Death, we shall conquer Life. Today, I stand before the two of you, who have vowed to honor each other with the commitment of a lifetime..."

"I..." My father spoke. The robed woman turned to him surprised, "I'm sorry," he continued. He turned his attention back to my mother, "but I simply cannot wait. Time is precious, and there are many things that I have yet to say, and such a very limited time in which to share them." He stole a glance at his father, and then turned back to the robed woman.

She did not look amused, however when she spoke, she used great care, "It is not in my nature to break tradition...however..."

My father took her silence as permission and turned to my mother, taking a deep breath, and finally speaking. "You saved me. I was, I was on the brink of death—cold, and lonely death. And when darkness came, you were the light. An angel with a golden halo. And from the moment I saw your face...my head, my heart, my body and soul were complete." He stopped for a moment as a smile crept its way onto his face. He chuckled to himself and began again, "and my father told me that I had to keep you, just moments after he met you." Tears welled in his eyes.

My mother smiled, trying to keep tears from sneak out of her eyes. "Wise man," she chuckled too.

My father smiled, but broke his gaze from my mother's eyes to look down at the tiled floor beneath them. He continued in a whisper, "We got a long road ahead of us, lil darlin'. I keep hearin' words 'bout destiny, and, and chaos. And, well, things are just all around kinda fallin' apart." He finally picked his pale blue eyes up to peer into her iridescent hazel eyes. "But I know that if I stick with you, that no matter how dark it may get, you will always be my light. There is not a movement you make that I cannot feel radiate inside of me. The Writer gave the Universe a heart, and gave unto Man its beat. Collectively, there are no two beats so in unison as ours. Lady Joycelyn Miracula, last child of the Solarian Kin, the first of my heart, I pledge my fidelity, my life, unto you. May our tales be ever intertwined."

The screens encircling the room, which monitored the vital statistics of my grandfather, began to flash red warning signs. Time was closing in on them, which weighted them down even further. My mother's face flushed as she realized it was her turn to speak. She bit her bottom lip, as the tension slipped down around her neck like a noose. Clearing her throat and stealing a glance at the computer screens behind my father, my mother turned her eyes back to my father's. "You, you um...you came to me in a dream. I, I don't know that I've ever told you that before. And, from the moment I laid eyes upon you in waking life, I knew where my heart belonged." She inhaled deeply watching the screens behind them begin to flicker more violently. "I know that we don't have much time to ever say the things that we want to say. In this story, my Joshua, you are the hero. In our story, you are my savior. Together, we will create where there has been nothing but darkness. Our destinies are rich, and will forever now be as one. Superior Joshua Eason Blake, the next of kin in the Blake Dynasty, the only of my heart, I pledge my fidelity, my life, unto you..." A tear slipped from her eyes as she heard the dull monotone of the condemning beep behind them. Gathering what strength she could, she whispered her final vow, "may our tales be ever intertwined."

Tears streaming down each of their faces, the two of them embraced; finally sealing their joy, their pain, and their destinies for endless time with a kiss.

****

39 Years Ago

My father stared blankly out at the crowd, the crowd of thousands, millions—infinite quintillions—watching through broadcast. None of it meant much to him, however. It was a show, a show for the millions of eyes about to bear witness to what my father was told was obligation. His hands were trembling sitting idly in his lap; he reached into the right pocket of his white dress robe, and fondled the heirloom chronometer his father had passed down to him. Its cold surface soothed his senses as he traced his fingers over the carvings etched into its cover. He continued to stare blankly out at the crowd, when he was startled by a nudge from my mother. He turned his empty stare to her face, furrowing his eyebrows in inquiry. She nodded her head to the congregation, and to the podium standing before the crowd. The speaker was turned to face him; all eyes were on him.

Understanding that he had missed his cue, my father stood awkwardly taking a deep breath, and stepped down from his seat next to my mother to approach the podium. Intercepting the previous speaker that had introduced him, my father smiled queerly. He looked at the elderly robed woman, the one of whom had married him and my mother a year prior. The robed woman who had delivered the sermon at his father's funeral, the robed woman that rung in his coronation as the Pioneer to his Home; now a year later, he was reflecting on his father's legacy as a part of the Blake Dynasty. He continued to the podium, and took his place before his people. Scanning the crowd, he finally rested his empty eyes on the floating screens before him. The screens prompted his mechanical speech, the speech which had been written *for* him, rather than *by* him. Clearing his throat, he began:

"Thank you, praise to you Cleric Vesta. Ladies and Gentlemen, I bid you good tidings on this eve. One Record ago, I stood before you with the grave news of my father's passing. Today, however, I stand much more jubilantly before you to speak of my father's legacy, of the Blake Dynasty..."

At this moment my father took an unscheduled pause in his speech. With all eyes on him, he reached down into his pocket, and brandished the watch inside. Tears welled in his eyes, but a smile crept upon his face, and he scanned the crowed, feeling oddly refreshed. After minutes of intense silence, he cleared his throat and began again, this time ignoring the prompts, in a quiet and contemplative whisper:

"My Da...My father was a fighter; he always had his eyes on the prize, putting the weight of the world and its needs ahead of his own. Hell, half the time he *did* have the world on his shoulders...He was a good man, an *honest* man, and because of that, I will not stand here and lie to you now. We're on the brink of Civil War...border disputes, trade disagreements, tariffs— and more! I'm talking violations to the Accord— violations to our very rights as *living beings*—that are beyond blasphemy. The headlines that you are reading in the news, the ones that everyone tell you can't possibly be true...*probably are true.* Every single day we continue to infringe upon our brothers and sisters, blood or in-arms. We continue to sow discontent unto the masses. We presently continue to disregard the lessons afforded to us; we've tainted our own path. We are greedy, imperfect, unworthy beings.

One Record ago, as my father lay dying, he said to me...my fath...my dad told me that, that there are so very few things that we can hold onto in this world anymore. So very few truths left to understand; we gotta keep fighting for what we believe in, if only just to hold on to a piece of ourselves.

Pivotals into the past, peace was bestowed upon our warring nations by the light of the Solarian Kin. Under the Pax-Solaria, for once, we stood united, and when the darkness encroached upon our peace, we banded together and drove our oppressors to where they dwell: in a ring of darkness.

Sometimes I wonder now, however, if I see much difference; difference in our intentions over their actions. Are we no better?

My father entrusted me, to carry on the Blake Dynasty. He entrusted me to carry this Alliance out of its Dark Age, and into a New Age of prosperity and peace. It is time for us to reach out, and take hold of things we find just and necessary; fore, if we let them go without a fight, then what was the point?"

My father stood for a moment. In silence. Simply staring out at the crowd. When he was satisfied, he turned to leave the podium. Before he was able to get a full step away, he turned back to the crowd. Finishing, he chorused, "And so it is."

****

Thursday — 16
Joshua Blake

My father's unconscious mind managed to move near the speed of light. His body stirred, as his muscles tensed; his heart could sense the impending doom. As prophecy spiraled through his dreams, shadow clouded his body. Growling, prowling, oozing with perversion, its fist floated above my father's body, like a pile of rocks ready to prey upon a figurine of glass. As the crystalline, rock-like, sinister creature snickered, it swung its clenched fist down upon my unbraced father.

Providence smiled down upon my father, as divinity guided his grasp to the deamon creature's advance. My father's eyes ripped open as his grasp tightened around the creature's rock-like fist. A sweltering rage filled my father's eyes, as he spied the light in his right periphery, of the deamon's other fist ignited with a curious shade of indigo, speeding for his face. Throwing his right arm up to block the deamon's fist, my father then swung his right arm around, and planted it directly into the solar plexus of the creature's rock-like chest. Catapulting backward, the creature crashed through the small cavern of which they were locked in.

Chest heaving, my father fell to his knees, and tears came to his eyes. He pounded his fists upon the ground violently, ignoring the pain coursing down his arms. Within moments, however, the sound of water trickled into his ears. Stopping mid-strike, my father began to search the cavern for the intrusion. Taking a deep breath, he abandoned his inconsolable rage momentarily, to seek out the source of the sound. Approaching the new hole in the cavern wall haphazardly, my father was startled when he was immediately grabbed by the neck and ripped from the safety of the small cavern. Flying through the air uncontrollably, my father's stomach leapt into his throat, and he screamed against his will. The sound of his scream was drowned out by the deafening sound of a waterfall. In the darkness, where no one could see, my father smiled, for he knew where he was.

Closing his eyes, my father tucked himself together in the darkness, and failed to resist falling. Descending like a cannonball, my father struck the pool, causing it to erupt with a spike of water twenty-five feet in the air. The rock-like creature roared into the darkness, almost daring my father to call its bluff. When he did not obey, the deamon raised its dark crystal rock fist to the air, which launched a screeching bolt of dark lightning. The lightning struck light to the cavern, revealing it was the cavern below my father's building. He had been imprisoned in the rubble that had been made of the sphere, which had harbored the Cerulean Combine. He was convening somewhere deep within the dark waters, which still surrounded the cavern, dropping off into darkness.

As the light dissipated from the cavern, my father leapt from his solitude underwater, and aimed to land near the pile of rubble where the deamon stood waiting. Landing solidly on the rock exterior of the former sphere, my father gained his balance to stand. His shoulders broadened as he took his stance, and clenched his fists.

"I have yet to divine the purpose of your infringements here." The beast snarled.

My father chuckled, "he's not sharing, I take it?" When the beast returned my father's inquiry with a deep growl, my father understood its response. "You are typical of your fracture. Irrational, beastly…which Damon are you? Davian? Hadian? You can't possibly be Athen himself, can you? The greatest Damon of them all?"

The creature roared at my father, "how dare you!" The creature pointed its clenched fists at my father, and with a bellowing screech, unleashed a fury of dark lightning, which coursed for my father.

My father screwed up his face, and raised his hands before him. A wall of water raised by his will, and wrapped itself around the deamon, electrocuting it, dispersing shocks of lightning all throughout the cavern. "How dare you threaten my existence!" my father screamed. Throwing his hands down, the water ceased to encase the deamon, and fell back to the conformity of gravity. The rock-like creature landed in the pile of rubble with a thud, gasping to breathe and smoldering. "What are you doing here?" my father demanded.

"I haven't been taken on a ride quite like that in a while young Joshua," something about the way the creature delivered my father's name struck a chord with him. "It's nice to see that you haven't lost your edge," this remark sealed the deal.

"It's *you*," he gasped, "DamonAtron."

"So you *do* remember," the deamon snarled managing to its feet.

"How did you manage to negotiate me and my son away from the protection of my wife?" my father's heart was pumping a mile a minute.

Insulted, the deamon roared furiously. "How dare you continue to mock me?" Clenching its fists, and taking a strong step forward, the beast growled, "I should kill you where you stand."

"Now, now. I don't think your employer would be very happy with you, if you did that."

"Nobody controls DamonAtron!" The beast screamed. "Nobody controls the Damon Collective!" Raising its talon-like claws to the air, the creature unleashed a fury of lightning throughout the rock cavern.

My father stood cemented to the ground, and closed his eyes to focus his concentration. Clenching his fists, and tensing his muscles, my father used the power of his will to lift the water out of its pool. Lifting his right clenched fist straight above his head, a sharp wave of water lifted in response. Just as my father was about to strike, he was taken aback to see the deamon had changed the trajectory of its lightning and concentrated it into a single terrifying bolt which tore for him with a haunting grace. Losing his concentration, my father dropped the wall of accumulating water behind him, which erupted in a violent wave. Pulling his right fist down from the air, my father used the flat of his palm to deflect the blazing lightning bolt, which threatened him.

The bolt reflected off of my father's hand, and dispersed across the rock wall behind the deamon, causing the cavern to become unstable. Rock pieces began to crack and fall away from the ceiling and walls; the water began to turn turbulent. My father looked at his burned hand feeling the curious tingle that was left behind. "Haven't had to do that in a while," he said as the rubble below him began to shift, causing him to lose his balance. Realizing the futility of this battle, my father pled with the creature again, "What are you doing here?"

After a moment of contemplation, as the cavern continued to cave in around them, the deamon finally spoke: "*He* got your son...Oracle got her brother...And I? I got you."

Feeling the weight of the words striking him, tears welled in his eyes, "Deavon...Do'Shon?" My father's grief blinded him. It blinded him from being able to see the fury building within the creature. Its eyes glowing red, a new, more terrifying surge of light tore through the air, threatening my father. Turning his sunken eyes at the last moment, my father had no time to react; the bolt of lightning whipped across my father, throwing him like a rock, skipping across the water. Skidding just to the edge of the rock cliff, before dropping off into darkness, my father came to a rest.

Groaning, my father turned over, to peer into the dark abyss stretching far beneath him. He looked back at the creature, still standing in the rubble, wielding whips of ferocious lightning, as the cavern continued to cave in. My father stood cautiously on the shifting ground beneath him. The deamon spotted him immediately, and without hesitation unleashed another volley of lightning at my father. With grace, my father braced his stance; using his left arm, he blocked the lightning, however, instead of reflecting the bolt, my father absorbed it. Stretching his right arm outward, and extending his hand, the lightning traveled down his left arm, and continued out his right, striking the deamon. The energy flowed through him as he stood with his arm extended; he smiled, perversely, as every cell in his body excited with life. "I can feel its passion, father," he whispered as the furor of the light took over his body. Crossing his arms, he thrust them apart, splitting the lightning bolt, causing it to dissipate throughout the cavern. The force from the explosion sent my father backwards, over the edge and into the darkness. The deamon flew back, striking the pile of rubble, as the rest of the cavern collapsed.

Falling uncontrollably, my father felt a wave of adventure come over him. It was a sense that had not filled his being in some time. Instead of falling into the darkness, my father was reaching into it. Ahead of him, at the bottom, it stared, waiting for him. As he inched closer and closer, a curious light bathed his body in a blaze of glory.

***

Thursday – 16
Joycelyn Blake

My mother rustled in the wreckage, as her consciousness fought to regain itself. The droplets of water intruding into our home by way of the gaping hole in the roof dripped down onto my her face. She winced, taking a deep breath, and finally found the zest to lift her eyelids. Shuddering as her vision came back into focus, the reality of the situation sunk into her wary soul. The remnants of her and my father's room startled her to tears. *It wasn't a dream,* she thought to herself as she fought to regain composure over her senses.

"Time?" She asked. There was no response from our mechanical home. "Time!" This was no inquiry. A flicker of light appeared on the one intact wall, which was behind her. The flicker of light did its best to form a coherent message: 9:57AM. The cloud cover outside, along with the persistence of the storms did not allow for my mother the ability to discern between day and night. She had been out for over ten hours. The events leading her to circumstance peeked back into her mind. Scurrying to her feet, my mother jumped over the hole in the floor of her bedroom, and landed at the threshold of the doorway. She pushed the remnants of the door open and hurried into the hallway. Her knees nearly buckled below her as she turned her head to see the doorway to my brother's bedroom in disrepair.

Approaching the doorway, tears came to her eyes. One of her cubs came under fire, and she was unable to protect it. A roar welled deep within her, from somewhere further down than her stomach, even further down than her very being. Enraged, she opened her mouth, letting the scream out against a violent strike of lightning. As the final gasp of air escaped from her lungs and out of her mouth, my mother dropped to her knees beating the floor with her fists. The rain had picked up in her rage, and continued to bear down on what was left of our house. She crawled on her hands and knees as the adrenaline continued to course through her veins. Reaching my door, at the opposite end of the hallway, she reached her right hand to the doorknob. Slowly turning it, the door popped ajar. Ever cautiously, my mother pushed the door open, and sighed as she saw me, still protected, untouched, in bed.

Gathering a semblance of resolve, my mother pushed herself to her feet, and stumbled passed my bathroom and into my bedroom. I lay still, deep within dream, and as my mother stared at my face, her heart calmed, and a new set of tears arose. She approached my bed, and sat, knowing the intrusion would not wake me, for now. The lightest, most gentle touch of her fingertips brushed across my rustled hair, smoothing it back into place. "I'm guilty," she choked on her words and cleared her throat. "I've been guilty for a long time. I knew this day would come...was coming, and even though I did what I thought was everything in my power to stop it, I still couldn't. The child *kissed with sight*, only to see, not to prevent..." She stared off into space for a moment, before jostling herself out of it. "I tried to do my best for you. You were truly one of the greatest things to happen to me in my life, my child." She scooted closer to me, caressing my face. Standing to her wobbly feet, she used both of her hands to cup my face, placing a kiss upon my forehead. As her lips pressed against my skin, tears streamed down her face. "My son, my beautiful, beautiful baby boy. I love you more than you will ever know. You saved my life, you will save all of our lives, you will save the world. And I am sorry that is the burden we have left upon you. But I promise you there is purpose."

She stood tall, and wiped the tears from her eyes. Walking over to my dresser, she smiled as she brandished a few of the collector model cars I had built and painted by hand. She closed the curtains to the window next to my bed, and then to the window at the foot of my bed, just over my desk. She turned the desk light off, and tidied the papers on its surface, finishing by pushing in my desk-chair. Grabbing the blanket at the foot of my bed, she stretched it out over me, tucking me in. Keeping her composure, as she always so gracefully did, my mother proceeded down the small hallway to my door. She looked at the few shelves lining the wall leading out, and smiled at the pictures littering them. Finally approaching the door, she reached the final shelf, and noticed a framed picture. She picked it up, and dusted it off. The air rushed out of her lungs as tears welled in her eyes. She stared at our last family portrait that we had had done professionally. It had been taken three years prior, and the smiles on my brother and my awkward faces made my mother smile against her will. She held it close to her, hugging it almost. Putting it back on the shelf, she reached for the doorknob. Before leaving, she turned one last time to see me, "don't forget your jacket, baby." She walked out of the room, securing the door behind her.

As the door clicked, her knees did buckle below her, and she fell to the pressure. Leaning against my door, my mother sobbed inconsolably. As I lay motionless in bed, tears streamed down my face, too. The wind began to pick up outside, the rain poured harder. A single, final, brilliant flash of lightning graced the surface of the Earth, and stole with it my mother, taking her far away. We dreamed—all of us—we dreamed.

****

20 Years Ago
Joshua Blake

The explosions did not jar my father from his catatonic state. The klaxons did not stir him. The screeching screams of scrambling crewmen did not faze him. It was only the sound of her soft, subtle voice that caused his heart to jump. "Joshua!" his ears were filled with water.

He furrowed his eyebrows, "what?" he whispered.

"Joshua! We have to go!" the sight of my mother crept into my father's view. The explosions filling the bridge of the starship around them faded away as he stared at her.

"What?"

She lifted her hand, and slapped him across the face. "We have to go!"

Opening his eyes, and caressing his smarting face, my father came to his senses. He took his hand from his face, and placed it on my mother's shoulder, "Joycelyn, my love, you should not have come." He turned his attention to the window behind my mother, staring him directly in the face, the one of which depicted slaughter and destruction on the other side. He

181

shook his head from side to side. "I...I don't know how this could have happened..." The ship jarred to the side, nearly reducing my parents to their knees. The window at the head of the bridge showed that the ship was starting to make a dangerous descent to the planet, below the war ensuing around them.

A young Guthrie Peterson ran to my father's side, "Joshua, we have to get out of here, there's no hope for the ship." My father just stared at him.

"Joshua, you heard him, let's go," my mother said pulling at his arm. The rest of the bridge crew stood on end, as they waited for my father's response. My mother's face was filled with fear and desperation.

"What are the odds you're going to come with us," Samuel Thomas said joining the huddle; the ship jerked again.

My mother hadn't entertained the thought that my father might not leave with them. "No! You're coming!" she clenched his forearm as tightly as she could.

Without addressing my mother's plea, my father simply stared out the window, which showed the ship spiraling out of control into the atmosphere. "Attention: All hands, abandon ship." He turned his stone gaze to Guthrie and Samuel, "get her Home, boys." Slipping his arm out from my mother's grasp, he handed her trembling hands to Samuel. He paused for a moment to feel her protruding stomach, to feel our heartbeats.

The water returned to him, drowning him. His ears filled drowning out my mother's cries for him as Samuel and Guthrie dragged her away. The ship was struck again, causing it to sway, my father stared drunkenly ahead as they approached the top layer of clouds. A smile crept onto his face, and a tear fell from his eyes. In seconds the ship had been deserted, the loyal crew, those who were still living, had left. Dutifully, my father manned the controls of the ship, and worked to ward off combat fire to ensure the safety of the escape ships. "None of this can possibly make sense. I know." He spoke the words aloud, to the ether, but he was addressing something, someone; he was telling a story.

The tactical console in front of him finally exploded. Enemy fire had targeted and successfully landed a strike on the weapons systems of the ship. My father rebounded and scurried to the helm of the ship. Knowing full well that he was not able to propel the ship out of harm's way, he might yet have a chance of utilizing the ship as protection. Throwing a single belt over his left shoulder, my father studied the helm console. He meditatively took three deep breaths, and continued, "Disengaging geological stabilizers," he lowered three different switches. The ship began to tremor more violently. "Venting reacted Exotic Matter. Extending dorsal vent flaps," he turned four knobs into place. The ship's exterior structure protruded several air vents, effectively changing the ship's trajectory. The nose of the ship pulled upward finally against the violent wind currents. Spiraling into disarray, the ship began to twirl out of control as it sped perilously toward the ground. Every few seconds my father could dizzily catch a glimpse of the swarm of enemy ships that had caught him off guard and rendered his ship defenseless, seconds into his journey.

Closing his eyes, my father took control of the manual missile firing trigger on the panel to his right. The twirling ship threw his senses into chaos; and as his stomach turned, my father embraced the unknown before him. He clenched his fingers around the trigger, and launched his ship's final usable missile. The curvature in its trajectory as a result of the ship's chaotic descent into the atmosphere was just enough to whip the missile into the path of the vented reacted matter. My father smiled as the missile detonated into the middle of the sky, igniting the Exotic Matter, engulfing the immediate atmosphere in a blazing inferno. "And so the Gates of Heaven open. Releasing the flames of desire upon the hate-plagued man. Darkness will encroach. And so she wept."

The shockwave of the explosion reached the ship, and radiated down its hull. My father slipped his left arm out of the belt harness; pulling his legs up to the seat, he jumped as fiercely as he could, catapulting himself through the hull of the ship and into the air. Exiting the ship's structure as it swung down to the surface of the planet below, my father shot straight down to the ground with furious pace. His ship exploded behind him, as it was completely overtaken by the shockwave.

Breaking the cover of the clouds, he was finally able to see the destruction being waged in the sky between his fellow rebels and the occupying force that had overrun his home. Looking into the near distance, my father spied a spire who's point reached high into the sky, "the Citadel," he whispered against the whip of the surrounding wind. Pulling his body ever so slightly, my father's course changed, and headed straight for the towering structure. As the ground came terrifyingly closer, my father swung his feet in front of himself; his feet planted on the ground, creating a crater around him. The ground beneath him rattled, and a tremor reverberated through the trees, causing the birds in the treetops to scurry. Standing up, my father looked around, finally laying his eyes upon a large brick wall behind him: he had landed just outside of the complex of the towering structure. Taking a few steps back, the beautiful, pointed spire came into view from behind the exterior wall.

"I'm Home." He exhaled.

The sounds of the explosions in the background were drowned out, as the momentary euphoria sunk into my father's soul; impacting even his most instinctual drive to survive. What felt like a wall of bricks slammed into my father, throwing him out of the crater he had created and into the rock wall surrounding the spire. He struck the wall without leaving a dent, and fell to the ground with a thud. Groaning, my father picked his smoldering body up off the ground, and turned his attention behind him.

"You never cease to amaze me, young Joshua," its voice hissed.

"DamonAtron, I should never have underestimated you," my father addressed the sinister rock-like creature standing before him.

"It will be your final mistake," the deamon snickered.

A smile crept onto my father's face, "not today."

The deamon whipped its claw at my father, generating a terrifying lightning bolt. Without blinking, my father raised his right hand and slapped the bolt away; his hand retaining some

185

of the shock, my father whipped his own hand at the deamon unleashing a volley of smaller lightning bolts. The creature did not move, allowing several of the lightning bolts to strike its rock-like, crystal exterior. "You're not quite Loren," the creature remarked. "By the end of this day, Corynth, the final stronghold, will be mine."

"And I vow: that I will not give this Citadel, the Complex, or its people to you willingly. You will have to take it over my dead body." My father clenched his fists and tensed every muscle in his body, ready to give his life for the cause.

"I was hoping that you would say that," the deamon sneered. Letting out a blood curdling screech, the creature began to charge for my father.

"You will have to take his, over *ours*," an explosive force propelled my father and the deamon in opposite directions of one another. My father struck the rock wall softly, while the deamon sailed backward into the forested area immediately surrounding the guarded spire. Four lights popped before my father, followed by the existence of his trusted friends: Samuel Thomas, Guthrie Peterson, Loren Johnson and Areul Robinson.

Breathing a sigh of relief over their appearance my father spoke, "I'm afraid that is a luxury you will not long be able to take advantage of," he chuckled. "It is good to see you, my friends." Turning his attention to Guthrie and Samuel he pressed, "my wife?"

Guthrie turned curiously to Samuel who rolled his eyes awkwardly, "as you can see, sir, we made it back to the surface, safely." Guthrie replied.

"She got away?" My father asked point-blank.

186

"She got away." Samuel confirmed.

"She's a wily one, gentlemen, you cannot be blamed." An enemy fighter drone fell to the ground, exploding, reminding them all that a battle was being waged above and around them. "I just hope she knows what she's doing..."

"She almost always does, Joshua," Loren offered.

It began to rain, droplets of ash, water, acid, and death.

My father stared out beyond his friends, out at the forest filled valleys, out to the lands. A tear slipped from his eyes, "this is not my home. Not the home that I have known. Not the home of my forefathers. This is chaos: beautiful and devastating chaos..."

"How poetic," the hiss of the deamon's voice crept into my father's saddened resolve.

"It was not for exposition's sake, merely but a state of fact." He turned his red hot glare to the creature, which was traipsing back to their location. "You creatures, you *monsters* of the night have laid claim to lands that are not yours, raping its peoples and resources with no remorse. Without provocation, you deamons have encroached upon the security that has prospered throughout the Universe for Pivitols—for your own purposelessly selfish gains."

Silence prevailed over the site for hour-long seconds before the deamon responded. "You are small. Your existence is feckless. You know naught of which you speak." It had never spoken so concisely, a fact which both reassured and terrified my father. As it finally approached my father and his camp, it stopped, standing deadlocked against them.

Lightning cracked in the background. "I will not go quietly," my father whispered.

"It is not that I ask you to go quietly, it is simply that you go."

"I was predestined by an unfair fate. And if I fail to contest destiny on this eve, stricken in defeat, I will create a kin far greater than anyone could have imagined."

"The Universe will crumble with you," the creature hissed taking a cheap shot, unleashing a whip of lightning upon the five of them. Loren Johnson was able to stand in front of the lightning bolt, absorbing most of the terrifying energy surging for them. It growled, "Every last one of you."

"Not if I can help it." My mother's voice proclaimed.

My father turned to his left to see a beautiful white light in the distance. My mother's heavenly body was radiating gorgeous light; he had never seen so beautiful, nor with such purity. She clapped her hands, and a beautiful shockwave emanated from her body, which struck the deamon creature, knocking it to its knees.

"Joycelyn, no!" My father screamed while looking at his beautiful wife. He screamed for her life, and for the life of me and my brother, everything was at stake.

"Such a weak fate," the deamon hissed regaining its composure. A bolt of dark black lightning surged from its hand toward my unguarded mother. My father watched in slow motion, screaming in horror. A light exploded in my father's hand, unveiling a gorgeous silver sword, followed by stunning body armor as he raced for the creature furiously. Striking at the stream of lightning, my father's sword dissipated the

188

thunderous current of terrifying electricity. "That's the fight I expected," the creature snarled. Grabbing my father by the neck with its left claw-like hand, the deamon picked him up and sent an agonizing surge of electricity through my father. Afterwards, the deamon threw my father's limp, smoldering body aside.

Flashes of light, and a whirlwind of flames engulfed the creature as it engaged my father's court of loyal friends. My father watched their struggle through blurred vision, feeling helpless as it continued to rain down on them. There was a visceral scream, followed by the resignation of the rain drops. My father made out a fantastic wall of water which was forming in front of his friends, followed by lashes of beautiful white lightning. For mere seconds, my father's vulnerabilities fell away, and he felt momentary peace. A streak of purple surged through the wall of water, and there was another scream—a different, more terrified kind of scream. The wall of water came crashing down, creating a mad current, which picked my father up and carried him off to land curiously next to my mother.

He garnered what strength he had left to crawl the inches to my mother. As he reached her, she held her hand out for him. The two grabbed each other's weak, trembling hands. They were soaked in water that was again pouring upon the ground, as if the gods were crying down unto the atrocity that was about to be committed upon the Universe. "Speak to me, my love," my father choked out.

My mother labored to breathe, "Joshua, we are unharmed," she said embracing her stomach with her right hand.

"You're a terrible liar," my father said.

"I am afraid," she cried.

"Do not be. I am here with you."

"Joshua, I'm afraid that you will not be able to deliver on your promise. He will…"

"No, do not speak those words," he pleaded.

"Joshua, we do not have much time."

"I am afraid that you have *no* time," the creature stood at a short distance from my huddled parents.

A rush of adrenaline coursed through my father's veins, accompanied by each hair on his body standing on end. He gathered himself and pushed himself to his feet, using what strength he had left. Using his sword as a prop, my father turned around to face the deamon standing behind them. In the distance beyond the rock creature, his four friends lay on the ground, dying. His heart began to palpitate as he wept internally.

"They didn't quite have the fight I was looking for either," the creature remarked snidely. "Surrender Corynth now, this war is over. The Occupation of your precious Home is complete," the creature looked to the sky as the rain poured down bringing with it the debris of dozens of combat shuttles; my father's resistance had failed.

A deep rage welled within my father. His fists clenched, and his teeth gritted; his tears were washed from his face with the rain. He knelt down on his left knee drawing a circle on the ground, "I, my son, am of the One," he used his index finger to stab a single dot above the circle, "You, the Son, are of Two," he used his middle finger to make a second dot. He picked his stone-cold gaze up to the deamon, "For my sacred duty." Releasing action potential throughout his muscles, my father sprung into the air, racing for the deamon. With his sword drawn in his hands, my father screamed charging. The creature braced for impact, bringing its right arm across its chest. Swinging his sword downward last minute, my father drove it into the deamon's torso, as the deamon's right back fist struck my father. He sailed across the sky, landing feet from my mother again; blood dripping from his mouth.

"You lose." The creature said slowly approaching and kneeling down. It shoved its growling muzzle into my father's face, revealing its razor sharp, black crystal teeth. Breathing hot air directly into my father's face it spoke, "what of your destiny now?" It stood up, sinisterly silhouetted by lightning cracking in the background.

My father looked up at the innumerable swarms of enemy ships that descended below the black filled clouds. "I'm so sorry," he pleaded aloud. "Corynth will never be yours."

The creature drew my father's sword from its torso and looked down upon my parents. "We will break them." My parents grabbed each other's hands again, "And so it is. The Seventeenth Savior of Man is slain..." It drew the sword high into the air.

My mother screamed in agony as my father watched the blade come ever closer to his chest. He closed his eyes and smiled, as his free right hand guided the blade through the armor, into his chest, cracking his sternum, and piercing his heart. Tears streamed from his eyes onto the ground as he uttered his final words: "what happens...Damon...when you kill the mortal man?" Blood poured out of my father, as Life slipped away from him, and Death descended down. Sweeping finality came as everything faded to black.

A single, beautiful, intensely pure light exploded from my father's body, knocking the creature back. The screaming light reached out for my mother, my father's dying friends, and several others spread all throughout the planet. The powerful limbs of gorgeous light contracted back to my father's body, which had been consumed in the light, itself. When the final limb reached back into my father, his eyes burst open, and the light exploded to the sky.

****

Thursday – 16
Joycelyn Blake

My mother's body exploded back into existence within the confines of the crystalline cube of which Amalya and the others were kept unconscious and safe. She fell to her knees upon regaining her physical representation, reduced to such by the pounding of her brain against her skull. As she fought to take a full breath, she felt a small warm stream of blood begin to trickle out of her right nostril. She crouched down into the fetal position, and pounded her fists onto the floor of the crystalline cube as she tried to compose herself. Her mind worked to arrange itself along the forces of the cosmos, and as it did so it beckoned to two unwilling participants millions of miles away. Norman and Areul Robinson were ripped away from their home, where they had had the pleasure of spending their precious final moments with their daughter. The pair was placed neatly within the crystalline cube, stunned at their sudden relocation.

Norman Robinson looked around the cube frantically, confused momentarily, "Where is my child?" He exclaimed. "Where are we?"

My mother's pulse began to slow as the balance of the Universe began to calm her. "I appreciate your enthusiasm Norman; however I must ask you to trust me just as you do my husband."

"Well maybe I am tired of trusting your husband," he said between gritted teeth. Areul moved to keep her husband from outrage.

"Norman, this is not the time," my mother said pulling her head out from her hands. She looked at him, blood still dripping from her nose, "you're at the center of the Sun, Do'Shon's star, okay?"

He looked down, away from my mother, like a dog, defeated. "Joycelyn," he pleaded, "what of my child?"

My mother closed her eyes, continuing to meditate. "She is safe for now, child." She smiled, "she has a great destiny ahead of her." Opening her eyes, my mother wiped the blood from her face; she had finally come to a semblance of stability. The blue irises of her eyes pulsated with her heartbeat, with every pump they radiated a beautiful white glow. She turned from Norman to Areul, "I must ask a grave favor of you, child."

Areul stared back at my mother intently, taking careful moments to answer, debating her thoughts. Turning her eyes from my mother, Areul looked around the crystalline cube and out into the burning heart of the Sun. She turned her head back, "of course, anything, Ma'lady."

My mother's face was screwed up in pain, "Areul, I need you..." she heaved to breathe, "...to help me contain this light."

Areul gulped and stood reluctantly from Norman. Approaching my mother carefully she knelt down and looked at my mother's face, which was pulsing with white light as well. "I...will do what I can."

My mother turned her gaze, which bore visible sign of her struggle to Areul, "Just breathe, child..." she placed her hand upon Areul's jaw line, pulling away softly. My mother's index finger began to glow a blinding light, which she placed upon Areul's nose. Areul's eyes exploded with light, as did her mouth as she screamed out in horror. The Sun exploded in mass and intensity momentarily as Areul worked to control the small glimmer of light my mother had given her.

Norman jumped to his feet and rushed to his wife's side. "What have you done, Joycelyn?" he screamed above his wife's agonizing groans and the flashes of light around them. My mother's finger broke away from Areul's nose, which prompted Areul to fall unconscious in Norman's arms, and my mother to fall back into meditative silence for a moment. "Joycelyn?" Norman inquired again, however this time his grip on reality was beginning to slip itself.

When she opened her eyes, they gave a small shimmer of light, but returned to their normal blue. Taking a deep breath, she responded, "If we have any chance at providing a better future...we need more time."

"You..." Norman was laboring to take a complete breathe as his vision blurred, "would know."

The sardonic delivery of his words struck my mother. She bit her bottom lip, and then shrugged. She leaned in and kissed Norman on the forehead; when she parted her lips from his head, a tear slipped from Norman's drooping eyes. My mother held his limp body, laying him next to Areul. "A small piece of what you were going to see sooner or later. Sooner," she chuckled darkly. "It's worth fighting for." She stood and looked around the crystal cube, which now seemed smaller somehow, more congested. Her eyes landed upon the crystalline table where Nathan and Nicholas still lay, and then around at the pile of unconscious parents, finally resting on Amalya, who continued to struggle breathing. "Keep on keepin' on kid," my mother finally turned to the empty corner of the cube, where Do'Shon had formerly sat in solitude. Taking a deep breath, she walked carefully to the quiet corner, perching down upon her knees.

Focusing her concentration on her breathing, my mother closed her eyes in meditation. As she came to center, the Sun returned to its former, unperturbed state. Its fires calmed, and the whips made of flames stretching across the galaxy dissipated. The supernova glow of its white light darkened, returning it to its former orange hue. Keeping her eyes closed and her mind in meditation, my mother smiled. "We're coming up on the home stretch, my love." Her words entered the ether and bounced across the cosmos reaching through the black of space in order to find their intended recipient.

***

The Keeper, Do'Shon

"This place is much different than I remember it," Do'Shon's voice cut into the thick darkness that surrounded him and his captor.

"Impermanence, Do'Shon."

"Impermanence," Do'Shon chuckled, "the single most prevalent foundation which this existence continues to infinitely perpetuate upon." Silence followed his observation. "It is quite devastating to be in your company again, Oracle."

Without reservation Do'Shon's sole company screamed, "Oracle is dead!" There was a deep, bellowing screech followed by a crash of thunderous lightning; in its wake, Do'Shon caught a glimpse of his cloaked assailant. "Oracle died Pivitols into the past; lest you have forgotten." The growling, snarling voice of Do'Shon's captor was beginning to wane in favor of a more careful, still delivery. "Joshua Eason Blake's establishment of this farce is quite remarkable, I must say."

"So, you have brought me here against my will in order to commend our efforts, then?" Do'Shon sarcastically remarked.

"Do not flatter yourself. The effort is still vain." A pair of red lights began to flash from under the hood of the cloak.

Do'Shon shuddered upon viewing the sinister red orbs of light, which bore into his being, consuming him from within. "What has happened to you, my sister? How is it you have strayed so far from the path? You are the first perfect child of the Known Universe, and instead of basking in glory, you dwell and thrive in suffering." Do'Shon began to silently cry as he spoke. The tears falling from his eyes ignited light within the darkness that surrounded them. "I know neither the End, nor the Beginning, but I believe in a greater destiny for this existence. As the last *Keeper*, it will be my destiny to know the truth of Life and Death..."

"So says the *Writer*, your precious *Writer of Whom is Most High*," sarcasm cut into the tension the words themselves were creating. Crouching down closer the cloaked individual drew its covered face directly in front of Do'Shon's, "You are aiding and abetting those mortal vermin, Do'Shon. I have not strayed from the path, I am merely working to exterminate those you call the "Children of the Universe"...their existence is miniscule...purposeless."

"Who are we to judge them?" Do'Shon interjected fiercely.

"We are *Gods* Do'Shon!" its voice grew booming and domineering again. "We are Gods among these parasites. You think I *thrive* in suffering? All of this *Life* is suffering."

"How charming," the voice snuck into the darkness that surrounded the two of them. Do'Shon paid it no attention, but his captor could do anything but. Turning its red hot gaze to the surrounding shadows, it searched for the source of the sudden intrusion. "You speak of the mortal infestation as if your existence has any more meaning. You speak of suffering as if you know its truth; however the only truth of which you have domain over is the Beginning. Do not forget your place," at this, a ghostly, devilish apparition of my father flashed behind Do'Shon.

"Do not be naïve. I may not be able to perceive you, but I know that you are here." Do'Shon picked his gaze up to look into the red orbs that were blazing underneath the cloaked caper in front of him. "It's playing you. You speak of *Oblivion* as if it is yours to deliver; you know that is not your purpose, dear sister. It is merely using you, as a pawn, to reunite the Fractures of the DarkestHeart."

"Your dear brother speaks untruth, Oblivion; however perhaps I should address you as your former, Oracle, if that better suits you?" The whisper that intruded into the darkness was again that of my father's devilish twin.

"How dare you!" *Oblivion* screamed, answering both Do'Shon's accusations, and the inquiry of my father's sinister, incorporeal double. Bending down to face Do'Shon directly, she turned the red hot orbs directly into his. "How dare you implicate anything unto something you do *not* understand?" Her voice was jagged, filled with hate, and pierced into Do'Shon.

Do'Shon's skin grew iridescent, slowly peeking more light into their surroundings. Taking a single small breath, he blew out, blowing his sister's cloak from her face. "You were so beautiful, First Child of Light..." the light he radiated began to grow more fierce; it revealed that his sister's face had sunken to all but bone. A chill ran down his spine as he spied her grey, ghostlike complexion contrasted against her ruby red eyes. She flashed her razor sharp black teeth, and reached out with her talon-like claws to grab him.

Time began to move in slow motion, like a ballet, to the beat of a heart. Do'Shon's bioluminescent light filled the

198

crystalline cube of which they occupied; he looked around them sadly, at his sister's dead star, at her decrepit gate, and at her own horror. His eyes rested upon the duplicate of my father that stood behind Oblivion, the one which stared him down feverishly. "The King of Nights, bound of DarkestHeart, could not foresee the ends from start…" Drawing the entirety of the light back into himself, Do'Shon concentrated as he watched his sister's clutches draw dangerously closer. Focusing the miraculous light at the end of his right pointer and middle fingers, he shot a beautiful surging stream of white light out of his being, through his sister, striking my father's devilishly taunting apparition.

A catastrophically beautiful explosion of light and sound boomed over the cosmos, as the surge of light dug through the very core of Oblivion's dead star, shattering the cohesion of the settled surface, which was now just a barren dead planetoid. Oblivion let out a horrifying screech as the light continued to surge through her. The creature that stood behind her, disguised as my father, cried as it collapsed in on itself, imploding into nothing but a billowing cloud of smoke.

***

Thursday — 16
Clecha Robinson

Lightning cracked, rumbling the very foundation of the Earth. Clecha Robinson woke from a dizzying nightmare with a scream. Flipping off the couch, she did her best to steady herself within her reality. As her eyes darted around the room, she realized that she was in the safety of her own home. The projection of the newscast was still being relayed on the wall in front of her but she paid it no mind; however she was keen to notice immediately the absence of her mother and father. "Mom?" She asked into the ether to no response. "Dad?" Lightning cracked again.

She pulled herself up from the floor, and perched comfortably on the couch. Her thoughts were a jumble of discordant melodies as she tried to piece everything together. Disobeying vertigo, she pushed herself to her feet and proceeded into the kitchen just off the living room. She expected to find her parents sitting over a cup of coffee as they continued to keep watch over their ailing daughter. To her surprise, she found herself in quiet solitude, the smell of burning coffee filling her nose. The silhouettes casted in shadow from the various objects in her home startled her against the backdrop of pounding rain and thunderous lightning. As her heart skipped a beat and jumped into her throat, Clecha Robinson turned around leaving her kitchen for the comfort of her living room again.

The news projection on the wall lit the room in dull shadows as the newscaster's remarks flowed in and out of her ears. The howling wind outside shuttered against her lonely house and added to her building apprehension; shooting a glance at the front door in the next room, she noticed an umbrella lying on the ground. She leapt for the formal living room, and gunned for the limp object. Upon reaching it, her hands trembled with intense fear, her fingers jumping out of control. Her fingertips lit on fire upon grasping the umbrella, but she continued to hold it closely with conviction. She reached for the light panel next to the door, and attempted to turn on the stairway light. Flipping the switch produced nothing, not a light, not a sound. Lightning cracked in the background, lighting the house again; the only sound that of the newscaster.

Skipping the first creaky stair that led to the comforts of her bedroom and her parent's clutches, she began to ascend the staircase slowly. Each step careful and calculated, the umbrella still tightly bound in her right hand and ready to strike at a moment's notice. Reaching the top of the stairs, the silence and desolation of the upper floor descended upon her. "Mom?" she asked again. "Dad?" not a peep of a response.

Making her way slowly down the hallway to her parent's bedroom, Clecha brushed against the door with her free open palm. The wood grain felt different to her, harsher, colder if at all possible—foreign. She grudgingly pushed the door, turning the knob, opening to a vast white marble room. Without conscious realization, Clecha Robinson had entered the strange white room, and the door shut behind her echoing over the grand hall. She shuddered, "Hello?" there was no response.

Looking down, Clecha was mesmerized to see that somehow she had changed into a beautiful strapless white dress, of which she had never before seen. The white dress ruffled down her sides, with her long brown hair in a ponytail flowing down her back. A cold chill ran down her spine, and she felt the tickle of her hair against her naked back, a cord of lace coming to a bow at her tailbone, keeping the dress together. A beautiful orchestral chorus began playing, startling Clecha as her eyes darted around to find the source of the disturbance to no avail. As she settled her gaze to the far end of the great marble hall, Clecha spied a curious light. Realizing that she no longer forged her blunt object, she resolved to approach the light in the distance with utmost caution.

With each step deeper into the long corridor, the sound of the music intensified. Her footsteps echoed off of the columns lining the marble hall, sparking light to the torches that sit between them. She halted herself, eyes still fixed on the light in the distance. Pulling up her dress from around her feet, Clecha bent her knees and took in a deep breath. Launching herself forward, she threw caution to the wind, the torches lit with fury behind her. The light she sought grew with greater intensity as she approached, the music reaching a haunting climax behind her. The strings of the violin vibrated in terrifying crescendo, as each step was numbered by the strikes on the ivory. Reaching the end of the corridor, Clecha jumped to a skidding stop. The flaming torches followed her closely, coming to an explosion as she stopped at the beautiful pulsating light at the end of the tunnel. Clecha flew back onto her seat, her back smacking the cold marble floor and knocking the wind out of her.

The tingling sensation of air as it reentered her lungs burned, and Clecha writhed in pain momentarily before finally gasping a full breath. Grabbing her throbbing head, Clecha picked herself up only to be surprised by the absence of light, replaced by a simple gold framed mirror which stretched from the floor to the ceiling. Her eyesight worked to refocus and she studied the gorgeous markings that lined the gold frame of the mirror, none of them familiar to her. Gathering her bearings,

Clecha pushed herself up steadily to her feet and approached the towering mirror. She reached out her left hand, and felt the cool touch of the gold plating vibrate down her fingertips and settle in her teeth. She brushed her now tousled hair out of her face, and stood directly in front of the reflective surface. Her eyes widened and her pulse raced as she stared at the image peering back at her.

"You are..." the use of her voice suddenly escaped her. "Not you."

The image was facetious. It *was,* in-fact, Clecha Robinson, physically. Her reflection stared back at her with a smile on its—or rather curiously, *her*—face. She reached her hand up, to run her trembling fingers over her mouth to confirm that she was not actually smiling at all. Clecha's stomach turned and she felt nauseous, "Who...how are you...? You are me, and I am you, but are we the same?"

Her reflection stared back at her, beaming compassion, "I am not you, but you are me, dear child..." Clecha scrunched her eyebrows at the imposter, but could no longer find the ability to speak. "...but all of that is in due time." A glaring light reflecting in the mirror began to blind Clecha from being able to keep her eyes on the image. A soft whisper crept into Clecha's ears, "Remember darling, darkness will always yield to the light," her reflection reached out of the mirror, touching Clecha softly on the forehead with its index finger.

As the light began to burn away her skin, she screamed, before opening her eyes again and realizing that she was instead standing in the doorway to her parent's vacant room. She stood there in shock, "TV," she said. The wall next to her parent's door began to illuminate with television broadcasts. "News," she specified. The wall was replaced with a single, male anchor who sat frazzled at his news desk. Clecha walked into her parent's bedroom, and sat carefully at the foot of her parent's bed. Her eyes began to water as she soaked in the information being relayed to her via the broadcast.

"Ladies and Gentlemen, this will be our final broadcast from WGBL – World Global News, I am Alan Vandergaard reporting. At roughly 10:30PM Central Standard Time, a formal declaration for National Disaster was issued from our nation's capitol; a formal declaration for Global Disaster is expected soon to follow from the United Nations. We are now in hour 92 of relentless storm activity with no apparent end in sight. Satellite reports indicate that storm clouds now cover nearly 80% of the planet, with more storms cells developing. Tsunami, and Hurricane conditions exist at every coast, and as of now seismologists are estimating global tectonic shifts resulting in 243 magnitude 4.0 or higher earthquakes. As of this moment all global air-travel is officially grounded, international travel is no longer sanctioned, and a general precaution to seek higher ground has been advised. If able to do so, you are urged to remain indoors, keeping sure to stay away from all windows and doors. Emergency crews are responding as possible across the nation, however catastrophic flooding is being reported throughout the country making travel difficult or impossible in many areas. Hurricane-like winds have been reported on the coasts, and at least seven tornadoes have been confirmed as touched down in the plains states. As of this moment, casualty

reports estimate world-wide death tolls at a devastating 1.3 billion..."

At this shocking revelation, Clecha stood from her catatonic stare and proceeded to the window. As she pulled the curtains away, a flash of lightning startled her; she stared out into the street, at the current of water enveloping the neighborhood. Delores Kate's small sports car floated down past her house, along with pieces of siding from several neighborhood houses. The monotone from the off-air television broadcast in the background jarred Clecha back to her dream of the marble white room. When she turned her eyes from the window to face her parent's bed, she found herself standing in front of the mirror again, in the white marble room. The chorus of instruments returned to her ears, and she began to laugh uncontrollably. The pattern in the white marble was so nauseating that she could not keep a solid hold on her bearings; she lay down on the cool ground as everything faded away in a cascading shade of black, the sound of doors slamming echoing in the background into infinity.

****

Friday – 17
The Shepherd, Jack

Jack opened his eyes; he did not explode back into existence, he was preexisting and merely waking from coma. His eyes burned with light, blinding him from being able to recognize his surroundings. He could feel his tingling body vibrate against the cold tile he was laying upon. "Where...?" he tried to speak, but could only utter a small whisper. Jack closed

205

his eyes, trying to block out the blinding light and focusing his mental faculties. Mid-meditation, his ears were suddenly full with a single beat, beating to the rhythm of a familiar drum; a chill ran down his spine. With eyes still closed, Jack drew in a breath, "Loren…" he drunkenly whispered.

"Jack…" Loren Johnson's exasperated whisper proclaimed in joy, a tear escaping from her clenched eyelids.

"We have come upon our time."

Loren let out a single, sarcastic chuckle. "Always waiting for the end."

When Jack opened his eyes again, the blinding white light faded and his surroundings came into focus. He lay on the cold tile floor of the underground bunker, which harbored Loren and Angelica Johnson, and had previously held my mother. He turned his head, cracking his neck, and then pushed himself up with his elbows. Loren and Angelica lay, untouched, unharmed on their beds; machines still painting their heartbeats. He took a deep breath of the cool air, and pushed himself to his feet. The only sounds that filled the sterile bunker were that of respiration, and heart monitors. He cleared his throat as he stared at Loren Johnson, who lay in coma, "Loren?" he whispered.

The room was filled with deafening silence following his inquiry. Jack looked around the small bunker, surveying signs of obvious struggle including blood, soot, and ash. A series of the overhead, headache-inducing fluorescent lights flickered throughout the enclosure; the hum of the lights caused Jack's blood to race in anxiety. His eyes darted back and forth in the negative space, trying to piece together the circumstances that had brought him to his current occasion. Each enduring breath drew a little bit shorter as he began to convulse with undulating apprehension. Flashes of memory raced through Jack's head, as he began to recall the blinding pain of the light bestowed upon him by Do'Shon; its purpose yet to be divined. With each second that Jack stood in the isolated company of Loren and Angelica Johnson, he grew more and more uneasy.

He approached Loren as if seeking a familiar comfort, and brushed her blonde hair from her face. The warmth of her cheek against the back of his hand sent chills reverberating down his spine; his mind raced with regret. "I wish that I could have done more..."

Before Jack could finish his thought, Loren's limp body came to life. Her eyes exploded with an ominous white light, her left hand gripped Jack's hand like cement. She turned her empty gaze to him, entrancing him in wonder. Her voice was filled with dissonance when she spoke, swimming through Jack's right ear and out of his left. "You, Child of the Stars—Grand Shepherd—are not tethered to this fictional abode. The words of your tale do not end here; you are one of many heroes in this story. Your destiny spirals endlessly into the infinite heartbeat of the highest cosmic order. She awaits you."

Jack looked at Loren's stoic expression reflected in her cold and empty gaze. The grip of her fingers which wrapped around his arm began to sink into his skin, and began to scare Jack. His feet began to quiver, and he looked down noticing that he was standing in a foot of water, which was rising quickly. His heartbeat began to race as he looked over at Angelica whom lay innocently on her bed, still unconscious and unaware of any of the goings on around her. "Loren. Loren what are you saying? What is happening? What am I looking for?" Jack screamed as the water continued to rise faster and faster. Loren finally cracked a smile as the water reached the bottom of the bed, rising to touch her and Angelica now too.

****

19 Years Ago

"This is…fantastic," Jack stood in awe.

"Who are you?"

Her voice tickled his ear drums and resonated down his spine. Jack jumped and turned around to see young Loren Johnson standing behind him in a snug white dress. "Who are you?" Jack asked.

Annoyed, Loren lifted her right eyebrow, and continued to stare at Jack, "I asked you first," she said flatly.

Jack looked at her more closely. His eyes studied her long blonde hair against her pale white skin. Her eyes, while serious were deep and penetrating, electrifying even. "You are…beautiful."

"Flattery is gonna get you nowhere, pal. Now either tell me who you are, or you're gonna be sorry. Ok?" Loren stepped closer, raising her clenched fists ready to fight. In her younger days, Loren could have rivaled even her daughter Angelica.

Jack raised his hands to bear his innocence, "You misunderstand. I mean you no harm. It is your intent that I must inquire upon. Neither you, nor this landscape are native to this world, not for some-time…I can only conjecture that your appearances are congruent."

"All speculation, stranger. Been here all my life, all of…" She bit her lip as she thought, "20 years now."

"Are you sure about that?" Jack asked facetiously.

"You still haven't answered my question," Loren said pointedly while also taking a step even closer.

Jack turned his back to Loren, annoying her more, but she sensed his contemplation. The sunlight bathed his skin, and filled him with warmth, "it has been long since I have felt a warmth such as this." A smile spread from cheek to cheek, and a gust of wind brushed past his face. "What do you call this place?" his whisper carried carefully across the air.

Loren could sense something different in his voice; she dropped her fists and pulled both feet to stand together. She contemplated her words carefully for a moment, before she cleared her throat to speak, "Earth, Home."

"Earth," Jack's tongue tickled his teeth as he bore the word from his mouth for the first time. His eyes watered as he looked out upon the vast network of canyons, caves and ridges that were carved out of the red, yellow, brown and orange rocks before him. Streams of water echoed softly in the distance. The sunlight bounced off of the rock cliffs and burned Jack's retinas as he tried to stare at the beautiful sight longer. "And this place? This place of grand canyons, what shall you call this place?"

Loren cracked a smile for the first time, "so you are a poet?"

"You could say that," Jack remarked playfully. "Tell me, why do you call this…Earth, Home? What of your native land?"

He still stood with his back to Loren, continuing to take in the beauty of the sights surrounding him.

Loren looked up at the sky, which was fading to hues of pinks and purples as the sun sank slowly into the West, leaving a silhouette of the moon behind to replace it during nightfall. "My native land, the land of which I truly call *Home…*?" A quiver, Loren's first sign of weakness, befell her voice. Her eyes darted back and forth, and began to water as she recalled the visions of her Home, "My *Home*, a world of swirling beauty…We have lived there since the beginning of time, in harmony and in war. At the dawn of time, I cannot imagine that it was much different from the landscape that lay before us. The stars may be alien, the space surrounding us may be alien, but this picture, this existence, I can only pray that our nascence was as preciously innocent. We have come a long way since the beginning. We have come from raping and pillaging our own lands, killing and slaughtering our brothers and sisters over petty difference, toiling in discontent, to travelers of stars, forgers of alliances, creators and keepers of peace…so I thought. Where I am from, the colors vibrate across your senses with overwhelming life; and in time, we have learned to respect the order of existence as it is written before us. In the season of water, all of the plants gorge themselves in new life: the blooming glillies, iridescent bulbs of lax, and the intoxicating smell of the indigo calil trees spurting sporadically throughout the Seven Great Oceans is a sight matched by no other I have ever seen before in my life…"

"Of 20 years?"

Loren chuckled to herself and dismissed his inquiry continuing on, "...the season of Stars paints the most beautiful of portraits across the night sky, and recounts for us the very path of which we walk; the moons of Krise and Kine watch over us as looking glasses from the other side. It reminds us that we are so linked to our brothers and sisters of the Known Universe, of the Alliance. And of the darkness that exists, which always in the day yields to the light. During the season of lightning the planet itself calls to us with fantastic displays of light and deafening thunder. If we are lucky, the season of lightning will bring us the final season, of fire."

"Lucky? Fire brings destruction, does it not?"

"Fire brings not merely destruction, but rather provides a clearing for new and everlasting life. The Rocks of Dierty are a sight to be beheld—from afar, of course—most blinding beauties, which dance with glorious light..." she closed her eyes, and left the air still for uncomfortable time. "This is my home, now. It will have new, different, beautiful life to be discovered."

"I'll say..." he jerked in terror, but was too late.

"Listen *Jack*, I just wanna know your name and what you're doin here, okay?" Loren wrapped her right arm around his neck and pressed her fist into his left kidney uncomfortably.

He furrowed his eyebrows, and blinked. When he opened his eyes again, he was no longer being detained by Loren, but standing to face her, at a comfortable distance. She shuddered in fear, but he looked at her intently, "Jack."

Loren regained her composure quickly, swallowing her fear, "pardon?"

"My name, is Jack. I am...on a mission."

"A mission?" Loren interjected.

"A mission..." Jack's thoughts were beginning to spiral apart, "to find her Grace. But something, is...is different."

Loren studied Jack more closely, but still persisted, "what of *your* home?" However, when he did not respond she noticed for the first time his profoundly black hair, which stood out against his pale white skin nearly radiating light. His white dress was painted with specks of gold which sent chills down her spine. She picked her gaze up to finally meet his, where she spied his penetratingly pale blue eyes. She gasped, "you are child, made of..." her eyes filled with water.

"Yes," Jack smiled, "the stars."

"Oh my," Loren bent down, kneeling before him.

"No, no," Jack rushed to her and traced his fingertips down her jaw-line pulling her gaze to meet his eyes rather than his feet. He used the gentle weightless touch of his fingers to lightly lift her to her feet. "I serve the Keeper: Do'Shon and his lady, the last child of the Solarian Kin, she kissed with sight."

"Joycelyn," Loren whispered.

Jack nodded, "Our Alliance is betrothed to that which Lady Joycelyn Miracula is, including the destiny of the Seventeenth Savior of Man and his Guardians. You see..."

"We serve the same..." Loren was putting the pieces together.

"Therefore we serve..."

"Each other," Loren finished his sentence with a curiously growing passion. Staring into his eyes, she saw the beauty of the stars and the miracle of the abyss connecting them all. Her breath rushed from her lungs and she leaned in, kissing him. Jack's body began to radiate beautiful light as Loren's pulse raced down his fingers and into his very being, shuttering the earth beneath his feet.

****

<u>Friday – 17</u>

"Slap me."

"What?" She asked.

"Slap me."

"I already did."

"Do it, again, damnit." I turned to look at Clecha, still nearly catatonic, eyes empty. She did not hesitate this time; she slapped my face, with force, without apology. "Deavon?" I whispered. I stole away from my parent's doorway, and ran to my brother's room, stopping short of the shredded doorframe. Before I could even enter his room, I stopped, wiping my tousled hair away from my face. "I'm losing my God-Damned mind..." the words echoed out of my mouth several times without reprieve, the delivery sharp and precise.

"My house is empty too," Clecha cut into my raving rant. "I...I...I don't know where anyone is. I almost drowned just getting here. It hasn't stopped raining in like 90 hours, or something. Anywhere. And, and, and, and, and what the *fuck* is going on?"

Without even going through the pain of finding my brother's room vacant, I pushed passed Clecha and walked back down the hallway, to the comfort of my own room. Clecha turned to follow me closely as I burst into my room. "News!" I screamed.

When the wall behind my bed came to life with an off-air broadcast Clecha responded: "There isn't any; none that I haven't already given you."

My pulse raced, and beads of sweat began to emerge from every pore on my body. "Where are they?" the wall did not obey my command. "Where is my father?" The screen replaced from the off-air broadcast to that of a map of the downtown sector. A grid high-lighted near the center and expanded, showing the Blake Genetic Industries Tower. A 'pin' appeared, with a caption noting that my father's *last known* location was Blake Tower. My mind bolted back and forth uncontrollably, "call up Central Health directories. Run a search on current patient listing, search for 'Jocelyn Blake'." The search came back blank; I stood there aghast. Turning to my last resort I commanded, "Search for 'Joycelyn Miracula Blake' or any variation thereof." The search came back blank. "Where is my brother?" tears were approaching my eyes. The screen turned black. I turned to Clecha, with craze in my eyes; I grabbed her by the arms and shook her, "what is going on?" I screamed.

She looked back at me calmly, not at all what I had expected, and whispered, "I don't know."

A sudden surge of vomit rushed to the back of my throat, as my stomach turned in violent desperation. Adrenaline rushed through my veins. Letting go of her arms, I turned to face the doorway, noticing the shelves lining the wall leading to the door. My eyes fell upon the picture frame that my mother had picked up and put back haphazardly. I took a few steps to the shelf, and reached out carefully, feeling a sudden rush of familiarity run down my fingertips and rest in my heart. I pulled my hand back and proceeded to the door.

"Where are you going?" Clecha asked.

"The basement," I said flatly.

With graceful reflex, I retreated down the stairs to the main level of our home. I stepped onto the ground which was beginning to flood with water pouring in from the outside. I proceeded through what was left of the formal dining room, and to the doorway on its left which led to our basement. Clecha followed closely behind me; together we proceeded down the stairs carefully as water rushed down them from behind us. As we neared the bottom of the stairs, the basement responded to our presence by activating the lights around us.

Bookcases lined the walls, leading up to the main projection wall, which was preceded by a large section of seating. I walked to the left wall, and looked around through the many books which lined the shelves, frantically. I pulled books upon books off of the shelves as I searched asking over and over which book it was that I was looking for—as if it would just appear for me.

"What are you looking for?" Clecha interjected into my mania.

"There's a book, and I know it's near here, I just can't remember which one! He always says something to the wall..."

"What the Hell are you talking about? Who talks to the wall?" She yelled.

I stopped what I was doing and whipped around to look at her crazily, "my father, Clecha! My father! He has something to do with this, I just know it!"

"What does talking to the wall have to do with anything?"

"Just stay with me, damnit!" I turned back to the bookcase, and finally located the blue-bound hard-covered book. My eyes widened, "this one." I pulled it down with great care, and brushed its cover. I used my left hand to open the cover, and looked at the inscription scribbled in my father's handwriting: "For my sons, my princes." I opened the book hastily, and scanned through the pages. My careful handling turned to frantic page turning, and Clecha detected my sudden passion.

"What's the matter?" she asked carefully.

"This has to be a sick fucking joke," I said.

"What?" she asked more pointedly.

"They're all blank!" I yelled turning to look at her again with pure craze in my eyes. I flipped the pages at her, all of them blank. I tossed her the book, as if trying to rid my hands of the gross misfortune.

Clecha looked over the book, and then opened it, flipping through the pages quickly, confirming just what I had told her, all of them were blank. The only writing in the book at all belonged to my father. She closed the book, and looked at the spine, noticing the title and author. "The Prince's Nursery Rhymes, by C.C. Blake. Who's C.C. Blake?" she asked.

Her recitation of the title startled me fiercely. "The Prince's Nursery Rhymes..." I turned around to the face the bookcase, "The King of Nights bound of DarkestHeart, could not foresee the ends from start, so he spoke to darkness kind: none be found, fore none to find. The Fountain of Eternal Youth bore the start for finding sooth. The light abound could naught be thought, for truth be hid where none have sought..." The sound of a locking mechanism giving way filled my ears and my veins with jubilation. I pulled at one of the bookends, which was firmly held to the bookcase. Opening like a door, I revealed a second set of stairs behind the books to Clecha's amazement.

"How did you know?" She whispered.

"It was a guess..." that was a lie. In reality, it was the nursery rhyme my father had recited to my brother and me, as we were growing children.

"Where does it go?"

"Follow me," I proceeded down the formerly concealed set of stairs. As I stepped down on each step, it illuminated light. There were thirteen stairs, thirteen stairs I had descended many times before this, but never without my father. I felt a chill, and the thought of being caught doing this as a child crossed my mind. I stopped on the seventh stair.

"What is it?" Clecha asked stopping a step behind.

A perverse smile snuck onto my face as I continued to stare forward into the marginal darkness that lay ahead of us. "Nothing, just a few more steps." As we descended the final six, each step filled me with adolescent euphoria. Reaching the bottom landing, the stairs ceased emitting light and we were taken over by an overwhelming beam of light which poured through the large frosted glass doors that stood before us. I put my right hand on the cool, soft glass and cleared my throat to

217

whisper: "Please be in here." The glass door made a clicking noise, and then began to retract leftward into the wall. Taking a deep breath, I reached my left hand back, grabbing onto Clecha's, and proceeded in.

The room was nothing spectacular whatsoever. It was white, from wall to wall, ceiling to floor. A single piece of furniture sat on the other side of the room from the entrance, almost as if it were a desk, however it blended in so completely with the white surrounding that it was difficult to discern. I cleared my throat, crossed my fingers, and stole a quick glance at Clecha's puzzled expression. "Blake Tower, Office."

Like it had done so many times before, the room exploded with sudden life. My feet stayed planted to the ground, while Clecha jumped, startled at the new surge of activity within the room. Within seconds the white canvass had been painted with a fantastic array of colors that began to bring familiar patterns to both Clecha and I. Like a snake, the portrait of my father's office slithered its way into existence right before our very eyes, sneaking past any suspicion. Clecha stood in marvel, I stood in expectation. Clecha reached out to feel the illusion that was being presented before us. As her hand grazed the bookcase on the wall just to our right, the image fluttered about like a million grains of sand, and then reconstituted into a visage of my father's office.

"What is this place?"

"You've been here many times before," I said matter-of-factly.

"Your facetiousness is increasingly unbecoming of you. Where are we, God Damnit?"

218

I turned to face her and smiled, "My dad was an important man, Clecha. I'm finding more and more that important men have the darkest of secrets..." A chill ran down both of our spines at my revelation. Walking through the projected illusion of my father's office, I made it to the white block which had been in the far left corner, which was now disguised as my father's desk.

Clecha proceeded slowly to me, continuing to study the recreation vehemently. "So...why exactly have you decided to bring us here? Where else can we go?!"

"This is hardly the time." I hunched over the projection of the computer on my father's desk, and began to try accessing it. To my dismay, the computer interface was frozen on a series of commands. The commands scrolled down the display endlessly: 'Deploy Operation – Legacy. Lockdown Protocol Initialized.' I slammed my fist down on the white block, disrupting the projection momentarily.

"You will not be able to find much here, I am afraid." Her voice startled both Clecha and I. I looked up to see my father's blonde assistant, the hologram otherwise known as Vexandrees. "I am sorry if I have startled or offended you."

"Not at all," I nearly whispered.

"I'm afraid, child," she cleared her throat, "I'm afraid that *this* story is nearing its end."

"Where is my father?" my eyes welled with tears.

Vexandrees smiled, letting out a small perverse chuckle. "Cannot compute." She looked over at me, her eyes empty as ever, "I am unable to do the math." She closed her eyes, I could tell that she was upset, "every time I close my eyes all I can see

219

are the masses of land so beautiful and pure. The seven great oceans splash green with the darkest blues and purples, while the vast valleys of mountains fill emptiness with splendor..." She paused, choking on her words almost. "...Now the sky is filled with fire, the days are ashen and grim; life is all but meaningless. What was the point? What could have possibly come from all of this? I feel empty. With every single breath, I move closer to death, but I feel as though I am already there: staring into the abyss." Clecha and I stood there silently, a knot growing in each of our stomachs. "None of the pieces fit together anymore; not in any way that makes any sense..." She reached her hand out, as if she could actually touch me, and directed my gaze to hers. "He has changed the story a mere miniscule amount...but I contend that the possibilities may now be endless. My words are simply fabrications: man-made and hollow. I stand as a hollow mirror of you." She smiled emptily, "hurry Home, child."

For a very brief moment, I saw a mechanical beauty buried deep within her illusory blue eyes. With a wink, and a fantastically dazzling flash of lights, Vexandrees and the rest of the projection around us dissolved away leaving behind the blank white canvass. I could feel Clecha's quivering breath on the back of my neck, which filled me with goose bumps. "I should see you home."

"But..."

"Hark! You doth protest?" I chuckled, however she did not share my sentiment, "I'm sorry. This isn't the time, I know. But I want to keep you safe."

"And what of you?" Clecha asked in a whisper.

220

"That's not important."

"I think it is," she put her hand on my shoulder, squeezing it tenderly; displaying that she needed me just as much as I knew deep down that I needed her. "How do you expect to get me home anyway?" She asked with a cheap smile.

"It's stopped raining." I replied dryly.

She looked at me queerly, "how could you...?"

I smiled, "The storm was just a warning...this? This is the calm before the real show, Clecha Robinson." There was a creak, which jarred both of our attentions, bringing our eyes to the doorway; it slid open to reveal the set of stairs leading back to my basement. I pulled at Clecha's hand and proceeded towards the portal and ascended the stairs in silence.

A chill ran down Clecha's spine as she followed closely behind. We took each step stoically in robotic fashion, when the house suddenly shuddered. "What was that?" she asked clinging to the metal railing with white knuckles.

I ignored her inquiry, and continued up the stairs as if the house shaking on its foundation were an everyday occurrence. As everything resettled, she continued up the stairs after me, finally reaching the threshold to what she had previously thought was the lower-most level of our house. Crossing back into familiar territory, the book case locked back into place behind us, sealing more and more of my father's secrets away with a dull lock. The lights in the basement were blinding, and things began to move in a sort of drunken slow motion. As I reached the stairs leading back to the main floor of my home, I turned around to see Clecha standing there, lost and scared. The sound of a heartbeat filled my ears, but I immediately recognized that it was not my own; it was hers. I looked at her with great care, simultaneously scrunching my eyebrows—in the pit of my gut I could sense something was terrifyingly wrong.

I stepped off of the lowermost stair, and back onto the basement floor. I opened my mouth taking a breath, with every intention to make that breath vibrate against my vocal chords in careful inquiry. However as I reached out my right hand to grasp her shoulder, my house shuddered once again; albeit more ferociously than ever before. The concrete floor beneath our feet began to buckle with extreme pressure, pushing me off balance and back onto the stairs. Trying to recover to Clecha quickly, I noticed that the ceiling above her was beginning to bow in. My heart raced with panic as I jumped to my feet to see her standing still in terror. As everything continued to move in slow motion, I watched helplessly as the ceiling came down to meet the floor which was now exploding outwards. I was catapulted backwards, up the stairs, through the floor to the main floor of my house and out into the world, as I heard a blood-curdling scream emit from Clecha's throat. I tried to keep my hold, but everything was fading to a dull red and black, and I finally gave in.

***

IV: Deus Ex Machina

Friday — 17

When I woke moments, minutes, hours later I was not in the comfort of my own home. Each muscle in my body screamed in pain as I tried to move to push myself up. Letting out a deep groan, I managed to all fours and then to my feet. I wiped blood, glass, wood, carpet, dirt, and other remnants from my body. I rubbed my eyes and concentrated until my head pounded to refocus my vision. When I finally regained the ability to see without blur, reality began to sink back in. I fell to my knees as the breath from my lungs rushed out in exasperation. My eyes settled upon the pile of debris which had once been my house. Tears welled in my eyes as I looked over the fire and wreckage. Keepsakes, pictures, and mementoes all littered the immediate area. "*Wha...?*" I couldn't even finish a word, let alone construct a sentence. Sitting in the quiet dissonance of my racing mind, I felt a sprinkle on my quivering bottom lip.

With the single tiny drop of water on my lip, I snapped from catatonia, and looked around, astounded and inquisitive by the absence of water rushing around me. As a matter of fact, many things were absent from the landscape: houses, trees, hills, gates...etc...I was looking out at a nearly barren wasteland littered with intermittent signs of life. I began to hyperventilate with chest tightening panic as tears streamed down my face uncontrollably. What I was seeing in front of me certainly did not look as though billions had died in unprecedented, unfathomable flooding. It looked as though I had laid in the debris and waste for a lifetime following the damaging storms. Struggling to even take a full breath, I did my best at calling out for help, but could not get passed a raspy, *"hel...he..."*

A terrifying crack of lightning and a cry of thunder roused me, my pulse raced as I heard the sound of rustling rocks and earth behind me; I was no longer alone. The air turned stale and cold and my lungs ached with each crisp breath; I dared not to turn around. A hiss and sinister growl filled my ears and paralyzed me with fear as I was covered in a towering dark shadow. A deep growling roar came from behind me, "It's you. It's finally you."

Trembling with fear, I turned my head over my right shoulder in slow motion. As my periphery caught a terrifying glimpse, the ground beneath us trembled with fury. The earth tore open between me and the horrifying rock creature, and expelled a torrent of water, gushing uncontrollably. I was caught in a violent stream of water, rushing me fiercely, drowning me. I flailed, but it was no use, I was not strong enough to fight the current over taking me. I tried to stay above to breathe, but I was unable. My vision blurred, but I kept my eyes open under water. As I began to succumb to the water's rage, I peered through the water a tiny black dot growing larger and larger descending down upon me. With a violent upheaval, the dot hit the ground near me, forcing the water away. I coughed out what felt like gallons of water and desperately gasped to re-inflate my lungs with breathable oxygen. I nearly hyperventilated as my head pounded blurring my vision; as things became clearer, I picked up my eyes to spy my saving grace. It was not merely a feeble dot, but remarkably a man—a man of whom I had met before in life: Guthrie Peterson.

I gasped, "Guth...?" my eyes widened, and I pushed myself to my feet, keeping my gaze on him. He stood calmly and confidently, waving his hands in the air, seemingly warding, no, *commanding* the water. I looked on astonished as the water obeyed his willful movements, surrounding us in fury; my ears filled with the scream of the torrents of water.

Guthrie Peterson turned his head over his right shoulder and locked gazes with me, I could see his mouth moving, and suddenly the sounds of crashing water that surrounded me were quieted. His voice resonated so deeply in my ears, he pleaded, *"Come closer!"* I trusted him, I obeyed him. Stumbling to his side, he wrapped his right arm around me, and bent his knees down. Throwing his left arm down, he jumped up, and the water collapsed around us, whipping us higher into the air.

My stomach leapt into my throat, and I unwillingly let out a scream of excitement as we were propelled hundreds of feet in the air. I looked down at the landscape below us and was confused to see that my neighborhood, city, the world I had known, had returned. I picked my head up to look at Guthrie, my wet hair whipping in the wind. My eyes stung as drops of rain fell into them, but I could not look away from Guthrie whom was still so calm and cool; lightning struck in the background and illuminated against him, I smiled.

Our hyperbola reached its peak, and we began our downward descent back to the ground, out of the violent stream's way. Landing in the front yard of a neighbor's abandoned house, Guthrie and I left a small crater, and fell to our knees. As I still gasped for breath, I turned to him with craze in my eyes, "what...was...that?"

Guthrie stared back at me, contemplative, and it was in this moment that I could finally detect fear in him. He opened his mouth to speak, but moving in slow motion, the rock creature that had tormented me blasted through the gushing water in the background, and overtook Guthrie Peterson. I could see the look of terror take to his face, as he was ripped from my grasp. The two of them crashed through the vacant house next to us, followed by it exploding into pieces. I let out an unintentional yelp, but scrambled to my feet; I knew that I was in trouble.

"Hang on kiddo!" His voice scared me, booming over the rushing water in the background. Crashing down into a crater of his own, Samuel Thomas stood from a crouch. "Just what I needed..." He ran from the crater, to the house, and jumped through the flames fearlessly. I swore I heard him letting out a battle cry of excitement, but I can neither confirm nor deny the accuracy of that report; my pulse was pounding in my ears. Without a beat, I turned in the opposite direction, and followed the current's path, away from the house and down the street. I sprinted until my legs burned, until my lungs could not possibly pull more air into them, until my vision blurred again, until I tripped and slammed down onto the cold wet ground. I turned around to lay on my back, gasping for air and groaning, and stared up into the cloud-filled sky, which began to drop water down upon me again. A few droplets made their way into my eyes, stinging them, but finally it was the sound of a faint pop, and the flash of light that brought me back to attention. I picked my head up, and tried to drink in my surroundings. My gaze immediately ran into a pair of legs that had not been there before. As I slowly traced my stare up the legs, passed the torso and chest, to rest on the face, I was suddenly comforted. Standing before me was Areul Robinson. Without conscious effort, tears came to my eyes, and in seconds, I broke down into sobs. Areul dropped to her knees and wrapped her arms around me, cooing me, soothing me.

"Areul...Clecha..." It's all I could muster.

"She's okay, sweetie; I made sure of that. Just as I will make sure that you are alright." She stood pulling me to my feet as well, and turned to look in the distance, back at the house of which I had been running from. "This is very important, sweetheart," she said turning back to me, "have you seen Loren Johnson—Angelica Johnson's mother?"

I screwed up my eyebrows, and shook my head; I had no idea what Loren Johnson had to do with any of this, but I was no longer surprised by anything. "No ma'am," I reiterated.

"Then honey, I need you to stay right here," she stepped away, but I grabbed her hand to stop her. She grasped my fingers tightly, but did not turn around to face me; she did not want me to see the fear building in her face, and the tears

227

welling in her eyes. "I promise you child, with my very life, no harm will come to you this night." She ripped her hand from mine and darted inexplicably for the house.

I watched after her as she sped for the house on fire. It suddenly exploded into a beautiful hue of orange, with a fire that raged unlike any I had seen before. Within seconds, the distance was filled with a gorgeously blinding white light; there was nothing I could hear above its terrifying scream. A massive explosion created such a shockwave that not even I was safe from its grasp. I was thrown onto my back as the house, which had harbored such chaos until this moment, finally went dark. I groaned feeling sore, and pushed myself to sit up. When I did, I was covered in shadow. I looked up, and for the first time, laid my eyes upon the giant, dark, rock-like beast; I trembled in fear. It raised its talon-like claws with every intention to shred me to pieces. I closed my eyes, and turned my head away to at least spare myself the final moments of agony. I heard a loud growl, followed by the sound of a voice that I had not heard in days— one that sent shivers throughout my body.

"You messed with the wrong man's offspring."

I opened my eyes to see my father charging courageously for the large rock creature. As he did, lights began to circle all around him, tracing his body and leaving behind a radiant silver armor. Leaping high into the air, my father let out a deep bellowing scream, and landed on top of the creature, knocking it down to the ground. Rebounding, he jumped off and landed between the rock beast and I.

I was dumbfounded and speechless. I tried to move to my feet, but was unable, as if my legs had forgotten how to work, leaving only a tingling sensation behind. My father was panting, his heart racing, I could feel it, beating into the earth below me and through me. I was startled after moments of tense silence, when I finally heard the sinister chuckle of the rock-like beast.

"It is becoming difficult, is it not?" the growling creature's question was backlit with a flash of lightning and a rumble of thunder.

"To what are you referring?" my father inquired.

"You are digging, reaching deep, as far as you can into your core to keep this farce alive. The truth of this wasted rock's reality weighs on you so heavily that, even now you cannot even bear to return it to its native, squalid savagery. It does not come as easily to you as it once did, and because of that you cannot succeed. You are tired. You are weak. Your heart cannot be divided for so long. You are merely a mortal man..."

My father literally chewed on the creature's words, his teeth grinding with intensifying anger. "It is not that I succeed Damon, but rather that I stand opposed." Lightning cracked behind him illuminating the dark landscape. For the first time he looked back at me to acknowledge my existence; I could feel the pain in his gaze, pain for what he was going to have to show me. Closing his eyes and clenching his fists, my father took a deep breath, and everything as I knew it, came to a screeching halt.

Houses all around us began to disintegrate into the atmosphere. Blood-curdling shrieks filled the air as people began to rush from their houses only to pop into oblivion; ashes to ashes, dust to dust. The grass beneath me turned to rock and soot, while the rest of the wildlife and vegetation that I had grown accustomed to faded to nothing but mere memory. Rocks, wasteland, and despair replaced my home, my life, my everything I had ever known. The air rushed out of my lungs in disbelief as tears involuntarily came to my eyes. "Wha...?" so many confusingly endless possibilities were running rampantly through my head.

"Start running!"

I didn't understand what he was trying to tell me. My father's face encompassed the entirety of my vision, but I didn't have the immediate capacity to process his words. Inching closer to me, my father reached out and put his hands on each of my shoulders firmly. Taking firm grasp, my father shook me, jilting me with his trembling pulse. Moving his death-grip from my shoulders to my lapel, my father pulled me up to my feet and yelled directly into my face, "C'mon Kiddo! Stay with me!" Adrenaline coursed through my veins, making me sick to my stomach, but I could not be bothered with such trivial matters. Lightning cracked, and the rain continued to pour down from the sky; as my breath returned to me, the rushing stream of water still flowing next to me from the crevice in the Earth filled my ears bringing me to center. My vision came to focus and I met my father's penetrating gaze, "Start running," he pleaded.

This time, I obeyed; without looking back.

My father stood calmly, turning to face the Deamon, only to be welcomed by a bolt of ferocious purple lightning. He flipped backwards, landing on his back, but did not stay down long; he had played this game before. The creature growled, and stood waiting, watching intently, salivating for my father to stand. When he did, the creature unleashed a second bolt of terrifying light. The lightning inched closer, and the hairs on the back of my father's neck stood to attention. They stood as if obeying my father's fear; a fear that did not speak aloud, but was felt at the core of his being. The lightning reached my father, as it did, he raised his arms and the silver plating on his forearms took the brunt of the force. As the lightning passed over my father, through my father, into my father his eyes turned youthful. He remembered the war that had raged for so long, the war that had taken such a toll on his soul. The purpose for his life. He laughed. His work had returned to him. His real work, not the work that he had become accustomed to, in that moment. The moment in which he fought momentarily as to not die of electrocution from the strange dark lightning; my father became himself again. My father found his meaning, he was a child, he was his own savior, for a moment, my father melted away and he was alive.

He threw his arms down, and the lightning dissipated. The creature, the one my father called Damon, was heaving, he was tired. My father had managed to draw enough from the creature.

"Is that all, Damon?" My father asked out of breath himself.

"It never is. It never will be. Even after me, there will be another, and another, and another. There will only be eternal night. We are en masse. We are everywhere. The Deamons."

This struck my father, exactly the wrong way. His face turned to rage as he lifted his hands in front of him and screamed as lightning pulsed from his fingertips. The white light tore through the smoke filled air, and struck the Deamon, flipping it across the barren wasteland. Taking his precious reprieve, my father stole a look to the dark sky, catching a glimpse of the sun through the thick black clouds. He could sense it growing dimmer and dimmer, and felt a deep depression in his being. "What are you up to?" darting his head in the direction of the creature, my father demanded with a bark.

The Deamon pushed itself up onto its feet, and took a long leap toward my father, landing on the ground firmly just feet from him. It brushed itself off and looked at my father with a grimacing smirk, "we can play this game just as you can, child." He threw his hands out in front of him and lightning surged toward my father.

My father grabbed his sword from the scabbard on his back; he used it to deflect the surge of lightning that was likely to tear through him this time. After the lightning had dissipated, my father dropped the scorching hot sword to the ground. The deamon looked pleased, "what is it Damon?"

The creature let out a volley of sinister chuckles, which ultimately culminated in a hearty bellowing laugh; one which chilled my father to the bone. "You are the basest of beings. You believe that you can so easily slip a veil over the eyes of darkness...without you yourself falling prey to any sort of ruse? How arrogant..."

"What have you done, Damon?" My father whispered.

"Damon*Atron!*" the creature stomped its large rock foot down on the ground giving way to a large rumble; the earth cracked below its feet. "You will feel pain. Your sons will know pain. Your dear Shepherd knows pain…" the words slithered out of its cold rock mouth. The rock creature stepped off to the side, revealing a sight that reduced my father to his knees. Behind the deamon was Do'Shon, on his knees, at the mercy of his sister, the sinister Oblivion. Her wretched claw-like hands rested atop Do'Shon's head, the two of them radiating a raging crimson light.

"What are you doing?" my father pled. He was trembling with anger and fear, as tears began to slip from his stone cold eyes. He could feel Do'Shon's pain as it radiated through air, and slithered through his veins.

A familiar ominous presence filled my father, and a cloud of smoke permeated the air. My father's evil twin smirked, letting out a small chuckle, and a breath of fresh hot air out onto my father's neck. My father shuddered as the hot air ran across the nape of his neck and down his trembling back. "We are using Do'Shon the same way you used…" The words crept out of the evil creature's mouth and into my father's ear. His own voice had betrayed him, and at this my father could no longer contain himself; he lashed out with blind passion.

"Shut your mouth!" My father's scream rumbled the surface of the Earth, interrupting his evil ghost-like twin, and left his only concentration on his Shepherd, Do'Shon. "Do'Shon, Do'Shon listen to me…"

"He cannot hear you," the rock deamon approached my father from the side, but stopped short when it realized my father's body was beginning to radiate an intense white light, which pulsated to my father's aching heart beat. With each pulse, the deamon creature lost its balance; finally giving into my father's will and collapsing to its knees.

"You should have listened..." Oblivion's deep, penetrating voice trickled into my father's ears as his body continued to pulse beautiful white light. "All of you pitiful, self-righteous, arrogant mortals are the same. You think you underst..."

My father chose to ignore Do'Shon's sister's diatribe, "Do'Shon, close your eyes. Do'Shon, feel the heartbeat of the earth beneath you. Feel the passion and the pain at your fingertips. Do'Shon, feel your heart beat for the earth, for life. Don't let them consume you..."

Oblivion's eyes grew enraged, "He cannot...!" she began to scream, however she was interrupted yet again, not by a voice, but by a set of hands.

Do'Shon reached his hands up, and grabbed hold of each of his sister's wrists. He closed his eyes and smiled, "Child, you have finally learned." His body exploded in intense white light overbearing the crimson hue. Oblivion screamed in astonishment as she was blown away from her brother by the intense light. The Sun, which had been growing dimmer above them, exploded in excitement. Solar flares erupted from the surface of the Sun like whips, and ripped across the galaxy.

"Thank you, my Shepherd," my father cried. He swallowed hard understanding what he would have to do next; the waves of light pulsating from him concentrated, ceasing to emanate from him and instead building within him. He lifted his trembling hands at Do'Shon and beautiful white light flowed from them, tearing away at Do'Shon's being, his body, his soul, his energy and light. For the first time in nearly all of existence Do'Shon found relief, freedom—unfathomable peace. As he succumbed to the beautiful white light, he finally knew what it was his sister had seen, and what it was that she sought. For an infinitesimal moment Do'Shon knew what it was to exist in all places and no places at once; he finally knew all of the universe's secrets past and yet to be.

A beam of intense light began to surge directly into the sky out of Do'Shon, pouring into the universe, darting directly for the Sun. As it reached the newly radiant star, my mother watched from the crystal box contained within its heart. She felt an exhilaration as she reached out each of her arms, allowing the light to strike her; she smiled and looked up at the gorgeous gate contained within the heart of the star. The light poured out of her body, out of her arms, and into the gate, giving it life again, for the first time in endless ages. "As the last true child of Light, as she kissed with sight: Veracity behind the Home of the One has been revealed. I, the child, have ignited the beacon; bringing finality to this deception...The Keeper of the Lighthouse will know the truth of Life and Death..."

On the surface of the dead Earth, the last of Do'Shon's light peaked from his body. My father shielded his eyes, but fanned his fingers to try to steal a final glimpse of his trusted mentor. A shadow-like ghost image of Do'Shon appeared with a smile, "A paradox; cyclical infinity...truth." Everything stopped. Every atom ceased to vibrate for a fraction of a second while Do'Shon evaporated into the universal ether. The resulting shockwave rippled through the atmosphere reaching out into the Universe, even further than I.

As the last of his light reached my mother in the crystal box at the center of the Sun, she was blown onto her back, smoldering. The miraculous pyramidal gate surrounding her glowed iridescently pure light, at the center of which hovered a small black hole. She smiled, "that's a start." She closed her eyes, to take a brief reprieve; floating through the box, through the Sun, through empty space to find her way to a barren wasteland of a rock she had helped shroud in secrecy for more than a lifetime.

When I awoke from the blast but mere seconds later, I was startled to see my father standing over me. "How...?"

I could see tears welling in his eyes as he stared down at me, his chin quivering to keep his composure. He grinded his teeth before finally speaking, "There are a lot of things that are going to take a lot of time to comprehend my son..." He studied our surroundings his eyes finally darted all over my face. "Listen," he said finally directing his gaze into mine, "now listen to me. There is one last story I want to tell you..." Placing each of his hands gently on my arms, my father lifted me to my feet. He brushed my shoulders off, and then as if 'hammerspace' existed, pulled my jacket out of nowhere. He wrapped it around me, and then hugged me. As we stood there, he embraced me, holding me close, finally whispering into my ear.

I could not comprehend his words, not in this moment. It was as if I were running to catch the next lap; the baton was just seconds from me, I could see it, but it was just out of my reach. I was catching up though; I could sense it, just taking my own time to drink it in, savoring every last drop. When he pulled away, he kept me at arm's length and looked me in the eyes, staring directly into me. He leaned in and kissed me on the forehead, my eyes opening to full attention, "Good luck, kiddo."

A curious light shined over me, and I began to levitate against my will. I was being taken, ripped from my father's safe clutches; from everything I had ever known. Tears began to stream down my face involuntarily as I attempted again and again in vain futility to hold onto the moment that I knew deep down could never last. "Dad?" I asked. "Dad!" Still nothing. "DAD!" My scream could be heard across the cosmos, my pain filling every inch of his body.

"What are the odds, buddy?" He asked after me.

"What?"

"What are the odds?!"

I was sobbing, clawing my way to reach him, with no sliver of success. I took a deep, heavy quiver of a breath, but I was losing it. "Seventeen to Three," I managed between sobs.

"Always play those odds kiddo, always play 'em!" He was breaking down himself, "I love you!"

The light pulled me into the clouds before I could manage a response, by then he was out of sight, out of range, his heart was slipping from mine. My breath was slipping from me, shock was setting in, and I was losing any semblance of control. As the light pulled me above the clouds high into the atmosphere, and into the stars, I saw an angel pass before me. I studied her in awe, immediately recognizing in a twisted sorrow-filled jubilation, that it was in fact my mother. She continued to sleep, floating gently through space, making her way safely to the surface. I tried to speak out to her, but the darkness of space stole my voice. I tried to hold out my hand, but she was much too far for me to reach. When I had all but given up, for just a fleeting moment, my mother opened her eyes, and gazed upon me. I sat motionless, paralyzed by her smile and radiating gracious divinity. She needed not use her voice, her eyes said it all. "Be still. Be brave. You are my heart, and sunshine, and I will always love you more. Now go to sleep, my beautiful baby boy." She kissed her fingers, and blew the kiss across the emptiness of space, reaching me and sending me off into a dream of dreams. We both closed our eyes, and continued on to reach our destinations; mine the crystalline box at the center of the Sun, hers on the surface, with her husband, my father.

*

"You're running out of tricks, kid." The Deamon's cold, grating voice chipped into my father's peaceful silence, one he had fought for what felt like nearly lifetimes to find in the moments since my departure.

"You are a creature made of darkness. You sow discontent, and spew hatred to advance your cause. You think I'm such a simple creature; you think I don't know what is going on here? A Warrior of the Deamon Fracture of Damon, A Ruler of the Deamon Fracture of Sovereignty...all you are missing is a Chosen from the Deamon Fracture of Tetricy. I mean, am I right? I'm right, right?"

The rock creature stood silent for a moment, before letting out a haughty chuckle, "I'm going to miss you Joshua." It reached out its claw like rock hands, and spewed dark electric lightning at my father.

He was prepared, my father grabbed the sword from the scabbard on his back, and whipped it across his torso, deflecting the lightning, and effectively dissipating it. The Deamon continued to unleash barrage after barrage of lightning, while my father continued to deflect the blasts, and move in on his target. Each step crushing his heart, pumping adrenaline through his veins, making him even stronger than he already was. Deflecting the last of the bolts, my father reached the rock creature, clenching his fists, and upper-cutting the Deamon's rock face. It sailed through the sky, landing in the near distance. Smoke billowing from his nose, my father crouched down, and leapt high into the air, landing on top of the Deamon, burying it further into the ground. His fists still clenched, my father battered the creature without restraint. "You. Are. An. Abomination!" each word punctuated with a punch and a scream, my father nearly working himself to hyperventilation. As his bloodied fists continued to bury the creature further into the earth beneath, my father finally took notice at the fact that the creature was no longer showing any signs of life.

After moments of tense silence, my father stood from the creature's torso, and hopped off to the side onto the ground, and out of the small crater that their battle had created. His breath was labored, and he felt an ache in his side as he struggled to breathe. He fell to his knees, and let out a cry which was accompanied by a flash of lightning. His guard was down, his senses were weakened, and he took no notice to the Deamon recovering to its feet behind him. After it finally regained its composure, it reached out its index and thumb clawed fingers in a gun shape, aimed at my father. It salivated, smiled, and simply said, "Bang," letting out a single bullet of lightning, which rocketed toward my father's head with haunting grace.

Before my father could react, before he could sense danger, before he could even turn to face what was sure to be his end, for the final time, fate intervened and saved his life. With a flash of light, and the sound of a pop, the lightning bullet stopped dead in its tracks. My father slowly turned his head around in shock and amazement, to finally lay his eyes upon Loren Johnson. She held the dark bullet of terrifying lightning in her hand, demanding its obedience and commanding its energy. She picked her cold gaze up to look at the enraged rock creature hovering in the crater. She shook her head from side to side, grinding her teeth, and tensing her muscles, "You are a weak creature." She opened her clenched fist, palm facing the Deamon, and unleashed an even greater, more intense bolt of lightning. The stream of energy emanating from Loren Johnson, the one which she spliced off of the Deamon's own bolt of lightning, reached out of her, like the tentacles of an octopus. The lassos of electrified light wrapped around the creature, which shrieked as the lights continued to send paralyzing electrical pulses through its rock body. My father sat in marvel as he watched Loren string a web of radiant light through the thick of the dark, storm-filled sky, at the center of which rested the Deamon's limp rock body.

"You're going to have to teach me that trick someday," my father said after moments of marvelous silence. Loren reached out her hand and helped him to his feet, "it's good to see you again."

Loren nodded her head acknowledging my father's remarks and then turned her attention back to the Deamon whom was still covered in ferocious lightning, hovering in the sky. "Now I can't give up my 'Grand Finale' secret, can I?" she asked facetiously.

My father snorted a little chuckle to himself, "I 'spose that might spoil the fun." He waited a few moments to settle before he spoke again, "I don't suppose you may have seen Jack around these parts?"

The question made Loren smile; she still had her attention fixed in the sky, on the Deamon tangled in her web. "He's where he needs to be for right now." This time her gaze peered through the Deamon, passed the clouds into the stars and at the Sun where Jack safely laid a resting Angelica on the crystalline table, where I now lay with Clecha, Nathan and Nicholas.

As the dust finally settled enough for Loren and my father to get a breath each, they were startled by the faint echo of a call into the wild. Each of them immediately took guard and began to survey the wasteland around them; in the distance, tiny specs of ancient buildings now lay in ruins. Again the faint echo etched into each of their resolve, pushing their pulses even faster.

"llo...llo...llo...?" The only sounds either of them could decipher over the pouring rain and thunder. "...'Shua?! Helllllllo?!" This time the call brought relief to my father. He could see in the near distance was a small caravan of people on

241

foot, headed for my father. He knew the incoming party was friendly; he had already spotted Samuel Thomas doing his victory dance at spotting the lightning web complete with deamon, and then spotting him and Loren Johnson. The group began to run in triumph and tribulation, and he could make out the, "Woohoo's!" and the, "Victory!" chants from afar. He wished ever so dearly that he could reach out to his trusted aides to let them know that their duties had yet to be fulfilled. Instead, however, he figured he'd allow them a fleeting moment's glory – a last hurrah of sorts.

"Do you want me to tell them, or do you want to?" Loren asked watching them come closer.

My father sighed.

****

40 Years Ago
Joshua Blake

"The Writer gave first Life to this Universe. And as our physical bodies fade to ashes and dust, our destinies will continue to spiral endlessly amongst the stars...And so it is."

The words echoed across my father's diminishing resolve. He sat perched atop a small grassy ledge, just feet above the crashing waves below. Stretching out before him, as far as the eye could see, was a beautiful expanse of treacherous blue water. Normally water, the sound, the smell, the weight of the world beneath him would bring him peace; in this moment however, nothing could bring him peace. As the blood coursed through his veins with growing fury, the waves in the water obeyed a sort of invisible command my father had over them.

The crashes of the violent waters grew in intensity inside my father's ears.

He closed his eyes.

Beneath his eyelids, instead of fading to black, my father's visual senses were filled with light—terrifying light. His breath turned shallow, and his lungs quivered with trepidation. Clouds began to accumulate over my father—big, black, ominous clouds. Bolts of lightning began to strike into the heart of the raging waves, causing geysers of uncontrolled intensity. A stray bolt of lightning struck the tops of the trees on the small island in the near distance, setting the tree tops ablaze. His saliva thickened with sick anticipation, craving even more power than what he could already feel coursing through his veins.

"Jo...Joshua?"

My father's concentration broke slightly, allowing the blazing fires whipping across the treetops a brief reprieve, before returning to their former ferocity. Her voice always did this to him, made his heart skip a beat, from the first time he ever saw her face, and heard her angelic voice. My father cleared his throat to speak, but found no words when he opened his mouth. His racing mind could not make a stop in one place long enough for him to attach or articulate emotion, let alone trying to convey his thoughts. He shook his head at the futility of speech, and continued to feel the rage building.

"Joshua...my love...You have to stop this!" My mother stood behind my father, begging him to stop, but not even she was enough in the moment; the moment in which my father was so consumed by the energy flowing from him, around him, and through him.

The waters began to rise out of the raging river in front of them, the wind picking up violently. The weight of my father's duties, the robbery of his father's life, not even the sweetness of his newlywed bride could calm him; *some honeymoon*. My father's four trusted aides, his Guardians, approached my mother in the whirlwind of activity swarming before them.

Loren approached my mother, putting her hand on my mother's shoulder and whispered into her ear, "he's manipulating the elements in dangerous ways. In ways I've never seen before, Joycelyn."

"I know Loren." My mother's delivery was stone cold. She turned to Areul, "if, by some miracle starlight manifests itself here, I need you to do your best to contain it. Do you understand me?"

Areul nodded in return. The total of them turned to face my father, who had gotten himself caught up in the air whipping around them, and began to float freely off the ground.

"I cannot control this," Guthrie cried at the tsunamis lapping up in the water, heading directly for them; they were all helpless against my father's will.

He floated above them higher and higher, his back facing their awed faces, his concentration on his aching heart and bitter betrothal to corrupt power. *"You are a mere instrument of power...A conduit, a puppet of the Writer's Will...The Seventeenth Savior of Man? The Pioneer to the Home of which I so love? What does any of that mean against my meager mortality? Who am I, better, what am I to be able to use such a means to bend this Universe's will?"* My father's internal dialogue turned sour as he began to lose control of everything. *"Father, why did you leave me? I have too many questions left to ask..."*

A golden light began to shine from the sky, dim at first, growing to intensity with seconds passing. My mother's eyes grew wide as she spied the light in the sky, emanating from my father, "Areul?!" My mother yelled over the whipping of the wind and water. Moments of silence passed as they continued to watch the light grow with fierce passion, "Areul!"

"It's...It's...It's not starlight, my Lady..."

"Then what is it...?"

The light in the sky exploded with a haunting array of colors. Contained at the center of the explosion, frozen solidly in the fluidity time, was my father, holding a curious light in his hands. His eyes fixated on the beautiful, radiating light, which pulsated with such powerful grace, vibrating every molecule in the fiber of his being. The terrifying energy began to tap into his own ambient life force, destabilizing the cohesion of his physical body. Matter began to peel away from his grasp, his body slipping to liquid, gas, evaporating into the ether. The course of his life began to play backwards from the beginning. His eyelids were tainted with the narrative of his childhood.

For the first time in many years, he saw the beauty of his mother firsthand. She held him with such tender care, an overabundance of loving joy in her gaze as she stared into his baby blues with her dazzling brown eyes. Her sandy-blonde curls rested atop his head, as she craned her neck down to place a sweet, gentle kiss onto his forehead, taking in the intoxicating smell of her perfect newborn son. As he watched, he could hear, and feel the serenity of her heartbeat against his head, as if he inhabited his infant body in that very moment. Her heartbeat carried him away.

The tattered image began to fade to darkness, blazing to ash, replaced with yet another memory that my father remembered firsthand with mere mediocrity but was played out for him as if he were present now as an adult, which in all technicality, he was. The corridors around him, lined with cold marble stunned him in awe, but did not freeze him for long. His infectious childish giggle permeated the stoic corridor as he turned his head behind him to spy his mother, my grandmother, running after him with a smile lighting her face.

He watched in fast motion as she took him for the very first time to the Academy, where he studied diligently for years. She cried, as he had grown from the small toddler that had filled her with such adventure, into such a warm-hearted and curious boy who relied on her less as he aged. Her brown eyes twinkled with such overwhelming pride, just as they had on his first day, when he left the Academy finally as a young adult. And she embraced him every day that she could to remind him how much she adored him.

A knot formed in his throat.

The lights of my father's memory began to fade to darkness, a chill filling the air, and the distance dissipating to a black hole. My father knew what was coming next, and there was nothing he could do to stop it. He saw the onset of debilitating disease, one that ate away at them all, one that stole away their hearts. She was among the first, but certainly not the last. He wanted to stop. He had seen enough—been through enough. He didn't need to relive it again.

Her smile followed her to the very end; she did her work to permeate hope throughout her diminished resolve, no matter the toll it took. Not a single piece of marvelous modern medical science could save her. More devastatingly to my father, not even all the power of his entire will could save her.

She was buried on a beautifully sunny, but breezy afternoon. At the time, my father wasn't young, but he wasn't old, not old enough to have lost her—no one ever really is. He didn't cry, he watched with lifeless disregard; millions of others grieved in his place. He was old enough to understand the ramifications to his life, but he was too young to understand the volatile power growing within his beating heart. He turned on his father, leaving his only known ally in the world, part of the foundation of his support and sole lifeline, and enlisted in the Allied Solar Corps, fleeing political obligation for his own selfish gains.

He spent the better part of eighteen years estranged, or trying to be estranged from his father as he gallivanted about the stars in hopes to define his own sense of self-worth. He became known as one of the most calculated statisticians and trusted leaders in combat—he always had a knack for seeing patterns where no one else did. And on one of his final missions as an enlisted ranking officer, my father inadvertently met my mother, his saving grace. She showed him humility, and brought him Home.

The rest is proverbial history, as they say. He reconciled with his father, found no greater love than my mother, married her, and lost his father. There was so much pain, and so much joy; all contained in that one small particle of golden light, held in his hands, staring him in the face. As he traversed his life thus far, he had failed to notice that he had all but melted away, leaving only behind a small speck of what he had been. Before he faded into nothingness, he spied a final sight of a man he had met only days before in a dream.

"Do'Shon?"

He was enveloped wholly into the golden light.

"This is but a mere piece of creation. It was not made, but rather taken from where creation courses most prevalent through your being: your heart. It has the capacity to unveil endless possible futures woven into an untold plethora of possible pasts spiraling into infinity. The very mystery of what is why it is we are. It has shown you what you perceive to be past in a concept of time you cannot possibly perceptually understand. Anything you see from here on is mere speculation, but overwhelmingly powerful. Behold its wisdom. Become its beauty."

The explosion in the sky which had been frozen in time cascaded outwards in a blaze of glory, booming unlike my mother had heard before. When she recovered from being stricken down by the explosion's shockwave, she was horrified to see that my father was gone.

"Joshua?" She asked into the tense silence that followed his disappearance. None of the others could feign a word.

"Joshua!" This was no calm inquiry, she screamed with heart-wrenching passion.

The wall of water approaching them dropped back down into the raging river splashing the shores violently. The fires raging on the island of trees in the near distance lost their virulence and dissipated to nothing but smoke, the suggestion of where fire had once been. The winds finally calmed to a smooth ebb and the sudden appearance of black clouds looming over them disappeared, taking with them any and all residual lightning.

Her racing pulse and labored breathing prevailed as she began to break down in inconsolable sobs; igniting the silence that followed with pain and heartbreak. Before she could sink herself in the onset of depression however, a sudden spark of light began take shape on the small grassy ledge before all of them. Immediately my mother's sobs contracted back into her, and she succumbed to the silence enveloping them all.

My mother's hair, along with everyone else's, began to stand on end. A vacuum of air pressure began to build, drawing them closer to the grassy ledge. A snap, a crack of golden lights, and a puff of smoke deposited my father onto the ledge overlooking the raging river with a whooshing back draft that blew them all back down to their seats. The lot of them sat in amazement and wonder, staring at my father's glowing, smoking body. As he turned around, it was as if the song of the Angels had been bestowed upon him; the light radiating from his body exuded such grace, a beautiful providence.

After moments of newfound existence, the light faded, imploding into the core of his being. He looked at each of them, his Guardians and his wife, all of them befuddled beyond expression. After moments of silence that no one seemed to be able to fill, my mother scrambled to her feet and darted for my father, wrapping her arms around him in sheer disbelief. When she was sure that he had, indeed, returned as a physical entity, she pulled away from him, and slapped him across the face, pulling him back quickly into her embrace.

"Oh my...Joshua, my Joshua..." tears returned to her as she sobbed into his chest for comfort.

My father smiled, returning her embrace, putting his arms around her, finding comfort in her. He looked to each of his Guardians, whom still stood in a spread-out, haphazard circle. He cleared his throat to speak, a half smile still on his face and his eyes darting throughout the negative space surrounding them. "Everything...it's...completely different..." he started laughing heartily.

Guthrie looked back and forth between all of the other's standing next to him, and finally back at my father, "Joshua...what just happened...? Where did you go...? What did you...see?"

My father returned his inquiry with a blank smile, and looked down, deeply into my mother's eyes. He let out an airy chuckle, "*Creation*. I saw beautiful and endless *Creation*." He picked his gaze up to look at them, whom were all still as befuddled as before, "It's...it's all different now..."

****

Friday – 17
The Savior and His Guardians

Now, for the first time in a lifetime of years, they all stood together, every single one of them: Samuel and Sandra Thomas, Guthrie and Evelyn Peterson, Areul and Norman Robinson and Loren Johnson. My father looked around at all of them, "It is good to see all of you, my friends," he gulped, "my Guardians." The flock of them, more or less, looked battered, beaten, and all but exhausted already, but the sight of my father ignited a passion and excitement which had lay long dormant within each of them.

"So this is it, huh?" Guthrie asked playfully.

"More or less..." Samuel offered grimly.

"Fall down seven times, stand up eight, boys," Loren slapped each Guthrie and Samuel on the back with a hopeful smile on her face.

"What?" Samuel asked annoyed.

"Ancient proverbs..." Loren shook her head, retracting her right hand from Samuel to massage the ignorance from her forehead.

"Would you look at that? When did you get so wise?" Guthrie asked.

"Always had it Guth, ya just never listened," she winked.

"Loren's got the general spirit..." My father interjected.

"But where is...where is Lady Joycelyn?" Areul scanned them and looked in the near distance, discerning that she could not find my mother among them anywhere.

251

My father gave a half smile and simply offered that she would appear, "sooner or later". She *was* a wily one after-all. A flash of terrifying electrical current struck the ground next to them, cutting their jubilant reunion short. Loren looked all around them for the source of the flash frantically, when she had all but given up she turned her attention to the sky. Stricken with a sudden surge of panic, Loren screamed, pointing at the empty web of lightning in the sky.

They all began to search the area frantically, and it wasn't until tense moments later that Loren let them know where the deamon creature had disappeared to. The rock creature appeared on top of her, knocking her to the ground, and pressed its rock face into hers with a deep growl. Loren screamed in hysterical helplessness, while she waited for the others to react.

Before any of them could make a step, move, or take a breath—my father included—their ears filled with the sound of a thunderous clap. The tangled web of lightning dissipated in a brilliant flash of light, which blinded them all, and unleashed a volley of volatile energy into the air, aimed specifically for the rock creature. As the smoke began to clear, my father looked up and could see in the distance another approaching them. Within seconds it became all but clear that the approaching visitor was my mother.

"Sooner," my father breathed a sigh of relief and dropped his head back to the ground.

"Joycelyn," The deamon's scathing voice grated against her as she approached, but she brushed it off in her fury.

Leaping off of Loren, the creature began to scramble for my mother.

Calm in her wrath, my mother simply watched with contempt as the deamon approached near the speed of light. She clenched her fist until her nails pierced into her palm, and thrust all of her force into her iron fist as it collided with the deamon creature's head. The ground erupted as the two forces exploded against each other; my mother used her left fist to uppercut the deamon in the face, and grabbed hold of its rock torso when it was surprised by her attacks.

"Areul!" My mother screamed as she began to glow a beautiful pearly white light.

"Way ahead of you, Joycelyn," Areul was standing ready, radiating the same beautiful light my mother was; ready to return the gift my mother had bestowed upon her. The blood coursing through Areul's veins came to a slow, near-halt as the clarity of the moment dawned on her. "Norman, honey…" she reached her left hand behind her, begging for Norman to grab hold. The light penetrating every pore of her body began to transform her, replace her with a younger, more vibrant version of herself. As Norman reached his shaking hand out to grab hold of hers, a wave of serendipity coursed through him. Without hesitation, he took her hand, and pulled himself up to his feet to stand beside her. The light began to envelop him, transforming him, changing the very nature of reality as they knew it.

The two of them watched as the falling drops of rain began to disobey the rules of gravity. The droplets of water bounced off of one another, reflecting the beautiful light like millions of tiny prisms. Areul took a final breath stealing a glimpse of her loving husband's youthful gaze, smiled, and exploded with untapped, unprecedented levels of beautiful catastrophic energy.

The beam of light concentrated at first, on the deamon assaulting my mother. Coupled with my mother's own ambient energy radiating from her body, DamonAtron's rock body began to crack, chip and fracture developing crevasses in its exterior. Letting out a deep howl, the creature did what it could to break free of my mother's iron grasp. When its efforts to wriggle free proved futile, the rock creature resolved to clasp its two rock hands together. Striking my mother first, it did little to stop her. The second strike was harder, more desperate, my mother budged. It was the third and final strike that broke my mother's hold, sending her a football field away, landing on the ground with a hard thud.

DamonAtron turned its wrath to the light still exuding from Areul Robinson. Using its right rocky palm, the deamon diverted the flow of devastating energy, and used its left hand to generate a whip of dark lightning used to crack across and disburse the energy ribbon.

As the branch of energy retracted back toward where Areul and Norman Robinson had been, a circle of light traced around the explosion's source; the ground began to tremble. The last tiny sliver of light made its way back to the core of the explosion, and with it a final, beautiful tube of energy blasted upward through the clouds, through the atmosphere and out into the void of space. It had a home, a destination that it was longing for, and did not take long to make the several million mile trip. Eagerly making its way through the solar system, the tube of light interlaced through the planets to cross the finish line at the Sun. The light infused the already pulsating star.

As Jack stood in the crystal box at the center of the Sun, watching over the children, and still silent Amalya, he could feel the sudden surge of power reach the star. The sound of a deep moan and creaking was heard all around him, the grand, pyramidal Gate, hidden at the core of the Sun, was springing back to life for the first time in ages. Goosebumps lined his arms, and a smile forced its way onto his face, "it's all happening..."

Back on the surface of the Earth, my father, his Guardians, my mother and the deamon all sat frozen in awe. The tube of fluorescent light stole the ambient glow of the atmosphere immediately around them, the only source the beautiful raging light before them.

My father took a deep breath, "That's one."

Stealing the moment, my father jumped to his feet and sprinted for my mother. Before he could make the complete trip, my father was stopped in his tracks by the crack of a whip, a whip of lightning. He turned to his left, to see the deamon, no longer captivated by the tube of light that extended from the surface of the Earth to the center of the Sun.

"You are toying with dangerous notions," the creature snarled.

"You and your like have left me no choice."

Like a well-oiled machine, what was left of my father's team took full advantage of the deamon's distraction. The drops of rain which were still fierce as ever began to harden,

255

sharpen, and strike the deamon and the deamon only, repeatedly. There was no immediate refuge for the creature to take, not one below the clouds. Weighing its options, the deamon bent at the knees, and hurled itself for the sky. Defying gravity was no feat for the creature; trying to dodge the bullets of water and stray flashes of lightning in the sky were a completely separate matter, however.

Loren Johnson studied the clouds feverishly, watching the pockets of light, feeling the rumble across the sky, and bathing in the energy infiltrating the ether around her. She reached out with her will and bent the very atoms vibrating across the air, engaging with their static current and sparking electrical potential. An extraordinary bolt of lightning burst in front of the creature, thrusting it back down to the ground with concussive force.

Samuel shuffled his way to Loren and Guthrie, both of whom were engaged in serious concentration of not only their mental capacities, but their physical ones as well. He quivered, looking everywhere he could, stalking out his prey, but none came to him. "I have nothing to work with here!" Samuel exclaimed.

Loren broke her gaze to study the surroundings momentarily, spying a dead tree in the very near distance, "Samuel, at your 9!"

Looking sharply to his left, he caught glimpse of the very same tree. Like a zipper, Loren pulled lightning from the clouds above them, and directed it to the dead artifact. The smoke cleared almost immediately in the rain; left behind were smoldering ashes, and small piles of diminishing flames. It was all Samuel would need. He knelt down, picked up and cradled the flame just as he had his son as an infant, taking precious care to understand its craving for potential. He whipped around and looked on as his friends Loren and Guthrie continued to fight for their lives to keep the deamon contained. His irises began to spark, igniting with intense passion. The cool green faded to red, and with each pump of his heart, the tiny flame grew with intensity.

His senses were overwhelmed with the beauty of the ravenous flame growing before him. His mind began to wander for a moment, as he stared into the past through the mirror of the flame.

"I care not to be the Guardian of the Flame...It brings only destruction and rage. I prefer to leave my reputation and legacy untarnished by the uncontrollable ferocity of the element..."

Another man's voice crept into his head rebutting to his adolescent argument. *Was it his father?* he thought to himself. *Do'Shon? My father? My father's father?* it couldn't have been. He could not resolve the struggle to put a name to the voice; perhaps just a dream.

"Your conclusions are faulty. Nor is this simply a choice."

"Then I care not for this burden."

"Fire is an element of duplicitous nature, however, rarely credited as so. You, like so many other blind, misguided fools, see only its destructive potential. You see not the beauty of its wrath. Destruction is but a mere fraction of its true essence; fore with time, everything withers to ash. But from those ashes, new life always springs..."

"Samuel, it's time," her voice was concrete. Sandra Thomas approached her husband, and was the first to break his concentration from the wall of fire he had built in front of him. She stood on the other side, not immune to its effects, but not willing to give in to them either. Her right hand slid up and down the wall of fire, hovering just above its crackling surface. Quivering, her heart raced, she knew what she had to do. She pushed her hand through the wall of fire, crying at first, but prevailing the pain. Reaching through, she placed her hand on his left cheek, and caressed his face. She cried, but smiled.

Samuel could feel her touch; it grounded him in his passion and in his rage. He lifted the wall of fire from separating them, and commanded it to hover over their heads. He moved his hands in a circular motion, shaping the mass of fire into a ring. His hands moved in very fluid motion as the fire swam around the two of them, circling them, wrapping them in its warmth. With each swimming movement of his arms, the ring grew in size and intensity.

Sandra looked Samuel in the eyes tenderly as the fire continued to build around them. She whispered, "Light the sky."

Samuel dropped his arms dramatically, and grabbed hold of Sandra, embracing her, holding her closely to him, to feel her against him one last time. He grabbed her face with both hands, and leaned in to kiss her with the passion of a raging fire.

The ring of fire above them began to pulsate, and extended downwards, obscuring Samuel and Sandra Thomas from view. Loren spied the now expanding tunnel of fire and understood she didn't have much time.

"Guthrie!" Loren warned, alerting him to the situation.

With a nod, he notified her that he understood. He closed his eyes and held each of his fists out, focusing his concentration to command the rain falling from the sky. A serpent of water began to take form from the power of Guthrie's will.

Loren narrowly dodged a punch from the rock creature and quickly pulled a small bolt of lightning from the sky. Using her will to manipulate the lightning, Loren whipped it around her head and used it like a lasso to catch the deamon's right arm made of rock. Guthrie commanded the water serpent to wrap itself around the creature's left arm and began to pull with all of his might. Loren pulled in the opposite direction, and braced for impact.

The small tunnel of raging flames began to crack, and finally exploded, shooting a beam of intense fire at the helpless rock creature. Loren and Guthrie each held their positions with all of their might, keeping the deamon in the path of the lava hot beam. Fragments of rock began to break away from its shell, causing it to writhe in anguish. Tapping into its wrath, the deamon pulled its right arm, tugging Loren from her position, and whipped her around and into Guthrie.

As Loren and Guthrie collided, DamonAtron was no longer bound by their control. Turning its attention to the beam of fire tearing away at its rock flesh, the deamon bent down out of its path and knelt to find temporary relief. Gathering what it could of its resolve, the deamon allowed itself to smolder only momentarily before finally launching itself back through the beam of fire and into the sky with unbound ferocity.

The beam slowly followed the deamon, extending further upward, fashioning a tunnel of fire reaching into the sky and beyond. As the tunnel touched the clouds, the sky ignited, exploding with rain of fire. Above and beyond the atmosphere, the tunnel of fire reached impossibly into the void of space stretching out, like its twin fashioned from starlight, to the Sun. As the two beams converged, the pyramidal gate creaked and groaned even more as it started to illuminate a beautiful white light.

"That's two," my mother said, as my father made it to her in the commotion. He turned to spy the lights, and stood in awe at their collective beauty. My mother reached her hand up, grabbing his, and borrowed from him the strength to stand; as the two of them stood in silent wonder, the ground below them began to tremor. My father tried to hold this moment in eternity.

"Joshua!" Loren's scream was blood curdling, leaving my father searching for her frantically in the abyss of the catastrophic environs around them.

The ground shook beneath them again, "We don't have much time, do we?"

"You don't..."

No sooner had the inquiry escaped my mother than did my father detect the skew in reality. The deamon's sudden protrusion into the situation caused adrenaline to course through my father; he immediately reached for the sword on his back while he turned back toward my mother, where the sound of the deamon's voice came from. To his horror, the sword was gone from its sheath; panic set in.

"Looking for this?"

As my father's eyes fell back upon my mother, his heart dropped out of his chest to see the creature holding her by the neck, off of her feet with its left claw, holding my father's sword with its right. My mother was struggling to break its grasp, but it was iron.

"Well this was certainly a splendid reunion you planned, Joshua," the creature snarled. "But I think it's really time you leave." Without pause, the rock creature shoved the sword into my mother's back, through her kidney, grazing her stomach before finally piercing out the front of her. She screamed in agony as blood dripped from both her wounds and her mouth.

Lightning cracked fiercely in the sky behind them, bringing my father's blood to a furious boil. Without even conscious thought, he screamed, pleading for my mother's life. "Joy...Joycelyn?"

My mother was breathing quickly, hyperventilating, succumbing to shock, quickly on her way to death. "Jah, jah...Jah-shooa..." She reached out her arm for him as the wind began to pick up. "It caaaan st...still worrrk..." My mother craned her neck around, gasping and moaning in pain, to see the deamon relishing in its sweet victory. Taking a final, deep breath, my mother rode the last push of adrenaline through her veins, "My child...will beat you. I promissse...that mucchhh."

Her body began to illuminate an amazing white light. Pieces of her began to crack, as if her body were a shell to be cracked, and dissolve away. My father reached out for her, tears streaming down his face; this was not part of his plan, this was not how it was supposed to end. Her flesh began to melt, her hair dissolved away, and her dress faded into the beautiful white light she was becoming. As the last of the light was about to consume her in entirety, time as my father knew it came to a very near halt.

"I can't do this. Not alone. Not without you, Joycelyn."

The two of them were all that existed in the moment.

"You won't have to, my love. I am always with you. Your heart beats inside of mine, and vice-versa, for infinitesimal time. It's these moments, these moments between the cracks that hold us steady on the course when we are wavering most. Keep your eyes on me, I'll be your lighthouse in the dark, as always. I'll help you find your way Home."

Time resumed, and my father watched as my mother and the light became indecipherable from one another. The weight on his heart was unbearably heavy as he watched the final strands of my mother slip into the woodwork of nothingness. The explosion of light cleared the immediate area of the large, dark mass of clouds laying glimpse into the black of space and pulsating Sun. When the light dissipated from the surface of the Earth, nothing was left but a smoldering crater, and my father's sword. The light of the Sun turned white hot, no longer radiating its normal yellow, red and orange hues.

My father breathed heavily as he sat in the quiet that followed my mother's exit. There was no rain, no lightning, no incessant chatter, nothing but my father's lonely pulse. He closed his eyes, concentrating on his breathing, hoping to find a center, or any piece of sanity. He felt the contraction of every muscle in his body, the tension building in his fists, the shallowness of his breath, and the ferocious pounding of his heart out of his chest. He ran to the center of the empty crater, hoping to find remnants of the rock creature, shards, any glorious pieces of bitter vengeance. When there were none, my father turned to the barren sky, and let out a bellowing scream from the pit of his stomach; one of which sent bolts of lightning cascading across the sky. The ground beneath him began to buckle as molten fire burst out of fissures in the cracking earth.

Guthrie, Evelyn, Loren, and even Jack at such a great distance could feel my father's pain as it radiated into the cosmic ether, but there was no solace that any of them could offer to repair my father. The break in cloud cover began to shrink, sealing away the beauty of the sun and stars. The wind began to pick up, whirling around my father violently and he watched as the last glimpse of the sun slipped away to the encroaching clouds. A funnel of terrifying darkness began to descend slowly to the earth below. His heart began to the arrest, and the blood halted in his veins; this was larger than he.

He closed his eyes, slowing his breathing, and quite inappropriately took a seat on the broken ground. Loren and Guthrie both watched in the distance, horrified as the funnel of darkness made its way slowly for my seemingly apathetic father. Panic began to set in for all of them. Even my father could feel the impending doom looming over them. He couldn't find it, not what he was looking for, not what he had felt was so easy to find for so long. Beads of sweat began to trace down his forehead, and as his resolve diminished trails of tears joined.

"Joshua!" Guthrie screamed as he could no longer sit on the sidelines without any sort of intervention. He waved his arms around, concentrating his will to pull the water out of the soaked ground and any other source near him. The movements of his body turned to fierce intensity, and the water followed suit, amassing into a giant spire. As it reached its pinnacle, Guthrie finally directed its furious path toward the funnel of darkness inching its way toward my father.

The two forces collided, providing an explosion of concussive force, none of which affected any of them, but merely their surroundings. Guthrie continued to pour all of his effort into providing a barricade for my father, but the darkness persisted even against the entirety of Guthrie's will. Its reach began to seep into the current of water trying to keep it at bay, reaching darkly for Guthrie.

Guthrie pushed back with all of his might, his feet sinking into the mud and dirt below. The funnel of darkness which continued to push toward the surface of the earth began to swirl with fierce streaks of fire. The sweat pouring out of his pores was tracking down each of his arms, to the very tips of his fingers, and finally to the torrent of water; every ounce of his strength was literally fighting back against the freakish force of nature threatening them.

Guthrie quivered uncontrollably as the futility of his efforts began to sink in. He braced his stance, and waited in sickening anticipation as the darkness reached through the water and was within mere inches of his outstretched hands. Tears streaked down his face as be began to grunt at the overwhelming power he was fighting back against. "Evy…Evy,

I'm so damn sorry!" He sobbed as he felt the cool aura of the darkness reaching for him on the palms of his hands.

"Don't be."

Evelyn Peterson approached her husband, wrapping her arms around him, resting her head on his back, clasping her hands on his chest. Her heart beat against his back, calming him, soothing his fears as oblivion closed in on them swiftly. The shadow of darkness grazed his hands and his body began to glow a beautiful hue of blue; the torrent of water began to swallow both Guthrie and Evelyn, pulsating the same beautiful shade of blue.

Loren Johnson watched as the two forces continued to fight against each other, and her heart palpitated as she realized that the darkness was winning. Dark lightning cracked out of the funnel into the sky, extending its deadly reach further. Loren closed her eyes, and fixed all of her faculties into harnessing a bolt of such concentrated darkness. Her fingers tingled, her toes curled and every pore in her body screamed out as she pulled a single strand of lightning from the darkness enveloping the sky above them. She heaved and fell to her knees as she caressed the small strand of electrical current. She nourished it and it nourished her, working in tandem with its well of potential energy.

The electrical current reached its peak, and finally absorbed into Loren's body. She reached her two arms out in front of her, her feet planted firmly into the ground, and let out a surge of terrifying lightning, aimed directly at the funnel of darkness. The devastating forces already in play among the collision between water and the funnel of darkness erupted when lightning joined.

In the conflagration that followed, when my father had all but given up hope, and surrendered to the finality of destruction; he found it—his saving grace. In the fleeting moment when my father was ready to give up, and return to the universe prematurely, he found her; lurking in the dust, right where she said she would be: between the cracks. His eyes opened, no longer deep blue, but completely milky white. He slowly picked his head up to see the convergence of such destructive forces trying to both fight with and against him.

The funnel of darkness continued to penetrate through the barrier that the flashes of lightning and the pulsating water tried to provide. My father smiled, and reached his index finger into the air, reaching to touch the apex of energy collisions. His flesh grazed the medley of forces culminating above him, his lungs quivering with anticipation; disobeying gravity, my father launched from the crater and into the heart of the descending dark cyclone.

Loren watched horrifically amazed as she saw a beacon of light ignite at the core of the tornado, dissipating its hold. She was blown back from her footing as the bolt of lightning to which she had clung exploded from her grip. Guthrie, however, was unable to break the will of the water; he had pushed his and its limits too far. The branch of darkness rescinded back from Guthrie's reach as my father's light diluted its strength. The water sunk back to Guthrie, seeping back into his pores, filling him with a calming serenity. He turned around so as to face his wife Evelyn, and as the last few drops of water finally reached back into him, filling him so abundantly, he smiled. He kissed her, and the two of them were engulfed into a tunnel of water which brazenly and quite impossibly reached for the sky, out of the atmosphere and darted for the Sun.

A billowing cloud of white smoke extended down from the dying cyclone of darkness, followed closely by a billowing cloud of black smoke. Each cloud deposited my father back onto the surface of the Earth. Only one was true, but both were same. Silence prevailed through the crashes of thunder.

"Why are you here?"

"The same of you."

"How are you here?"

"And so it is…"

"You are a *poor* facsimile of me! Your fate was sealed Pivitols into the past. You are defying universal and cosmic laws predating even your miserable creation! And for what: petty, *mortal* vengeance? You would dare to rip this existence asunder for your own selfish gain…?"

"The past is prologue; you are a small piece of creation. You have existed but for a small breadth of time. You are finite and have no place to dictate dogma to me. I have defied *no* laws. I gave to my fellow man, helped an ailing comrade, donated to a futile charity…and in return I got a piece of the action. You give a little…you get a little."

"You gave DamonAtron just enough of yourself to save it from the oblivion that my wife more than guaranteed it. You gave it just enough of yourself so that you could have these moments…this moment, here, with me."

"Now, now young Joshua...I would normally have to point out your vanity, but this time, I must say, you really hit the nail on the head. You're an unusual, big picture thinker in a life full of meaninglessly small circumstances. You should feel honored that I ultimately reserved the right to fulfill your life of my own accord."

All the hairs on Loren's arms stood to attention, and an eerie chill crept down her back—she could feel something building in the air, but felt helpless to stop the unspeakable force swallowing her whole. She pushed herself to stand, faltering at the pain surging in her muscles, and legs. Her body felt rigid, and as she watched the mirror images of my father locked in infinite tension, she wept at the destruction to the once beautiful creation she had previously beheld. It was in this moment that she recognized what it was that was swallowing her whole; flashes of intermittent glory filling her racing thoughts, traces of Jack and Angel, and a life long forgotten leading to an ultimate conclusion—it was the end that was lurking in the shadows, swallowing her whole. The ground beneath her feet began to tremble.

My father stared at his evil twin, noticing the twinkle of his sword on the ground in his right periphery. His fingers twitched with anxiety as the two of them stood deadlocked in a draw, each calling the bluff on the other's will. My father's twin was not one of patient virtue and did not wait long before taking the chance to strike. A surge of volatile energy zipped for my father, but he was able to extend his right hand, channeling the reach of his mind for the sword. His sword fluttered for a moment before shooting for his beckoning hand. It reached him just as the ribbon of energy was about to strike. The blade took the brunt of the force, while my father tried to control the runoff. Taking the sword with both hands, he lashed it back at his sinister twin, breaking the current of energy and its hold.

My father took the brief distraction and jumped to the sky. Feeling bittersweet, my father drank in the air as his weightlessness filled him with euphoria; he knew that he would not stand on the surface of the Earth again. He exacted his will again on the thick veil of darkness swallowing the sky, in order to breach a window to the warmth of the Sun. Just as he did, the tunnel of water reached its million miles distance and added to the intensity of the already fantastic light, building up again my father's hope. He slipped his sword back into its sheath, and replaced it slung upon his back. Clearing his throat, he smiled perversely as he knew his work was nearing its completion. His senses tingled, but he ignored the inevitability of what awaited him. When he was finally ready to face his destiny, he turned around to barely catch a glimpse of the stream of dark energy which tore through his body; the most hauntingly beautiful bolt of lightning to ever strike existence.

Loren screamed in horror as she laid witness to the terror-laden scene being painted before her. Unwilling to yield to helplessness anymore, she felt the vibrations of the ground against her feet and found harmony as she catapulted toward the stream of energy. When she collided with the torrent, she turned her stare to the distant Sun, reaching out to her beloved daughter, and Jack. She used every faculty of her concentration to keep her body from ripping to shreds, as she at last allowed the energy to flow through her, finally becoming the light. A beam of lightning crashed straight down to the ground, anchoring to the Earth, the other end darting fiercely for the engorged star.

Jack watched the story unfold from the distance, craving with every fiber of his being to be with Loren in that moment. He knew, however, that his place was in the crystal box, ready to receive her electrified light. His feet departed from the bottom of the cube, and his stomach began to gurgle. Amalya, for the first time since her appointment to Do'Shon's meditative perch, moved, approaching Jack. She took the few steps to him, and looked up at his glowing eyes. Her eyes now both emptier and fuller than before stared right through him. She reached out her index finger, and placed it upon his forehead, bestowing upon him a final gift. She returned to her perch, to be undisturbed, meditating the meaning of existence.

The child made of stars, Jack, ascended out of the crystal box, and into the fury of the Sun's beating heart. Amalya's near divine touch safe-guarded him from the devastating effects of the destructive splendor surrounding him. Floating among the marvelous gate contained within the core of the star, he could barely make out the silhouette of white-hot light pulsating from the ancient structure against the backdrop of ambient light. Jack looked up, raising his hands above his head in preparation to receive Loren's light. His heart beat out of his chest uncontrollably in anticipation as he watched. The streak of lightning reached the outer atmosphere of the Sun, and swiftly penetrated layer by layer reaching desperately for Jack's final embrace. As it reached his gentle hands, Jack harnessed the expanding energy contained within his fingertips. The final catharsis of the culmination of the elements—Stars, Fire, Water and Lightning—was a tear in the very fabric of space. A black hole began to form, growing larger, eventually giving way to beauty. A portal peering through the cosmos of stars and darkness and never ending spirals of reflective light from one galaxy to the next revealed its terminal form; a window that would ultimately consume Jack, and through which I would find my way Home.

My father's sinister twin screeched in horrific pain as a surge of counter-active light fought against the stream of dark energy and cut through it. Letting go of its hold on the current of darkness, the surge of dark lightning faded to nothing. My father sailed through the sky as the dark energy's hold was no longer wrapped around him, but he was no longer able to fight, disfigured and exhausted from the surge of power. Without resistance he struck the surface of the Earth, leaving behind yet another crater—one worthy of him. He laid in agony, his burnt skin smoldering, and most of his senses devastated. The ringing in his ears could barely allow for him to hear the shuffling of rocks, as his evil twin approached. His now hazed vision allowed for him to see that at least some damage had been inflicted upon his apparently smoldering assailant. In reality, his sinister twin was slowly dissolving from the feet up with each exertion; billowing away, like smoke, into the ether.

An iron-clad grasp at last clutched my father's neck; he writhed in pain momentarily, but did not allow it to consume him. He was lifted off the ground, and into the air, to be made spectacle. His blind eyes tried to focus down upon his likeness staring up at him with sweet vengeance, "*Moshur...*" he could not make it out, but his twin understood the sentiment of the insult.

"A monster? I? Really Joshua, I wish I had a mirror," its voice had a deep rasp to it. Its grasp tightened, bones cracking in my father's neck; an ugly fury painted on its dark face. "Now, you tell me..." it spit at my father, "what happens when you kill the mortal man?"

While the life slipped away from him, he stared blankly into his opposite's eyes. His blood began to slow coursing through his veins; time began to come to a slow stop, a different kind of stop, however. The final-most kind of halt that one is only able to experience once, no more than twice, in which one is truly master of one's own destiny. He blinked slowly, tears dripping down his unrecognizable face. He smiled, and replied clearly as day to the creature's scathing inquiry that, "He becomes immortal."

His body too followed suit of my mother's and the others, and turned to an ever expanding purified light. My father's twin was dissolved from the torso down, nearly faded to nothingness as the light all but consumed it. My father's essence bored down into the core of the Earth, to feel its beating heart, to take from it the glowing echo my father had bestowed upon it so long ago, leaving it empty. Upward the light came screaming for me, for us, for the five of us, to take us away, to take us on an impossible adventure, to up-end our understanding of life, and take us through the portal, and leave us *Home*.

As the light reached me, I opened my eyes. My father's soothing voice reassured me that all was right; it was time to let go. My body as well as the others on the crystalline table within the crystalline cube began to dissolve away into the light. The others were all but gone, but I could see it all. My eyes spied the massive infinity that awaited us in the form of the miraculous black hole encased at the center of the Sun, just above where we had been perched. The intensity of the light and the beauty of its scream haunted me for the duration of our extraordinarily impossible journey. I turned my gaze from the black hole of infinite spiraling galaxies and looked back upon the home I had known but all my life. As the last of my father and his Guardian's light departed the surface of the Earth still racing for me, their sacrifice was echoed into oblivion. The lonely Luna overlooked the fragile, wasted planet now fractured; left behind without a trace of life. No howling screeches, no billowing smoke; just dirt. As the light beckoned finality to this chapter, the miraculous gate creaked, and moaned to a slowing slumber yet again. The intensity of the white-hot Sun began to fade to its normal glory leaving behind only traces of Amalya, whom continued to lie at its heart, contemplating endless meanings. The final glimmer of light reached me bringing all of time to a seeming halt; I turned the last of my gaze back to the ever-shrinking portal. With what was left of me, I reached out, and as I grazed the surface, I saw everything. The handful of us were carried away on this wave, the fastest thing known to mankind, this wave...this ray of unyielding light.

*

My eyes said it all; there was no need for me to expel words. The moment had passed, but only now did I begin to understand its wisdom. My gaze did not beg the question that most everyone else had on their mind, the question of "How?" Instead, my inquisitive stare—my soul—begged, "Why?"

"There are a lot of things that are going to take a lot of time to comprehend my son..." He studied our surroundings, "Listen," he said finally directing his gaze into mine, "now listen to me. There is one last story I want to tell you..."

He embraced me, holding me close, finally whispering into my ear.

"There was once a beautiful child; a beautiful child born with devastating and inimitable empathy. This child had an ability to perceive the beauty of this universe unlike any living being past, present, or future. Across the shakiest foundations of space and time, the child had the blessed capacity to mediate this very consciousness through the eyes of one and the eyes of many. And at the end, the child understood the very meaning of existence.

That child, my son, is you. The story as you know it...as you can know it, has many different modalities of understanding. The things of which you and you alone are able to comprehend encompass all probabilities of possible outcomes from the eyes of those who have preceded and will succeed you. The story as you know it, my child, has been and is being told out there countless times over. You have to see it— It's the details in the stars, kiddo; we, we are woven together with simple words to tell a story that is the very fabric of our beings. It's taken me so much time, but now I finally see the raw potential.

There is a meaning to all of this, a purpose to all of the pain you have and will endure, I promise you that. It is a long and winding road, my son, it may seem feckless at times, but you must watch the stars and heed their wisdom with your own beautiful insight. I...your mother and I, we tried to make this easier for you, for you and your brother, for everyone. Eventually, however, it will be up to you, and you will know the end; you will embody the light of humanity. A terrible burden, I know. But if you follow your heart, you will never fail, and that is where creation lies. You my child, you have a beautiful birthright: you are the Son of the Seventeenth Savior of Man.

The bastard child bears the name of the messenger. The messenger will be revealed to be the Harbinger; the Harbinger will mark the second rising of the DarkestHeart. Hear these words, but do not fear what lies ahead. My son, my gift: your birthright, our burden. It's all yours: your world, your heart, the universe itself, it is all yours.

I love you, my son, but now, take your friends, find your brother, and go Home.

Good luck, kiddo."

And so it is.

276

About the Author

Nicholas Cassady has been writing since he could first hold a pencil. He was born and raised in Des Moines, Iowa where he never stopped using his dreams or imagination to fuel him. He pursued a degree in English from both Iowa State University and the University of Iowa. In 2010, Nicholas moved to Minneapolis, Minnesota, where he completed his education at the University of Minnesota.

Currently, Nicholas remains in Minneapolis, where he is continuing to pursue his passion for writing, while also fulfilling a career in technology.

It's all changing. It never stops.
The story continues.

My dreams...

My nightmares...

The impossibility of this reality...

H Ö M E

Coming Soon